Sign up for our newsletter to hear
about new and upcoming releases.

www.ylva-publishing.com

Other Books by Quinn Ivins

The Love Factor

Worthy of L♥ve

Quinn Ivins

Acknowledgements

I wrote my first book alone, not knowing if my frantic revisions were making it better or worse. This book was a completely different experience thanks to the support I received from my publisher and the FF romance community.

I love writing for Ylva to a degree that is probably unsettling for everyone involved. Thank you to Astrid Ohletz for giving me the chance to be an author and for putting up with my neuroses ever since.

Ylva's senior editor, Sandra Gerth, has been a wonderful teacher and friend to me. She has helped me so much that even if she were to sabotage my future books for some unlikely reason, she would still have my unwavering loyalty for life.

The cover is the result of a collaboration between Astrid, Jenny Spanier, Glendon from Streetlight Graphics, and an email from me announcing that I found "the perfect models" after spending the duration of The Queen's Gambit scrolling through thousands of photos. I don't know if any other publishers accept design suggestions from writers, but I am grateful to Ylva for making it work.

Good editors are worth their weight in scrunchies, and I was fortunate to work with three of them on this book. Miranda Miller pushed me to improve the story and gave me technical tips I will use forever. Julie Klein brought order to the chaos of my sentence and paragraph structure, while Michelle Aguilar refined the wording. Every one of my editors caught errors that would have tormented me for years.

My awesome beta readers—Abigail, Angeli, Chris Zett, Lola Keeley, Mary, and Melanie—provided invaluable feedback on everything from

Filipino grammar to life after prison. Thanks also to the federal probation officer I met on Reddit, known to me only as Super Ballz, who answered my questions about supervised release.

Thank you to Lee Winter for writing a blurb that condensed my convoluted story into a few enticing paragraphs. Thanks also to Glendon for formatting the book and to Daniela Hüge for overseeing the final production and, crucially, for reminding me to submit these acknowledgments.

Finally, this book would not exist without my wife. Intrigued by my first novel, she began to pester me to write a romance about a "hot Filipino lesbian" who coincidentally looked like her. She got her wish…sort of. The character Nadine came to the United States from the Philippines, just like my wife. However, Nadine's story is fiction. My wife inspired some of the Filipino food and language in the book, but she has never gone to prison for campaign finance crimes (or anything else).

The scandal in the story was loosely inspired by Michael Cohen, the former president's personal lawyer. As of this writing, he remains the only person indicted for illegal hush money payments made on behalf of "Individual-1."

Dedication

For my wife. Mahal kita.

Chapter 1

"I SEE THAT YOU CHECKED the box."

He didn't need to say which one. Nadine clenched her fingers under the table.

The franchise owner stuffed his face with French fries while he interviewed her at a plastic table in the dining area. "Now, it's not automatically disqualifying. I get a nice tax break for hiring felons. So if you're committed to turning your life around, I'll consider you like any other candidate. But I need you to tell me what you did." He slurped his soda and peered at her.

Nadine glanced out at the arches towering over the parking lot. *Fucking hell.* Third in her class at Yale, a top corporate attorney, senior advisor to a presidential nominee—and now she wasn't good enough to flip burgers.

No point in stalling. "I coordinated illegal campaign contributions to a presidential candidate."

The man's mouth fell open, revealing a half-chewed fry. "Wait. You're—"

"Yes. I'm *that* Nadine Bayani."

Nadine steeled herself. Whatever his politics, the reaction would be bad. Republicans hated her because they viewed her as the mastermind of a corrupt—if ultimately unsuccessful—scheme to elect a liberal Democrat to the White House. Meanwhile, Democrats blamed her for the election scandal that led to their defeat.

The disgust in his beady glare suggested the Republican variety. "I didn't recognize you with short hair."

That's the idea.

"I watched you testify on TV. You said Alyssa Jackson didn't know anything about your little scheme. Is that true?"

She met his gaze. "That's what I said."

Red splotches appeared on his pockmarked cheeks. "That damn socialist almost became president because of you. We let you come to this country from—where was it, Vietnam?"

"The Philippines."

"Whatever. Same thing. We let you come here, and you crapped all over our democracy." He smashed a fry between his fingers. "Why?"

I did it for you, jackass. "I wanted to win."

He snorted. "Well, that didn't work out, did it?"

"Obviously not."

"You know, when you came in here, I figured drugs, maybe vehicular manslaughter. Something like that. But what you did..." His nostrils flared. "Honestly, I can't believe they let you out of prison already."

Already? She'd like to see him last two years in a cage, subjected to daily humiliations—as if losing one's entire life weren't punishment enough.

"If you ask me, you're not fit to scrape shit off the bathroom floor."

His haughty sneer was too much. Another minute and she'd shove fries down his throat till he choked.

Nadine pushed herself to her feet. "I think we're done."

"Yeah, don't call us. We'll call you."

She strode to the exit. When she glanced back, he crumpled her application and tossed it onto the tray with the rest of his trash.

Shit. What the hell am I going to do?

Half an hour later, Nadine returned to Renn House, the transitional housing facility she shared with about twenty ex-offenders. Her two suitemates, Jenna and Jodie, were exactly where she'd left them—lounging on the beat-up couch in front of the television. The judge on *Divorce Court* rapped her glossy nails on the bench while a schlubby husband complained that his soon-to-be ex had failed to lose the baby weight.

"He did not just say that!" Jenna slapped her leg. "Oh my God."

Jodie looked up as Nadine walked past them. "Hey, how did it go? You get the job?"

She stopped and faced them. "No."

Jodie frowned. "Was it because you're a felon?"

"Something like that."

"Well, fuck them!" Jodie raised her middle finger. "You're too smart for fast food anyway. I mean, you're a damn lawyer. So you fucked up once. So what? You're still too good to work there."

"Yeah, fuck 'em all," Jenna said.

Touched by the genuine support, Nadine calmed down a little. "Thanks." She trudged upstairs to her closet-sized bedroom and sat on the lumpy twin bed. The cramped, colorless room was like a five-star hotel compared to prison, and she'd been lucky to secure three months of free housing. But where would she go when her time ran out? Landlords would never accept a felon with no source of income. She pulled her phone out of her pocket and scrolled through her contacts, looking for her probation officer.

Nadine had imagined that supervised release would involve frequent meetings in person with her assigned officer, but Michaela had simply told her to text with any problems. Nadine tapped out her message: *I'm having trouble finding a job.*

She set the phone down, expecting to wait for a reply, but it rang almost immediately.

"What's going on?" Michaela's deep voice boomed over the rumbling of an engine.

"No one wants to hire me. I hardly get any interviews, and the one I just had was over when he realized who I am. I'm running out of money, and I'm getting worried."

"I know it's—shit!" A car horn blared. "Sorry. I know it's hard when you have a record. How many applications have you filled out?"

"God, it feels like a hundred." She massaged a knot in her shoulder. "I promise I've been applying all over central Virginia. I have another interview on Monday for a retail job outside of Richmond. Some tiny town called Cheriville."

"Retail?" Michaela sounded skeptical. "You need at least thirty hours to satisfy probation. Most retail is part-time—so they don't have to offer health insurance."

"The ad said it's forty hours per week. And I'm sure the health plan is abysmal."

"Okay. I hope it works out. If not, you gotta keep trying."

"I will." As if she had a choice. "Listen, I need to talk to you about my housing situation. I'm halfway through my stay, and my caseworker said I have to leave when it ends no matter what—even if I don't have anywhere to go. They already promised the bed to someone else."

"That's right. Renn House is ninety days max. No exceptions."

"But how will I find an apartment with no income?" Even in prison, Nadine had never imagined she would struggle to find a place to live.

"Let's take it one step at a time. Fuck!" Brakes screeched. "Not you… Look, I know it's hard with your notoriety. But you've got a lot of advantages even as an ex-offender. You're educated. You're not on drugs. And you have all your old friends and contacts. Something will turn up."

At least the first two were true. She hadn't heard from her so-called friends in years. "Okay."

"I gotta go. Hang in there, okay? Keep me posted."

Nadine flopped back on the mattress. Grimy mini blinds split the sunlight into bright diagonal lines on the ceiling. The familiar antiseptic scent stung her nose, and the bass from the TV boomed through the floor. Taking slow breaths, she tried to process the possibility that in six weeks she would be evicted with nowhere to go.

Nadine tilted the rearview mirror until she could see her face. She smoothed her short black hair and checked her teeth for visible food. That's what passed for getting ready these days, now that it no longer mattered.

She donned her oversized sunglasses and exited the car, taking in the prosaic strip mall before her. The Overstock Oasis sat sandwiched between a liquor store and a Food Lion, and—judging from the distribution of cars in the parking lot—it was significantly less popular than its neighbors.

The glass doors whooshed open. Four checkout registers sat at the front of the store; only one was occupied. A fair-skinned, curvy woman leaned over the counter, her honey-blonde hair falling forward in loose strands. At first, she appeared to be writing, but when Nadine moved closer, she realized the woman was doodling on receipt tape.

Nadine tapped on the counter. "Excuse me."

The woman jumped and lifted her head. "Oh my Lord. I'm sorry. I totally spaced. How can I help you?" Smoky eyeshadow and thick mascara accentuated her golden-brown eyes, and her voice was sugar sweet with a buttery Virginia accent. Aside from her unflattering polo shirt—royal purple with *Overstock Oasis* embroidered on the lapel—she looked like a stereotypical Southern belle.

Did this girly small-town cashier watch the news? Nadine removed her sunglasses. "I have an interview with the store manager. Grady Sanders."

The woman nodded, then froze as recognition dawned on her face. She stepped back and bumped into the cash register behind her.

Great. Nadine arched an eyebrow. "Is there a problem?"

"Um...no problem." Biting her lip, she picked up a telephone next to the register. Metallic-purple fingernails caught the light as she dialed. "It's Bella. There's, um, someone here to see you... Yes... Okay." She hung up. "He'll just be a minute."

"Splendid."

Bella stared at Nadine, clasping and unclasping her hands as if she didn't know where to put them.

Nadine sighed. "I'll just wait over there." She turned away.

"Are you...? Do you mind if I ask you...?"

Christ, were they really going to do this? Nadine faced her. "Look, you obviously recognize me." She held Bella's gaze, challenging her to disagree.

Bella nodded meekly.

"That means you have an opinion. Everyone does. But I can assure you, it's nothing I haven't heard every day for years. So if you already know who I am, and I already know what you think of me, do we have anything to say to each other?"

Bella blushed. "Oh, I didn't mean..." She glanced around and seemed to spot something in the distance. "Oh, thank the Lord. I mean, Grady's coming. He'll be right with you."

A slim older man with frizzy gray hair ambled to the front of the store. "Hi there. Are you Nah-dine?" He regarded her with curiosity, but his blue eyes were free of judgment, confirming Nadine's guess that he had no idea who she was. *That's why I got the interview.*

Nadine stepped forward to meet him. "Yes, I'm Nadine."

5

"Grady Sanders." He extended his hand.

As she accepted the handshake, she snuck a glance at Bella, whose mouth hung open.

Oblivious, Grady smiled. "Nice to meet you. Come on back."

Nadine followed him to the back of the store, passing the bath and housewares sections on the way. She had never been to an Overstock Oasis before and would never have visited one voluntarily in her former life. The store seemed to specialize in tacky clutter. Mismatched merchandise crowded the shelves, and many items were marked with neon clearance stickers.

When they reached the back, Grady ushered her into a tiny office with a desk and two metal folding chairs. A flat-screen monitor set on a CPU occupied the center of the desk, surrounded by precarious stacks of papers, folders, and binders. One wrong move would topple the piles.

"Have a seat." He gestured at the chair across from his desk as he plopped into the one facing the computer. "I have your application around here somewhere."

Nadine waited as he shuffled through the mess. *He really doesn't recognize me.* She braced herself for the question and the inevitable rejection that would follow. Soon she would be another day closer to losing her housing, with no source of income in sight.

"Ah, here we go." Grady held up a set of papers. "Nadine Bayani." He pronounced her name with twangy drawn-out vowels. "You're interviewing for the store associate position."

"That's right." Inside, she cringed at the job title. *Associate* made it sound as if she were applying to be a business partner rather than a minimum-wage lackey.

Grady leaned back in his chair. "I'll tell you a little about the job. You'll be working the register, stocking shelves, and cleaning up after customers. Is that the sort of thing you're looking for?"

Sounds delightful. "Yes."

He scanned her application. "Now, it says here you don't have any retail experience. Where did you work last?"

Here we go. "I was a lawyer."

"A lawyer?" His head jerked up. "Why the hell do you want to work here?"

6

"I lost my license to practice law. If you look at the end of the application, you'll see—"

When he found the relevant section, his eyes widened. "I'll be damned. You checked the box. I didn't even notice. What'd you do?"

Nadine considered her answer. "I coordinated the transfer of funds from a large corporation to...a highly regulated entity in violation of federal law." This, technically, was true. Except that it was completely false.

"Ah, I see." He nodded. "White-collar crime."

He still didn't have a clue. Was she going to get away with this? "I suppose."

Grady's face brightened. "You know, we get a tax break for hiring ex-cons. Corporate loves it. But normally, when I see a felony, I think trouble. I don't want to hire someone who is going to steal and shoot up in the bathroom. But you're not like that, are you?"

Nadine thought about Jodie and Jenna, who had both been convicted on drug charges. That's what he meant by *trouble*.

"And you're Asian." He smiled. "Asians are good workers. I bet you're good at math too. Won't have to worry about your register coming up short." He steepled his fingers and tapped his chin. "Are you a US citizen?"

"Yes. For twenty years." She pulled her passport and her Social Security card from her bag.

"Outstanding. Well, listen, Nadine, I'm going to make copies of your documents and send them to corporate. You'll need to take a drug test. I assume that won't be a problem."

"Not at all." Drug tests were part of her probation, one of many humiliations that had become routine.

"That's what I figured." He sat back and crossed his arms. "It takes a few days to get the test results and for corporate to process your paperwork. You should be able to start...let's see...next Thursday. That work for you?"

That's it? She had the job? Nadine's throat tightened as she said, "Yes, that will work."

Grady gave her some forms to fill out and left to copy her documents. She half expected him to barge back in and withdraw the offer, having realized who she was. Instead, when he returned, he gave her a toothy smile and asked if she had any questions about the forms.

When she had finished the paperwork, Grady escorted her to the front of the store. "Bella! Come over here."

Bella approached warily. She did a double take when she saw the employee handbook in Nadine's hands.

Grady beamed. "This is Nadine... What was it?"

"Bayani."

"Right. She's our newest associate. Used to be a lawyer, if you can believe that." He winked at Nadine. "Maybe she can get me out of my next speeding ticket."

Bella gaped at Grady. "A lawyer?"

"Yup. She worked in corporate law," Grady said, leaving no doubt that he still didn't know Nadine was world-famous and universally despised.

"Oh. Okay." Bella glanced between them with troubled eyes.

Nadine held her breath. If Bella told Grady what she knew, her employment would be snatched away before it began. She cursed herself for snapping at Bella when they first met. If Bella gave her away, it was Nadine's own fault for being rude. Time seemed to stop as she waited for Bella's decision.

Bella parted her glossy lips, then closed them. At last, she smiled and extended her hand. "Great to meet you. Welcome to the team."

"Thank you." Nadine accepted the handshake, noting Bella's soft skin and gentle grip.

As their hands broke apart, Bella met Nadine's gaze as if to remind her that she knew exactly what was up, even if she hadn't said anything.

Nadine walked back to her car in a daze. The job wouldn't last, of course. Once Grady found out who she was, it would all be over. But for now, she had an actual job.

Chapter 2

OMG. Bella tapped her phone furiously. *Nadine Bayani just left the store. She got a job here. Grady doesn't know who she is.*

The sound of a squeaky wheel interrupted her typing. Bella looked up to see a woman steering a packed shopping cart toward her register. *Crap.* She wanted to know Raelyn's reaction before she got sucked into helping customers.

At last, bubbles appeared in the window.

The customer slapped a set of sheets onto the counter. "I hope I'm not disturbing you." Her words dripped with syrupy sarcasm.

"Not at all." Bella set her phone down and plastered a smile on her face. "Did you find everything okay?"

Bella scanned and bagged the woman's items as fast as she could, but another customer pulled up with multiple vases and wineglasses. By the time she finished wrapping each item in packing paper, two more customers had joined the line.

As soon as the last customer left, she lunged for her phone and read the string of texts from Raelyn.

Are you shitting me??? Why the fuck would she work there? Are you sure it was her? Maybe it was someone who looked like her? Shit, I have to go to a stupid meeting. Call me tonight. Better yet, come over. You have to tell me everything!!

Bella wasn't surprised Raelyn doubted her. After all, she hadn't been sure herself when she first met Nadine. At first glance, the woman who walked into Overstock Oasis bore little resemblance to the cutthroat lawyer with long, shiny black hair and tailored power suits. Still, Bella had watched enough news coverage to recognize Nadine's round face, flat nose, and arresting brown eyes.

Bella typed back, *100% sure. Yes, I will come over. What time?*

No reply. Raelyn's stupid meeting must have started. Bella sighed and pocketed her phone. Just a few more hours of tedium to go.

Gravel crunched beneath the tires as Bella guided her Honda Accord up the long, narrow road to Raelyn's house. The air buzzed with a symphony of cicadas, reminding her that she was way out in the country. The porch fixture was the only light for a mile.

The front door was always unlocked, and Bella hadn't knocked since elementary school. It creaked as she pushed it open. When she stepped into the kitchen, Raelyn's mom, Kathy, stood to greet her.

"Hi, sweetie! Come here and give me a hug." Kathy's gray hair was pulled back in a low ponytail. She wore her usual retirement uniform of baggy sweats and fuzzy slippers.

"Hi, how are you?"

"Fine, just fine, darlin'. I just made water for tea. Would you like some? I've got lemon, pomegranate, and that fancy chai Raelyn likes."

"Thanks. I'd love some pomegranate." Bella opened the cupboard and helped herself to a tall ceramic mug with daisies painted on the rim.

"Oh my God!" Raelyn entered the kitchen, flush with excitement. "You met Nadine Bayani!" She was still dressed for her job as a bank teller in navy dress pants and a crisp blouse, but she had washed off her makeup.

"You did?" Kathy asked. "Where? I thought she was still in prison."

Bella reached for the teakettle. "Nope. She served her sentence. She applied to work at the store, and Grady actually hired her."

"Wow I can't believe it. Isn't he a Republican? I mean, I'm just assuming because it's Cheriville."

"Yeah, but Grady didn't recognize her. When he introduced her to me, he only said she used to be a lawyer. Like he just learned that today." Bella still couldn't believe it.

"Whoa." Raelyn moved to stand at the counter where Bella was stirring sugar into her tea. "What did you say when he introduced you?"

"I just said it's nice to meet you. Something like that." Bella would never forget Nadine's penetrating eyes.

"Damn. You still haven't told anyone?"

Bella shook her head. "You're the only one I've told."

"Goodness gracious," Kathy said. "Your coworkers are in for a shock."

"I'll say." Raelyn leaned back against the counter. "Wait until they realize they hired someone everyone in America hates. I mean, it's the one thing Republicans and Democrats all agree on: Nadine Bayani is a piece of shit."

Bella frowned. "Yeah. I mean, I guess."

"You guess?" Raelyn raised her eyebrows. "Do you have amnesia? I seem to recall you bawling your eyes out on election night and calling her all sorts of unladylike names."

Right. That was true. "I remember."

"It's *her* fault Rob Gunn is president." Raelyn narrowed her eyes. "Maybe Nadine was trying to help Alyssa at the time—in her twisted, criminal way—but all she did was cause a scandal that threw the presidency to the Republicans. Don't forget that none of these terrible things would be happening if it weren't for Nadine."

"Yeah. I know." Just last night, Bella had watched a gruesome report about the humanitarian crisis at the border, a result of Gunn's anti-immigration policies. Families had been living in makeshift camps for months without adequate food, clean water, or medical care. Anyone with children who crossed the border risked being separated from them. Gunn's election was the darkest day Bella could remember.

"So why didn't you say anything? Your boss never would have hired her if he knew the truth. You could have stopped it."

Bella had asked herself the same question all evening. Like most Democrats, she had spent the past two years hating Nadine. She had never dreamed she would do her a favor, let alone one that allowed her to get a job at Bella's own store.

"I guess I felt sorry for her." Bella stared into her tea, now the color of dark magenta. "I don't know why. She wasn't even nice. She bit my head off when I tried to ask her a question. But there was something about her..." Bella paused, considering how to explain it. "She just looked like she'd been through hell."

"She deserved to go through hell. She still deserves it."

"Maybe." Bella took a sip of the tart, fruity tea. It needed a little more sugar. "But you know, working at Overstock Oasis—it's not exactly heaven."

Bella peered through the glass door as she fumbled with her key in the lock. No sign of Nadine in the front. Maybe she was in the back? Or maybe she'd already quit, a prospect Bella found strangely disappointing.

"Excuse me, are y'all open?" A middle-aged woman with a tight gray bun had appeared beside her, clutching a canvas shopping bag.

"Not until nine, ma'am." Bella continued to fiddle with the lock.

"Oh, but I just want to browse. Can't you let me in early?"

"Sorry, ma'am, it's store policy." *What is wrong with this damn door?* Bella looked down. She was using her apartment key.

The woman stepped closer to Bella, crowding her. "That's ridiculous. I don't see why I can't look around—"

"Come back at nine!" Bella slipped through the doors and quickly locked them behind her, ignoring the woman's scowl. She hurried to the back of the store to punch in for her shift, then froze in the doorway to the break room.

Nadine Bayani, recently released from federal prison, stood at the far wall, reading the OSHA *Job Safety and Health* poster. She wore plain black pants that hung loose on her slim hips. The mandatory purple polo shirt exposed brown arms thick with defined muscles. Bella imagined Nadine doing push-ups in her prison cell, skin gleaming with sweat. She shook her head to banish the image. *Focus.*

Bella padded up behind Nadine, her ballet flats muffling her approach. She cleared her throat. "Hi."

Nadine whirled around and met Bella's eyes. She lifted her chin and squared her broad shoulders. "Hello."

Bella opened her mouth to speak, but Nadine's defiant gaze bored into her brain, scrambling her thoughts.

A pair of voices sounded in the hallway. Ashley sauntered into the break room, followed by Kenny.

"Hey!" Ashley pointed at Nadine. "You're new."

At the sight of Ashley's leopard-print leggings and bright pink lipstick that clashed with both her purple polo and her red hair, the hostility in Nadine's gaze gave way to bafflement. "I... Yes."

Kenny stepped forward and offered his hand. "Good morning, ma'am. I'm Kenny. What's your name?"

Nadine took in his slight build, blond hair, and earnest smile that seemed to fill his cherubic face. After a long pause, she accepted his hand. "Nadine."

Ashley cocked her head. "So what are you?"

Nadine blinked. "I'm sorry?"

"You know, where are you from?" Ashley asked, seemingly unaware that anyone might find the question rude.

"I'm...I'm Filipino."

"Oh wow." Ashley grinned. "We never had one of those."

God, she must think we're all hicks.

Grady appeared in the doorway. "Oh good. Y'all have met our new associate."

Bella guessed from his relaxed demeanor that he still had no idea he had hired the woman at the center of a national scandal. *Damn.* Usually, Bella arrived for work feeling sleepy and finished her shift in an exhausted stupor, numb from endless hours of boredom. Today, she quivered with anxious energy. Whatever happened, this was sure to be the most eventful workday in years.

Grady turned to Nadine. "You can shadow Bella today. She's our third key. She'll show you around and teach you how to use the register. I'm sure you'll be a quick study, you know, given your previous occupation."

He smirked, but Nadine didn't react, and only Bella knew what he was talking about. "All right. It's almost nine o'clock. Kenny, you're on register. Ashley, stockroom. I'll unlock the doors."

Grady, Ashley, and Kenny filed out, leaving Bella with Nadine.

They stared at each other.

"What's a third key?" Nadine asked.

"Oh, that. It means I have a key to the store. I can also act as manager when Grady isn't here, but I'm not the assistant manager—that's Jason. You'll meet him later." Bella winced as she recalled the slew of right-wing bumper stickers plastered all over Jason's pickup truck promoting gun rights, the Confederacy, and every Republican who had graced the state with their candidacy in the past decade. He would recognize Nadine from Fox News, and he'd hate the woman who had made a dirty deal on behalf of a Democrat—even though the scandal had benefited his party in the end.

"Anyway, I started as a store associate like you," Bella said. "But then a few years ago, I got promoted to third key."

"A few years ago? How long have you worked here?"

"Um, about ten years. Since I was twenty."

Nadine looked appalled.

She thinks I'm a loser. Bella felt her cheeks warm. She wanted to explain why she'd stayed at a crappy store with incompetent managers for a decade, but what could she say? *I'm afraid I'm not capable of anything better, and I'm too scared to find out for sure.* Instead she said, "I'm supposed to show you around."

"I heard." Nadine waited expectantly.

Crap. Get it together, Bella. "Okay. Cool. Let's get started."

Nadine followed her out of the break room with a weary sigh.

Bella led Nadine up and down the long, narrow aisles of the store. As she pointed out the different product categories, Bella searched her brain for information she could convey beyond the obvious.

"Oh, towels are the worst," Bella said when they reached the bath aisle. "We have to fold them into neat stacks, and the customers rifle through them and destroy it all in seconds. Sometimes they do it right in front of us."

"I see." But Nadine wasn't even looking at the towels.

Bella pulled on a strand of her hair. "Sorry. This must be the most boring tour ever."

Nadine didn't respond, which Bella took to mean that she agreed. It figured. Nadine was used to legal drama and presidential politics. Compared to her former career, the Overstock Oasis was nothing.

When they'd gone through all eight aisles, Bella looked around for something else to explain. "Oh, the music." She pointed at the ceiling where speakers piped out a bubblegum pop track. "It comes from corporate, and we don't have any control over the playlist. It's the same thirty songs over and over, so it can get really irritating. Just try to tune it out."

"Noted."

"Um, do you have any questions about the layout of the store?"

"No."

"Well, if you can't find something—"

"I'll consult the great big signs hanging from the ceiling." Nadine pointed to the one above them.

"Oh, right. Great."

"Do they really not know who I am?" Nadine asked quietly.

Bella glanced around to make sure no one could overhear. The only visible customer was several yards away, rooting through the gardening tools. "They really don't know. Ashley spends her free time with her loser boyfriend, Tino, and I doubt either of them could name the current president. As for Kenny, he just graduated from his mom's Bible-based homeschooling program. Neither of them is likely to be caught reading the news."

"Well, it won't be long before they find out. I doubt I'll last the day." Defeat clouded her eyes.

Bella couldn't help feeling sorry for Nadine. "Why did you take this job? If you don't mind telling me."

Nadine looked away. "I'm required to work while I'm on supervised release. And even if I weren't, I need the money."

"That's rough." The store barely paid above minimum wage. If Nadine was desperate for income, it meant she had lost everything—her friends, her reputation, and even her savings. "It must not be easy to find work when you're…"

Nadine's mouth quirked as she met Bella's eyes again. "A convicted felon and world-famous pariah?"

"Yeah." What could she even say to that? "Well, the only thing left to show you is the register."

At the front of the store, a line snaked out from Kenny's checkout counter. As soon as Bella approached the second register, the woman who was last in line steered her shopping cart triumphantly to the open counter and began to unload an eclectic array of items.

"I'm training a new employee," Bella said. "This may take some time."

"Oh, that's all right." She tossed her brown hair behind her shoulder. "I just hate waiting in line."

Bella showed Nadine how to operate the barcode scanner as she rang up the woman's purchases. The last item was a large pig-shaped lawn ornament with an upturned snout.

"Hold up." The woman pointed at the pig. "That's supposed to be half off."

An orange 50-percent-off sticker adorned the pig, but that didn't mean much. Customers swapped the stickers all the time. Bella checked the date code on the price tag to confirm. The customer was right—it really was on clearance.

"Oh, I'm very sorry, ma'am." Bella pressed the void key and turned to Nadine. "This happens every so often. The computer is supposed to discount the product automatically, but sometimes there are errors. We can't change the price in the computer, so you have to use a dummy SKU and calculate the correct price yourself."

Bella typed "99999999" for the bar code and then checked the price tag: $37.99. She hesitated, worrying her lower lip while Nadine and the customer watched.

Bella stared at the tag. She had memorized the most common discount prices, but $37.99 was unusual. *Crap.* Nadine was going to think she was an idiot in addition to a loser and a hick.

Her face burning, Bella pulled her phone out of her pocket. She opened the calculator app, multiplied the price by .05, and keyed the result into the register. She avoided eye contact with both women as she wrapped the cursed lawn pig in a large sheet of paper.

She turned back to the register. "Your total is $163.88." She should have taken the opportunity to show Nadine how to process a credit card payment, but she wanted to end the transaction as quickly as possible. She grabbed the card and punched the buttons without a word. A moment later, the terminal spit out the receipt.

After the customer left, she turned to Nadine to offer an explanation, but Nadine was staring at the next customer—a bearded man in a camouflage T-shirt. His eyes were glued to Nadine. *Oh no.*

"Hello?" Bella tried to get his attention. "Did you find everything okay?"

The man dropped a set of barbecue tongs on the counter and pointed a bony finger at Nadine. "What the hell is she doing here?"

Chapter 3

"WHAT DO YOU MEAN I can't just fire her?" Grady's voice boomed through the wall. "She cheated in the goddamn presidential election!"

Nadine waited in the break room, her chin resting on her clasped hands. In the next room, Grady was shouting at someone from the Overstock Oasis corporate office. The call was on speaker, and Nadine could hear every word through the flimsy wall.

"You knew she had a record when you hired her," the woman said. "You'll have to manage her out. Document examples of poor performance. Give her a chance to improve, then document again if she doesn't perform. *Then* you can fire her. If you fire her right away, she could sue."

"Customers will boycott the store," Grady said. "You should have seen the guy who just left. He told everyone else in line who she was, and two people walked out without buying anything."

"Why not keep her in the back? She can work in the stockroom."

"Trust me, she'll be working exclusively in the stockroom. Plus cleaning toilets. And doing every other miserable, dirty, humiliating job I can find until she quits."

"Just remember to document," the woman said brightly. "Every time she's late or insubordinate or screws something up, you write it down."

"Fine." There was a banging sound and then silence.

A moment later, he appeared in the break room. "Corporate says I can't fire you—at least not today. But if you stay, I will make your life miserable. This is your chance to walk out of here before that happens."

Nadine met his gaze. "I won't quit."

"Well, in that case, go sit your ass down in the stockroom. There's a truck coming in half an hour, and you're going to unload it. By yourself." He stomped out, slamming the door behind him.

The stockroom was dusty and dark, the only natural light coming from a small window next to the delivery door. A single lightbulb hung in the center of the room. Unmarked cardboard boxes were stacked on the cement floor in a configuration that appeared both inefficient and structurally unsafe. A few tall stacks threatened to collapse despite a sea of empty space on the cement floor.

Nadine perched on a large unopened box and contemplated her situation. She couldn't afford to quit, not when she was losing her housing in a month. She would have to submit to whatever degrading tasks Grady could devise, do the work without any mistakes, and hope she could find another job before he concocted some bullshit reason to get rid of her.

As she waited, she thought of Bella and her confusion when confronted with a simple math problem. How did a woman reach thirty years old without learning to divide by two? Were the schools in Cheriville that bad?

Bella didn't strike her as someone who lacked intelligence. Plus, she seemed to be the only store employee who followed the news. She wondered if she would be at this miserable job long enough to learn more about her.

Why do I even care?

The delivery door screeched and lurched upward, revealing the back of a massive freight truck. Grady stood next to the truck with his arms crossed over his chest like Mr. Clean, watching as the driver secured a loading ramp to the truck.

When the driver finished, Grady walked up to Nadine and shoved a scanner at her. "You're going to scan the boxes in that truck and carry every last one of them into the stockroom."

He turned to the driver. "Don't help her."

The man pulled a cigarette from his shirt pocket. "Weren't planning on it."

Nadine stepped outside, wincing in the sunlight, and walked over to the base of the ramp. The truck was crammed floor to ceiling with boxes, some marked *heavy* and others marked *fragile*. Unloading the truck by herself would take hours.

Bile rose into her throat. She wanted to tell that asshole where he could shove his scanner and then march straight to her car and drive fast and far away from the hell her life had become. Instead, she just stood there.

Grady shot her a satisfied smirk and then walked back into the store. She was powerless, and he knew it.

"I still don't understand." Ashley's frown cracked the orange foundation on her forehead. "What did she do wrong?"

Bella, Ashley, and Kenny were huddled at one of the registers, discussing the scene that had erupted in front of them. Bella had tried to explain the scandal to her politically unaware coworkers, but their expressions remained blank. While Grady had realized who Nadine was as soon as the customer pointed it out, for Ashley and Kenny, there was no bell to ring.

She tried to think of another way to explain. "Okay. Let's say Overstock Oasis wants the government to pass a new law, like—"

"A law to ban stickups," Ashley said. "You know, *give me all the money, or I'll shoot.*" She made a gun with her fingers.

"Well, that's... Okay, sure. So the company can give money to a candidate who wants to ban armed robbery, but there are limits on how much it can give."

"Why would there be limits?" Kenny asked.

Bella marveled at his innocence. With his lack of civics education or cognizance of current events, he was like a boy in a bubble, pure as virgin snow.

"Because if Overstock Oasis gave a presidential candidate a million dollars and that person got elected, they might end up serving the company instead of the people."

"Oh." He frowned. "I guess that makes sense."

"Anyway, there are limits. But when Alyssa Jackson was running for president, Atlas Health Source—that's the health insurance company—really wanted her to drop her plan to cap insurance premiums. So, Atlas used the names of their subscribers to donate more money to Alyssa Jackson—a *lot* more. And Nadine is the one who bribed them to do it. She told Atlas that when she became White House chief of staff, she'd get the cap dropped from Jackson's healthcare bill."

"So *that's* why everyone hates her?" Ashley twirled her ponytail. "Jesus. It's not like she killed someone."

"Well, it was more than that. People thought Alyssa was involved, and it really hurt her campaign. So when she lost the election, her supporters blamed Nadine." Bella paused. "Honestly, I blame her too. Rob Gunn wouldn't be president if it weren't for what she did."

"Damn." Ashley clicked her tongue. "That chick is famous. How do you know all this, anyway? You watch the news?"

"Yeah, and I get alerts on my phone. I like to know what's going on."

Ashley straightened, her attention drawn to something behind Bella.

Bella turned to see Grady walking up to them with a pissy scowl and his hands balled into fists. She stepped back from the register and looked for something she could pretend to be doing, but Grady didn't seem to notice or care that nobody was working.

"Nadine is unloading the truck," Grady said.

Nadine still has a job? "Um, okay. I didn't realize the truck was here." Bella turned to Kenny. "Do you want to stay on register while I help her unload?" Usually she tried to get out of truck duty, citing cramps or some other ailment, but this time her curiosity outweighed her distaste for manual labor.

"No, you don't understand." Grady held up his hand. "I want you all to stay on the floor."

"Wait," Bella said. "She's unloading the *entire* truck by herself? It's ninety degrees out."

"Hell yes, she's doing it herself—and every truck from now on until she quits or croaks." The sadistic glee in his voice made Bella feel sick.

"But she could get hurt," Bella said. "Or she could get heatstroke and pass out or something."

"Well, tough shit." Grady glanced at Kenny. "Sorry."

Bella had to try again. "I don't mind helping. It would still be hard with two of us."

"No way. None of you are helping that criminal. Kenny, you stay on register. Ashley and Bella, start on the shelves. Garden looks like crap." He turned and stalked off.

Ashley shrugged a shoulder and headed for the garden section.

Bella turned to Kenny. "Are you okay with this?"

Kenny's face was pale. "Well, uh, Grady is the manager, so we have to do what he says."

"I know, but do you think it's right to punish someone at work for what they did in the past if they already served their time? Because that's what this feels like to me."

Kenny squirmed. Finally, he said quietly, "That's not what Jesus would do."

"I agree." Unloading the truck was, at minimum, a two-person job. Bella would never be okay with what Nadine had done, but this was cruel.

Bella wasn't about to risk her job, especially not for Nadine Bayani, but maybe there was something else she could do.

Nadine spent the next two hours hauling box after box into the stockroom. She found a rusty handcart that helped, but some of the boxes were so heavy that even loading the cart strained her back. As she ground through the punishing task, rivers of sweat soaking her clothes, she was thankful she'd stayed in shape while in prison. It was the only reason she had the endurance to finish the job.

After she dumped the last box onto the floor with a graceless thud, Nadine collapsed against the pile. She was covered in dirt and sweat. For several minutes, she lay panting from exertion while her body cooled down.

The doors to the stockroom swung open. Nadine's shoulders tensed as she imagined Grady arriving to mock her exhaustion, but instead Bella appeared.

"Hi." Bella sat on a box next to Nadine. "I heard what happened. Um, I brought you a Coke and something to eat." She reached into her purse and produced a bottle of cola and a glazed doughnut poking out of a paper bag.

Nadine's instinctive reaction was suspicion, but Bella's eyes were kind. She accepted the drink. "Thank you." Her voice cracked from hours of heavy breathing. She twisted off the bottle cap and poured the cold, fizzy drink down her throat.

She drained half the bottle before she paused to breathe. "God, that's sweet. I can't remember the last time I drank soda."

Bella looked down. "Oh, sorry. You probably wanted something healthy. Sugar is my biggest vice, mostly because it's the only vice I can afford on ten bucks an hour. That's why I need to lose twenty pounds."

Nadine scoffed. "Don't be ridiculous." Bella had to know she was beautiful. She had an hourglass figure with a round bottom and large breasts. Her hair caught the light when she moved. Even in her shapeless purple polo, she was stunning.

Bella blushed. "I can't believe Grady made you unload the truck by yourself. Usually we leave one person on register, and everyone else helps out. Even with a team, it's hard work, especially in the heat."

"It's my punishment for being who I am. The first of many until he can concoct some excuse to fire me." Nadine took another swig of soda. "Welcome to my life as the woman everyone loves to hate." She studied Bella. "Why are you being nice to me, anyway? Don't you care about politics?"

"I do." Bella shifted. "I, um, supported Alyssa Jackson. I was upset— devastated, honestly—when the scandal happened. I don't understand what you did, and I probably never will. But that doesn't mean what Grady did is okay. I just felt like I had to do something to make up for it."

"Well, I appreciate that. And if you don't mind, I'll take the doughnut."

Bella broke into a smile. "Of course."

It was soft, fluffy, and coated in gooey glaze. Her empty stomach growled as she swallowed.

Bella stood. "Anyway, I should get back on the floor before Grady catches me in here." Her hair swished as she walked away.

Nadine tried to remember the last time a stranger who wasn't a fellow ex-con or a social worker had treated her like a human being. It had been a long time.

Chapter 4

BELLA CLOSED THE DOOR BEHIND her and dropped her purse at her feet. As she entered the living room, she took off her shirt and flung it onto the couch. She groaned with relief as she unclasped her bra, which followed the shirt, then peeled off her khaki pants and left them in a heap on the floor.

In her bedroom, she pawed through the overflowing laundry basket that was full of clean clothes she hadn't bothered to put away. She pulled on a pair of sweatpants and a wrinkled oversized T-shirt, then settled on the couch with her laptop. It was time to check in with her side hustle.

She had two notifications on GigLife. The first was a review: five stars from a customer who loved her custom portrait. Bella grinned. Some clients wanted realistic portraits, flaws and all, while others preferred a more flattering interpretation. Bella had guessed correctly that this particular client was the latter.

The second notification was a request for a full-body character. The requester had attached a rudimentary sketch of her concept: a woman dressed in a skimpy bra and miniskirt brandishing a sword. Piece of cake. Bella accepted the request, promising to deliver the drawing within a week.

She clicked over to Google, intending to search for images of swords, but when the search bar appeared, she couldn't resist a more compelling subject.

The letter *N* was enough to bring up Nadine's full name, thanks to searches she had done the previous week. She had practically memorized Nadine's Wikipedia page, which detailed her crimes but said little of her life before the scandal. The Personal Life section merely stated Nadine's age (forty) and her place of birth (the Philippines), and noted that she had dated Mark Graves—now a congressman from Connecticut—during law school.

She clicked on an old video of Nadine from cable news in which she responded to allegations that Alyssa Jackson had used her position to secure an internship at the State Department for her teenage daughter.

The interviewer asked, "Are you claiming it's a coincidence that Senator Jackson's daughter was chosen out of thousands of applicants?"

"Absolutely not." Nadine wore a crisp blood-red blouse. Her eyebrows were heavily penciled, and her straight shoulder-length hair gleamed under the studio lights.

He peered over his glasses. "I'm sorry?"

"It's not a coincidence. The senator is an exceptionally dedicated parent who worked hard to instill an appreciation for education and public service in her only child. It's no surprise, at least to me, that Jenna earned the internship on her own."

"But—"

"But what, it's not fair?" Nadine scoffed. "Spare me. It would be unfair to *dis*qualify Jenna because of her mother, and the senator's political opponents know this. Perhaps they are insecure because they are not as attentive to their own children's education."

Bella marveled at Nadine's ability to dominate the conversation. She seemed to know exactly what to say without thinking.

There was no doubt that Nadine was smart—brilliant, even. After all, she had arranged and conducted a secret meeting with the CEO of Atlas without a trace of physical evidence connecting her to the crime. Without Jack Ritter's testimony, she never would have been caught. That took skill.

When it ended, she clicked on another video—highlights from Nadine's testimony before the US House of Representatives.

Nadine faced the panel alone at a table, her hands in her lap, rows of blank faces behind her. She wore her hair in a severe bun, and her flashy clothes and bold makeup had been replaced by a simple black suit and muted lipstick.

Representative Allan Evers, Republican from Texas, leaned forward to speak into his microphone. "When you arranged for these fraudulent contributions, Senator Jackson was in third place after the Iowa caucus, and the campaign was broke. Then out of nowhere, she had enough money to air commercials in New Hampshire and South Carolina. Did you discuss this sudden groundswell of financial support with the senator?"

"Yes, I did." Nadine spoke in monotone, a hint of her Filipino accent shading her speech.

"It's unusual for contributions to increase after a big loss. Did she ask how the campaign had managed to raise so much money?"

Nadine's face remained neutral. "No, she did not."

Evers shuffled his papers. "Let me put it another way. Was the senator surprised that after spending her entire campaign budget on the Iowa caucus, she suddenly had enough money for a major ad-buy in two additional states?"

"I can't speak to that."

Evers frowned. "What do you mean?"

Nadine folded her slender hands on the table and leaned closer to the microphone. "I can't say whether or not the senator was surprised."

"Let me put it another way. Did Senator Jackson express surprise to you?"

"No, she did not."

Bella stretched out on the couch and balanced her laptop on her stomach. Nadine's steady performance under scrutiny was mesmerizing. The Republicans kept prodding her to implicate Alyssa Jackson, but she never gave an inch.

At the time of the scandal, Bella had been furious at Nadine, just like every other Jackson supporter in the country. But now she decided there was something honorable in Nadine's refusal to blame an innocent person to save herself. Or was she clinging to anything that would allow her to see some good in her new coworker?

She kept returning to the image of Nadine slumped against a box, her soaked shirt clinging to her skin. There was something about her that Bella found hard to resist—her strong body, her refusal to quit. Now, watching Nadine hold her own against members of Congress, Bella felt drawn to her even more.

She didn't want to think about what it meant that she was so fixated on someone she was supposed to hate. She only knew she didn't want to stop watching.

When the video ended, almost forty minutes had gone by. It was long past time for dinner. She snapped her laptop shut and started toward the kitchen. Then she backtracked and grabbed the laptop.

She could always watch more while she ate.

When Bella arrived at work the next morning, Jason's hideous pickup truck was parked right in front. Her pulse accelerated as she walked to the doors. *This won't be pretty.*

Sure enough, she entered the store to find Jason pacing in front of the registers, ranting at Nadine.

"You know, liberals always try to say Republicans are corrupt, but really it's the Democrats who are crooks. Y'all like to go on television and act morally superior—calling the rest of us racist—when you're the ones cheating."

Nadine endured the scolding with total composure, hands clasped behind her back.

Meanwhile, Ashley watched from her perch on one of the checkout counters, swinging her feet as she gawked.

As Bella slipped past them to clock in, she flashed a sympathetic grimace at Nadine. She swiped her badge, stashed her purse in a cubby, and hurried back to the front of the store. If something happened, she didn't want to miss it.

Jason continued his tirade. "I'd like to know how you got only two years in prison. It seems awfully light for fraud and bribery. Actually, I already know. Alyssa Jackson probably paid off the judge—and the prosecutors too. I bet she's dirtier than you."

"Hey, Jason." Ashley pointed at the doors. "I think it's time to open the store."

Two women were peering through the windows and rattling the locked doors.

"It's after nine," one of the women shouted through the glass, tapping her watch for emphasis.

"Welcome to Overstock Oasis," he grumbled.

They waited in silence as the customers perused the endcap displays. Jason scowled at the floor while Ashley scrolled through her phone. Nadine didn't move. At last, the women disappeared down one of the aisles.

"Y'all need to get to work," Jason said. "Ashley, you're on register. Bella, markdowns. As for you, Nadine, you're mopping up the spill in aisle one."

What spill in aisle one?

Bella was about to ask when Jason picked up his coffee cup and poured its contents onto the floor, locking eyes with Nadine as the puddle expanded.

Oh shit. This could be the end. If Nadine refused, Jason would fire her for insubordination.

Bella didn't want her to go—not yet. She was curious about Nadine despite her feelings about the scandal, and she wanted to learn more about her. Besides, this was the most interesting thing to happen at Overstock Oasis in at least ten years.

More importantly, it just wasn't right to bully someone at work. Grady and Jason were managers, and they shouldn't be allowed to mistreat any employee, no matter what she had done in the past.

Nadine's gaze was hard as she turned and walked toward the back of the store. No one moved until she returned with the mop and bucket.

Bella exhaled. She nodded at Nadine, attempting to communicate support with her eyes.

Jason stepped in front of Bella, glaring. "I said you're on markdowns."

"I know. I'm going." Bella headed to the stockroom to grab the stickers. She started in lawn and garden and worked her way around the store.

When she reached the bath section, Nadine was sitting on the floor, surrounded by piles of towels. Half of the shelves were completely empty, their contents strewn cattywampus throughout the aisle. Nadine folded a single towel in her lap.

"What the hell happened?" Bella asked.

"You did mention the towel section could be trying," Nadine said, her expression deadpan. "You weren't exaggerating."

"But how... Oh. It was Jason, wasn't it? He dumped everything on the floor and told you to clean it up."

Nadine nodded. "Something along those lines."

Bella sat a few feet away and folded a towel. "I don't know why he bothers. There are plenty of demoralizing chores in this job. He could at least make you do something that helps the store." She placed the towel on the shelf and reached for another one.

"I don't think you're supposed to be helping me," Nadine said softly. "Not that I don't appreciate it."

"I'm not helping you. I'm working on markdowns like I was told." Bella held up a sheet of stickers. "Normally, I'd apply these stickers to towels in the clearance section, but as you can see"—she gestured at the mess around them—"there really isn't one anymore. So I need to search through these piles anyway, and it's best to put them on the shelves so I know which ones I've checked."

"I see. Well then, carry on."

They worked in silence. Bella searched her brain for appropriate small talk. "Do you live around here?"

Nadine shook her head. "I'm staying in Richmond in transitional housing. It's called Renn House."

"What's that?"

"Temporary housing for prisoners rejoining society." Nadine's words were blunt, but her tone was subdued.

"That's cool." Bella cringed. *That's cool? She must think I'm so stupid.* She searched for something else to say. "Is that like a halfway house?"

"Something like that." Nadine picked up another towel. "But it's not run by the state. It's a private foundation. They offer counseling, employment resources, things like that."

Bella tried to imagine Nadine living with other ex-offenders. "Um, do you like it there?"

"It's better than prison."

Bella wanted to ask what prison was like. Everything she knew came from *Orange is the New Black*, but the reality was probably nothing like the quirky show. And judging from her stiff posture, Nadine didn't want to talk about it.

Instead, Bella held up an army-green towel with yellow flowers stitched in a chaotic swirling pattern. "Yuck. Look at this one. No wonder it hasn't sold."

Nadine's mouth quirked.

Pleased that she'd almost earned a smile, Bella placed the folded towel on the shelf and then reached for a bright orange one with gold zigzags on the border. "If someone tries to buy this, we should call 9-1-1."

This time, Nadine's smile was unmistakable, but then she turned serious. She tightened her lips and shook her head.

"What?" Bella asked. "What's wrong?"

"It's not right." Nadine held up a baby-pink towel covered in purple roses and silver sparkles. "They sent me to prison, yet whoever made this monstrosity walks free."

Bella threw back her head and laughed.

Chapter 5

NADINE WAS ON HER KNEES, restocking toilet bowl brushes, when a bright white light surrounded her. "What the...?"

She whirled around. A news crew barreled down the aisle, led by a blonde in a hot-pink pantsuit and chunky heels. Right behind her, a bearded man in a black T-shirt and Bermuda shorts aimed a bulky video camera at Nadine.

Nadine's whole body clenched. She curled her fingers into fists and crouched lower as if she could somehow disappear through the floor.

They were in her face within seconds. The woman held out a microphone. "Nadine Bayani, do you work here? Can you tell me about your job?" Her mauve lipliner was two shades darker than her lips, and her fake eyelashes opened and closed like claws.

Nadine jumped up and strode toward the stockroom. Her heart pounded, but she kept her pace steady.

"Nadine!" The woman's heels clicked in a rapid sequence as she followed. "Nadine, we want your side of the story."

The double doors swung shut behind her. She stepped away from the window, hugging her abdomen as though bracing for impact. When no one followed, she let out a shaky breath.

After a moment, she peeked through the window. Grady was blocking the path to the stockroom while gesticulating wildly at the camera.

She sat on a box and tried to steady her breathing. *Three days.* It took them all of three days.

Now she would be on the national news—again. *Former lawyer Nadine Bayani now works for minimum wage.* She imagined people celebrating, laughing at her, turning the image into memes on social media.

After several minutes, Nadine checked the window again. No sign of the crew. Grady must have gotten rid of them, but it was too late: they already had their shot. Why did she have to be restocking toilet bowl brushes, of all things?

Nadine stayed in the stockroom, opening boxes and organizing merchandise. Thankfully, Grady left her alone, taking a break from his mission to humiliate her at every opportunity. Or maybe he just didn't want negative publicity for the store.

Hours later, her stomach growling, she ventured out to retrieve the stale cookies she had stashed in the break room. The store was quiet. She grabbed them and cautiously made her way to the front.

Bella slouched at one of the registers, staring at her phone. She looked up. "Oh, hey. Don't worry—you're safe. Grady left twenty minutes ago, and I haven't seen a reporter for a couple of hours."

Nadine exhaled. "Grady's gone for the night?"

"Yep, it's just you, me, and Ashley. I'm closing. You're closing with me, right?"

Right. For the first time, she was assigned to stay for closing, a duty they rotated among the employees. One manager or third key and one associate closed each night. Nadine was grateful to be paired with Bella instead of Grady or Jason. "Yes, I am."

Nadine was about to return to the stockroom when Ashley bounded up the aisle, waving her phone.

"We're famous!" Ashley set her phone on the checkout counter. "Y'all have to see this." She tapped the play button on the screen.

The video clip was from a local Richmond station. The anchor reported that Nadine had been sighted at a suburban Overstock Oasis. He spoke over wobbly footage of Nadine retreating to the stockroom, then announced that a correspondent was "reporting live from the scene."

The woman who had accosted Nadine stood in front of the store, her blonde hair blowing in the wind. "Nadine Bayani was once a powerful attorney who seemed destined to be the next White House chief of staff. Now, after two years in prison, she works at an Overstock Oasis in Cheriville, Virginia."

They showed the correspondent's interview with Grady, who turned red when the reporter demanded to know why he had hired her. "We can't discriminate against felons. Well, we can, but not after we've hired them. Look, I doubt she'll be here long."

Next was an interview with a customer, who declared in a nasal voice that she would boycott the store until Nadine was fired. The studio anchor closed the segment by speculating that this must be "an embarrassing day" for Nadine.

When the video finished, Bella and Ashley turned to stare at Nadine.

"Well, that's some shit right there." Ashley popped her bubble gum. "People really hate you, huh?"

"Thank you, Ashley," Bella said. "You can return to…whatever you were doing."

As Ashley walked away, Bella turned to Nadine. "Honestly, that clip was really offensive. If it's embarrassing for *you* to work here, what does that say about the rest of us? I mean, this is my life. Not everyone goes to college and gets a fancy lawyer job." She let out a huffy breath. "Someone should write a letter to the network."

"It's true. No one should insult honest work." Nadine hadn't missed the bitterness in Bella's voice when she'd said *college*. She asked carefully, "Did you ever think about going to college?"

"I went for a year." Bella looked away. "But it didn't work out."

Nadine wanted to ask why, but a customer wheeled up with an overflowing shopping cart.

Appearing relieved at the interruption, Bella shot Nadine an apologetic look and turned her attention to the customer. "Hi there."

What happened to you? Nadine wondered. *I know why I'm stuck here, but why are you?*

Nadine deposited another broken-down box onto an already enormous stack, causing the ones on top to spill onto the floor. She had been avoiding going to the dumpster all day, not wanting to risk contact with any reporters who happened to be lurking.

As she reached for the box cutter, she heard Bella's announcement crackling over the speakers. "Attention, Overstock Oasis shoppers. The store is now closed. Please bring your items to the front for checkout."

Nadine made her way to the front of the store where Bella was assisting one last customer. He didn't look like the political type, but Nadine hung back in the aisle until he left the store.

"Hi." Nadine stepped into view.

"Oh, hey." Bella locked the glass doors with a sigh. "Long-ass day, huh? It must have felt even longer to you with those reporters stalking you. I wish we could ban them from the store. I asked Grady, but he said no."

She did that for me? Nadine wasn't used to having someone look out for her. "That's kind of you, but they would just wait for me in the parking lot. There's nowhere to hide. Not after my face was all over the news for weeks."

"Well, I'm sorry you have to deal with it." Bella slid the cash drawer out of her register. "Have you closed before?"

"No, this will be a new experience."

"Okay. It's not too bad. I count all the money in my register to make sure I'm not short. Then we both count the cash from the safe. We have to count it separately and sign the bag."

Bella used her key to open the safe and placed two thick stacks of cash onto the counter. "Could you start with this? Just write the amount somewhere. Here, you can use this sticky note."

"Sure." Nadine quickly counted the cash and jotted down the total. When she looked up, Bella was still counting the coins. She whispered to herself and made notes on receipt tape. She seemed flustered, even a little angry.

Bella finished counting and looked at Nadine. "I'm over. Two dollars and ten cents."

"Well, that happens. It's better than being under, right?"

"I guess. But I'm still an idiot who can't count." Bella smacked two dollar bills and a dime onto the counter.

"Bella, look at me," she said, more sternly than she'd intended. "Why are you being so hard on yourself?"

Bella looked at her with turmoil in her eyes. "I suck at math. That's why I have to use a calculator. I can't add, subtract, multiply, any of it."

Nadine opened her mouth to speak, then closed it, fearing the wrong response would end the conversation.

"I mean, it's not like I'm completely stupid." She tugged at her hair. "I'm just not good with numbers."

"Well, it's not too late to learn. You can take online classes for free. I could get you the information." Jenna, Nadine's suitemate, used the Renn House computers to work on her GED.

"Yeah, maybe. Anyway, I need to count yours." She counted silently, then checked the total Nadine had written down. "They match." She signed her name on the bag, then passed it to Nadine.

Nadine scribbled an illegible signature, figuring it might prevent the bag from popping up on eBay. "So that's it?"

"Almost." Bella sealed the bag of cash. "You still need to follow me to the bank."

"Follow you?"

"Yeah, in your car. You have to drive behind me and then watch while I deposit the cash." Bella slung her purse over her shoulder. "That way there's a witness, you know, in case something happens to the money."

It had never occurred to Nadine that such a precaution was necessary. This was one of many aspects of retail operations that had been previously invisible to her. "Someone does this every night?"

"I know it seems silly, but it's important. We once had an assistant manager tell Ashley, 'Oh, you look tired. Why don't you just go home?' And of course, she jumped at the chance to leave early. The manager stole every cent and blamed it on the bank."

"Really?"

"Yeah. He got fired, and Ashley got written up. There are a lot of dishonest people in retail. You have to be careful who you trust."

Nadine laughed. She couldn't help it.

"What?" Bella furrowed her brow.

Nadine clutched her side, unable to contain herself.

"Oh, right." Bella smiled. "I guess you've seen worse in politics."

"You have no idea." Nadine regained her composure. "Well, then. Should we get going? I don't know about you, but I'm ready to get out of here."

Nadine tensed as they walked toward the door. She didn't see anyone through the glass, but reporters could be waiting out of sight, ready to pounce with microphones drawn.

The moment they stepped outside, there was a blinding flash, then another. Nadine slid her sunglasses over her eyes. A lone photographer was snapping photos from a few yards away.

Bella raised her middle finger directly between his camera and Nadine's face, blocking his next shot. "You're about five hours late for a world exclusive. So, not only do you have a scumbag job, you suck at it." She whispered to Nadine, "Don't let him get to you."

Nadine walked quickly to her car, staring straight ahead. As she slid into the driver's seat, she realized she *was* okay. Her breathing was steady, and her hands were still. She wasn't nearly as shaken as she had been when the TV reporter found her earlier in the day. The difference was Bella. For once, someone had stood beside Nadine and defended her.

As she drove behind Bella to the bank, warmth trickled through her belly. She recognized the feeling—trouble.

Surely it was no more than a natural reaction to the situation. Bella was the only person in this strange new workplace who made an effort to be kind. And she was undeniably gorgeous. But she was almost certainly straight, given her penchant for heavy eye makeup, pink lip gloss, and sparkly nail polish. Gay women didn't care about that girly stuff, right?

Not that it mattered. Nadine's life as a world-famous felon meant that, once again, a meaningful relationship was off the table. The reasons were different, but the reality was the same.

Chapter 6

BELLA SPOTTED HIM RIGHT AWAY—A slim white guy wearing a T-shirt with a Confederate flag. She watched as he canvassed the aisles, barely glancing at the merchandise. He wasn't there to shop. He was there to start shit.

Ever since the news had broken about Nadine's new job, the store had been plagued by gawkers hoping to catch a glimpse of her. They were bad enough. But employees also had to contend with a handful of people who came looking for a confrontation.

Luckily, Nadine was in the stockroom, where she worked most days.

Bella hoped she could get rid of the guy before he even saw Nadine. "Hi there. Can I help you find something?" She used her chipper salesgirl voice.

"No." He flinched and moved away.

Bella got right back in his face. "Let me tell you about our specials today. Hand towels are 30 percent off. And decorative flowerpots are on sale too—buy one, get one free." That was all bullshit, but she knew he wouldn't check.

"Okay." He tried to walk away, but Bella kept pace beside him.

"Do you like scented candles? We've got some new fall and winter scents: pumpkin spice, gingerbread, and peppermint. They smell delicious—"

"I'm just looking." His eyes were pale and angry.

"Oh, you're not a candle guy. That's cool. But I hope you check out the flowerpots because…uh."

Bella saw Nadine walking toward them, pushing a shopping cart full of merchandise. *Crap.*

The guy followed Bella's gaze. Then, he broke into a wide, wicked smirk. "Hey, Nadine!" He strode toward her. "Are you enjoying minimum wage?"

Nadine froze in place.

Bella scrambled after him. "Hey! Leave her alone."

"How was prison, Nadine?" He was almost directly in front of her now, his posture menacing. "Were you someone's bitch?"

Bella beamed silent messages at Nadine. *Walk away. Go back to the stockroom.*

Nadine either didn't get the message or didn't care. She remained silent, her posture indicating she had no intention of retreating.

"Sir, you need to leave." Bella caught up with him and reached for his arm, breaking his stride. "We don't tolerate abuse of our employees."

He shook her off. "Back off. This is between me and her."

Customers were gathering, but no one moved to intervene.

Bella's heart pounded. This asshole was not going to hurt Nadine. Not on her watch. She pushed in front of him. "I am the third key. This woman is *my* employee, and if you want to mess with her, you're going to have to go through me."

"Bella, don't," Nadine said softly.

"What the hell is going on?" Jason rounded the corner, trailed by Kenny.

Bella pointed. "He's threatening an employee."

Jason rolled his eyes. "Just go to the back. Both of you."

"You're scum," the guy spat at Nadine. "You should be deported."

"I agree with you, man," Jason said, "but this ain't the time."

Bella glared at them, then turned to Nadine. Her eyes were fierce and unrepentant. She still hadn't moved.

"Come on." Bella tugged on Nadine's arm.

Finally, Nadine turned and followed her to the stockroom. The metal doors swung shut behind them.

"Fuck." Bella sank onto a box. "Are you okay?"

"I'm fine." Nadine sat across from her, rubbing her arms as if she were cold. "You didn't have to do that."

"Of course I did. He can't just come in here and harass people."

"He came to harass *me*. I don't want you to get hurt trying to defend me. You don't deserve it."

Bella heard the unspoken words. *Like I do.*

"We don't allow harassment at the store," Bella said firmly. "I won't stand for it."

Nadine looked at her curiously. "You know, when you told him you were the third key, you said it like you were the president of the United States." A smile played on her lips. "Surely you know nobody knows what that means?"

Bella grinned. "Well, I thought if I sounded confident enough, he would think it meant something badass."

Nadine shook her head. "You're really something."

Bella wasn't sure what Nadine meant by that, but at least they were both calming down. "I wonder how long we should stay in here. I'm getting hungry."

"I have granola bars." Nadine pointed to a canvas satchel on top of another box. "They taste like cardboard, but you're welcome to have one."

Bella wrinkled her nose. "Thanks, but I'm going to need something more appetizing after what just happened. You should get something good too."

Nadine rubbed a spot on the floor with her shoe. "I don't like to go out for lunch. Especially not since the media found me. I get recognized even more now that people know where I work, and it's easier to stay back here."

"Oh gosh, I didn't think of that." Bella tried to imagine spending the entire day in the stockroom, knowing that if she showed her face, it could trigger someone's aggression. "Hey, what if we went together? There's a deli at the end of the plaza, and the booths are pretty private. I could even order for both of us."

The words spilled out before she thought better of them. *What am I doing?*

A few weeks ago, Bella would never have invited Nadine Bayani to lunch. Standing up against workplace bullying was one thing, but lunch implied actual friendship. How could she be friends with the woman who had plunged her country into a four-year nightmare?

Nadine appeared caught off guard. "Oh. Hmm."

"No pressure," Bella said quickly. "It was just an idea. You don't have to come."

"It's just that I...hmm." Something flickered in her eyes, a mix of vulnerability and longing that broke Bella's heart.

She wants to say yes. The realization filled Bella with shame. Who was she to think she was too good to be friends with Nadine? She had no right to judge someone who had served her time, someone who had never been anything but nice to her—well, except for the day they met, but now Bella understood Nadine's distrust of strangers.

"Come on. It'll be okay," Bella said. "I bet you won't be recognized if you're with someone. And if anyone tries to mess with you, well, I'll…"

Nadine raised an eyebrow. "You'll drop your credentials?"

"Damn right."

"Okay." Nadine's lips curved into a tentative smile. "Let's wait a bit longer, though, to be sure our friend is gone."

"Sounds good. We can go in ten minutes or so." Bella knew she had made the right decision. If nothing else, the gesture would cancel out some of the harassment Nadine received at work every day.

Besides, coworkers went to lunch together all the time. It didn't mean that Bella condoned Nadine's past actions. *It's just lunch.*

So why did she feel so nervous?

When Bella and Nadine entered the break room, Jason was sitting at the table, gnawing on a chicken wing.

"Hi, Jason. We're taking lunch." Bella strove for a casual tone as she walked past him to clock out, Nadine right behind her.

"Both of you?" Jason narrowed his eyes. "You're going together?"

For a split second, Bella considered pretending it was a coincidence, but she didn't want Nadine to think she was embarrassed to associate with her. After all, lunch had been her idea. "Yes, we're going to the deli." She swiped her ID on the time clock, then stood back so Nadine could do the same.

"Huh." Jason stroked his stubbly chin. "I'm surprised you're associating with a convicted felon."

Bella pretended she hadn't heard him. "Back in thirty." After Nadine clocked out, they walked past him without a word and made their way to the exit.

Outside, Nadine slipped on her oversized sunglasses, the ones she had worn the day she interviewed. They crossed the parking lot, Bella keeping close to ensure anyone watching saw them as a pair. That way, anyone who recognized Nadine would think twice before engaging. *She's not alone today.*

They arrived at the deli without incident and snagged a booth in the back corner.

"I'll order," Bella said. "Just tell me what you want."

"I appreciate that."

Nadine studied the menu, then pointed to the plain turkey sandwich, the cheapest item on the menu. As she walked up to the counter, it occurred to Bella that Nadine hadn't received a paycheck yet. Maybe she ate granola bars for lunch because it was all she could afford.

Bella ordered the sandwiches, along with chips, fruit cups, and sodas. She piled everything on a tray and returned to the table.

Nadine's eyes widened. "Did the sandwich come with all that?"

"No, but don't worry about it." Bella split the items between them. "Lunch is my treat."

Nadine shifted. "You didn't have to do that. I brought money."

"I know, but I'm the one who invited you to come. Besides, I've got a little side hustle going, and business has been good lately."

"Side hustle?" Nadine raised an eyebrow.

"Yeah, I draw. Portraits, characters, stuff like that. People send me requests, and I get paid commissions."

"Interesting." Nadine unwrapped her sandwich. "You must be a good artist."

"I'm okay. And it's not much, but anything helps. I'm trying to save money to go back to school." Bella raised her sandwich to take a bite but then paused. "Not that I'm anywhere close to having enough."

Nadine tilted her head. "I imagine you'd qualify for aid, considering the pittance they pay us."

Bella had flunked out and didn't qualify for financial aid anymore, but she didn't want to explain that to Nadine, a graduate of Yale and Northwestern. "Aid doesn't cover everything."

They ate in silence for a few minutes. Bella searched her mind for something to talk about but came up empty. If she were out with Raelyn, she'd ask her about work, dating, and television shows, but she already knew Nadine's work life was a disaster, and Nadine didn't seem to have a personal life.

Just as Bella opened her mouth to say something, Nadine slid her sunglasses over her eyes. Bella turned to see a customer walking toward them. He passed their table and continued to the restroom, never glancing in their direction.

Bella pierced a piece of pineapple with her fork. "It really sucks that you have to live like this. Do you think it will ever get better?"

"No." Nadine looked down at her food. "There's something about me... It's hard to explain, but it's more than what I did. People want to see me suffer. It's not enough that I went to prison. They want me to pay and pay and pay."

Bella thought about the man who had accosted Nadine in the store. White, male, brimming with rage. "Maybe it's because you're a woman. Plus an immigrant and a minority. That could be part of it."

"I suppose." Nadine resealed her fruit cup and folded the bag of chips, apparently ready to go.

"I'm sorry." Bella didn't know what else to say.

"Don't be." Nadine balled up her sandwich wrapper. "I deserve it, right?"

There was that word again. Bella didn't understand or approve of what Nadine had done, but the bullying Nadine endured at work wasn't helping anyone. It certainly wasn't justice.

They tossed their trash and returned to the store. Ashley stood near the only open register, absorbed in her phone. She looked up and waved hello before returning her attention to the screen. If she had an opinion about Bella and Nadine taking lunch together, it didn't show. The break room was empty when they clocked back in.

"Well, see you later." Bella turned toward the main floor.

"Wait." Nadine stopped her. "I just... Thank you for lunch. For the sandwich and for going with me. I appreciate it."

"Of course. It was fun."

Nadine nodded and returned to the stockroom.

Inviting Nadine to lunch had been the right thing to do. Despite her past, Nadine was a person with feelings—a person Bella was surprised to find she actually liked. And the more she got to know her, the more Bella realized the countless ways Nadine continued to suffer the consequences of her crimes.

There was no harm in being kind to her. In fact, it was good to have compassion for ex-offenders. Bella hadn't been to church in years, but she recalled that Jesus had advocated something along those lines.

Chapter 7

NADINE WOKE UP GROGGY AND stressed. It was her day off, but she had to deal with something almost as bad as work—looking for housing. She was over two months into her three-month stay at Renn House, so she couldn't afford to waste a day.

Nadine dragged herself out of bed, catching a glimpse of her face in the small mirror on the otherwise bare wall. Her eyes were puffy, and her hair lay flat on one side. Her T-shirt and boxers were a far cry from the pricey pajamas she'd worn in a previous life, but they were infinitely better than what she had worn as a prisoner.

Downstairs, she had the kitchen and living room to herself. Jenna slept late, and Jodie was gone. The new suitemate, Kendra, was a skittish young woman who spent most of the day in her bedroom.

Nadine brewed grocery-store-brand coffee in a single-cup brewer, then sat with her mug at the shared desktop computer to check her email. Since starting work at Overstock Oasis, she had applied for every apartment and room offered for under five hundred dollars—and there weren't many. Her email contained the depressing results: a few rejections. Otherwise, silence.

Maybe she should start applying under a false name. If she could visit in person, she might make a good impression before they realized who she was. But if the reactions of managers and customers at the store were any indication, that would probably end in disaster too.

Nadine swiveled around at the sound of creaking floorboards. Jenna was making her way down the stairs in yoga pants and a sweatshirt. Her blonde hair was tied up in a loose bun.

Jenna nodded sleepily. "Hey."

"Good morning. You're up early."

"Yeah. I have a job interview." Jenna couldn't hide her shy smile.

"That's great. Where?"

"At a hotel. You know, cleaning the rooms, changing the sheets, stuff like that. My caseworker set it up. And they already know I'm a felon, so I might have a real chance."

"Sounds promising." Nadine hoped the job worked out; Jenna was a good person who had been working hard to turn her life around. She deserved a break.

Jenna reached for a coffee mug and powered up the single-cup brewer. "What are you working on?"

Nadine glanced back at the screen. "Just sifting through rejections from landlords."

"Oh, that sucks. Even studio apartments are so expensive these days. I'm probably going to have to move in with my ex." Jenna mimed a gag.

"Your ex-boyfriend?" Nadine sipped her coffee. "Are you on good terms with him?"

"I guess." Jenna shrugged. "But I know he's going to want me to fuck him as long as I'm staying there. And if he gets a new girlfriend, I'm out on my ass."

Nadine clenched her jaw. She wanted to say, *No! Don't go there. You deserve better.* But it wasn't as if she could offer an alternative. She couldn't even find housing for herself. "Talk to your probation officer. They're supposed to help with housing. Maybe if you—I'm not saying to lie, but if you imply the situation would make you more likely to end up homeless or even to reoffend, they might be more willing to help. Your ex isn't a convicted felon, is he?"

"Nah. I'm the only one who got caught." Jenna retrieved her mug from the brewer and added powdered creamer.

Wonderful. "Well, maybe you'll get this job, and maybe it will pay enough for your own apartment. You never know."

"Thanks. I hope things work out for you too." Jenna touched Nadine's shoulder, then walked back upstairs with her coffee.

That was the nice thing about talking to other felons. Most of them didn't feel entitled to judge others, something she had learned to appreciate.

Nadine was powering through a set of push-ups in her bedroom when her phone buzzed. Panting, she sat back on her heels and checked the screen. It was her sister calling on Skype.

She sat on the bed and accepted the call. Patricia's round, suntanned face filled the screen. "Hello?"

"Good morning." It was evening in the US, but the Philippines was twelve hours ahead.

"*Ate*, are you okay?"

"I'm fine," Nadine answered reflexively. "The same."

Patricia's hoop earrings wobbled as she shook her head. "I know that's not true. I saw you on television. It made the news over here, ate, those shameful reporters following you to your job." Her sister spoke in rapid Filipino peppered with English, the language they had shared growing up.

"Yes, that was… unpleasant." While Nadine understood her sister perfectly, her Filipino speaking skills were rusty after two years in prison. She had to strain to remember some words.

"The store can't keep them away?"

"No." Nadine sighed. "This is just my life now."

"Unless you tell the truth," Patricia said quietly.

"Must we do this again?" In prison, all communications had been monitored, and she hadn't allowed Patricia to talk about what really happened. Now that she was out, Patricia had picked up where she left off two years ago.

"I don't understand. You took the blame for Alyssa because you didn't want Rob Gunn to be president. Personally, I think she's just as evil—"

"She's not."

Patricia scoffed. "Oh God. Don't tell me you still have feelings for her."

"I don't. I really don't. But Alyssa Jackson as president would have been the lesser evil." Nadine still believed this to be true. Sure, Alyssa would have watered down her supposed policy agenda with loopholes and corporate giveaways. But at least she wouldn't have cut benefits for children living in poverty. She wouldn't have rounded up immigrants for deportation. She wouldn't have been openly racist—and she certainly wouldn't have packed the courts with forty-year-old fascists.

"Fine." Patricia waved her hand. "Alyssa would have been better than Rob Gunn. But it didn't work. Gunn is the president, so what's the point of protecting Alyssa?"

"I'm not protecting Alyssa. I'm being realistic about my own situation."

"Realistic? What do you mean?"

Nadine rubbed her temple. Patricia didn't seem to realize what she was asking her to do. "I already confessed. I said in court that I did it, and I said it again under oath before Congress on national television. The whole world thinks I'm guilty. If I tried to walk it back... First of all, no one would believe me. They'd call me a liar in addition to a criminal. And then it would all start again. The media shitstorm, the death threats. Instead of one reporter chasing me, there'd be a hundred."

She flashed back to the days before prison. Reporters had swarmed around her, pushing microphones at her no matter where she was. Cameras flashed in her face like strobe lights in a nightclub from hell. Sometimes she thought she saw guns instead of cameras. So many people had wanted her dead, she had drained her retirement savings to pay for private security.

If she recanted now and accused Alyssa—still a powerful senator and party leader—it would start all over again. And for what? Her prison sentence was finished. There was nothing to gain. "Look, it's over. I made my choice, and I served the time."

"But it's not over. You lost everything. You were a lawyer, and now you work at a cash register."

"I know where I work." Grady had actually banned her from the register after learning who she was, but Patricia didn't need to know that.

"How is your job, anyway? Aside from the bad press?"

"It's..." Nadine paused. She wanted to say *It's hell*, but she didn't want Patricia to seize the opportunity to return to the previous subject. "It's fine. I mostly work in the back, away from customers. It's not glamorous, but it's a job."

"Are your coworkers nice? Or are they jerks too?"

Jason's snarling face popped into her head. "The managers give me a hard time, but the others are okay. One of them took me to lunch last week."

"Oh, that's good. So you've made a friend?"

Had she? Going to lunch together didn't mean they were friends. But Bella had jumped in front of the man who was harassing her. *You're going to have to go through me.* Bella had no reason to put herself on the line for Nadine, and yet she had without hesitation. "I suppose I have."

"Well, good. You deserve to have friends—real friends, not like those hypocrites you used to work with."

A voice off camera said, "Nanay!"

Patricia looked down. "Come here, sweetie." She lifted her son onto her lap. "Say hi to Auntie Nadine."

Little Miko waved at the screen, then leaned forward to touch it.

Patricia moved her phone out of reach.

"Hi, sweetie." Nadine waved back. "You're getting so big!" At eighteen months, he still had chubby cheeks, but with his new grown-up haircut, he was starting to resemble a little boy. "He's the perfect mix of you and Brian."

Miko shoved his hand into his mouth.

Patricia kissed the top of his head. "He's teething again."

"Poor little guy. Hang in there, buddy. Auntie Nadine loves you." Her voice caught in her throat. "I wish I could give you big hugs and kisses."

She felt the loss of her former life most intensely when she saw her nephew. She couldn't travel outside the United States without permission from the judge, not that she could afford a plane ticket anyway. It killed her that her first and only nephew knew her only as a face on a screen.

"I wish you could meet him." Patricia squeezed her son's belly. "I wish you weren't so far away."

"I'll meet him one day. I promise." Nadine's voice cracked. "I'll save the money somehow."

Miko reached for the screen again, fussing when Patricia moved it away from him. "I'd better go. But I'm glad you're okay. I'm glad you found a job and made a friend."

"Thanks, Patricia. Me too. Keep sending me pictures of Miko."

"I will. Every day. I love you, ate."

"I love you too." She ended the call before her sister could see her cry.

Chapter 8

THE AUTOMATIC DOORS WHOOSHED OPEN, welcoming Nadine to another crappy day at work. *Eight hours to go.*

"You're late." Jason leaned against the checkout counter, arms crossed over his chest. Kenny stood behind him at the register, openly staring.

"Excuse me?" Nadine checked the time on her phone. "I'm fifteen minutes early." She knew Jason and Grady were looking for any excuse to document poor performance, so she arrived early every day.

"You were scheduled to start at ten, not eleven. You're late."

"I was scheduled for eleven." Nadine struggled to keep her voice even.

"Nope. I checked the schedule this morning. It says your shift began at ten o'clock, plain as day. I'm gonna have to write you up for this. And next time it happens"—Jason jerked his thumb toward the doors—"you're outta here."

That was their plan? Lie about the schedule and then fire her? "I checked before I left last night, and I'm sure it said eleven. Shall I bring you the schedule so you can see?"

"So you can doctor it?" Jason scoffed. "No way. I'll show you." He turned and walked toward the back of the store.

Nadine followed, her mood sinking with each step. She hated working there, but she couldn't afford a gap in employment. Her first paycheck after all the deductions for taxes and health insurance had been barely over two hundred dollars.

Bella sat at the table in the break room, eating strawberry yogurt. She waved her spoon at Jason. "I'm still on my break. I have five minutes left."

Jason ignored her and walked up to the printed schedule on the wall. "See?" He jabbed a finger at the grid. "Nadine, ten o'clock."

"That's not what it said yesterday. Someone changed it."

Jason's smirk told her everything she needed to know. "Nope. It says ten right here. I'm writing you up."

"Excuse me." Bella held up her phone. "I take a photo of the schedule every week so I don't forget when I'm supposed to come in. Otherwise, I'm always doubting what I wrote down, no matter how many times I checked. Anyway, here's the photo from yesterday."

Jason snatched the phone from her, while Nadine craned her neck to see. The photo showed the schedule for the week with yesterday's date at the top. Sure enough, the box next to Nadine's name was marked for eleven.

Relief washed over Nadine. *I could kiss Bella.* Then she turned to Jason and said sweetly, "Was there anything else, or shall I get ready for my shift? I believe it starts in about ten minutes."

Jason's face flared red. He glared at Nadine, dropped Bella's phone on the table, and stomped out of the break room.

Bella squinted at the schedule on the wall. "Did he seriously change the schedule just so he could write you up?"

"It looks that way."

"Damn." Bella shook her head. "What an asshole. Maybe you should take your own photos in case he tries that shit again."

"I will." Her smartphone wasn't worth much, but the camera still worked.

"Good. I'll keep taking photos too. You know, to make sure you're covered if you forget or if you have the day off."

Nadine opened her mouth to tell her not to bother, but then she remembered her bank balance. "I'd appreciate that. Thank you."

Bella picked up her spoon. "No problem."

Nadine swiped her badge and left the break room, allowing herself a private smile as she recalled the look on Jason's face when Bella had shown him the photo.

For once, the day had started out okay.

Bella had just returned from her lunch break when Grady called out to her.

"Yes?" She swiveled around to his office.

Grady sat at his desk, a half-eaten banana in his hand. "Come in here for a minute. Close the door."

Uh-oh. Had she done something wrong? She had closed two days earlier. Was the bank receipt off? Was money missing? She shut the door and sat, crossing and uncrossing her legs.

Grady leaned forward. "I talked to Jason."

Oh great. Jason had been pissy ever since Bella had proven Nadine right about the schedule. "Yeah?"

"I want to talk to you about Nadine."

"What about her?"

He looked at her gravely. "I know you don't follow politics, so I want to make sure you know what all the commotion has been about."

Seriously? "I already know."

"You do?" Grady frowned.

"Yes. I'm extremely familiar with the story."

"Huh." This seemed to unsettle him. "Well, I've seen you getting friendly with Nadine—chatting in the stockroom, that sort of thing. Jason said you two even went to lunch together. So I thought you might not be aware of what she did."

"I am aware."

"Then maybe you should be more careful. After all, she's a convicted felon."

What the hell? Did he think Nadine would tempt Bella to violate campaign-finance laws? "I'm not sure what you mean."

Grady grunted. "What I mean is you're a good girl. If you associate with someone like her, people will talk."

As far as Bella knew, nobody was talking except Grady and Jason. Ashley was fascinated by Nadine's notoriety but had little interest in the details of the scandal. Kenny was skittish around Nadine, but he didn't have it in him to judge Bella by association.

"Thanks for your concern," Bella said, "but I'm not worried about what people think. Nadine and I are friends."

Grady studied her. "I suppose it's up to you."

"I'm so glad you understand. Excuse me, I've got to clock in." Bella jumped up and left the office before he could object.

Out in the hallway, Bella allowed her face to make the disgusted expression she had suppressed during their little chat. He thought *she* was clueless? That was rich, coming from the man who had interviewed and hired Nadine Bayani without even recognizing her.

She thought back to what she had told Grady. *Nadine and I are friends.* Bella had never thought of Nadine that way before, and she wondered if Nadine would agree.

A tiny part of her was pleased that her relationship with Nadine was significant enough that her boss had called her in for a talk. It made her feel as if something real—maybe even something important—was happening between them.

Nothing romantic, of course. Sure, Nadine was hot, smart, and mysterious. Of course Bella was drawn to her. But she wasn't going to crush on a woman whose crimes had harmed the United States.

Besides, Nadine was probably straight. Her only relationship on record was with a man. A past boyfriend didn't rule out bisexuality (as Raelyn was always quick to remind her), but there was zero evidence that Nadine had ever dated women. Bella had no reason to even think about it.

But they could be friends, right? Ever since their lunch, they had talked more at work—no serious discussions, just commiserating about customers and managers. Bella enjoyed their chats, and she sensed that Nadine did too.

In fact, having friends was probably an important part of reintegrating into society. It might even reduce the odds that a person would commit more crimes. Hell, befriending Nadine was practically her civic duty.

Fuck Grady and Jason.

With that settled, she swiped her badge and headed to the stockroom to say hi to her friend.

"Todd is totally in love with you," Ashley said out of the blue.

"What? Who's Todd?" Bella stepped out from behind the checkout counter.

Nadine looked up from the endcap, where she was restocking cookware.

"You know, Todd, from Food Lion. He was in here the other day with Tino. Apparently, he can't stop talking about you." Ashley grinned. "He said you were flirting with him."

Bella scrunched her face, trying to place the name. "I have no idea who that is."

"Here, I'll show you." Ashley scrolled through her phone and presented it to Bella. "That's Todd."

The photo showed a middle-aged man with a sandy-brown goatee wearing rectangular glasses. He looked familiar, but she couldn't remember ever speaking with him.

"Todd is delusional." Bella handed the phone back. She caught Nadine looking at her and shrugged.

Todd appeared in her checkout line later that day. Kenny was on the other register with only one customer in line, while Bella had two people waiting, but Todd planted himself right behind them and leered in her direction.

Lucky me. Bella kept her eyes down as she helped the other customers.

When Todd reached the counter, he set down two items: a tin of tea cookies and a bag of red licorice. Food sold at Overstock Oasis was dicey from the moment it arrived since it had already languished on another store's shelves for months. Todd's items were on clearance, which meant they were guaranteed to be stale—not that Bella cared to warn him.

"Ah, the lovely Bella," Todd said with a sticky smile. "You look magnificent today."

"Thanks." Bella stiffly scanned the items. "Your total is $4.03."

Todd leaned in closer, resting a hairy arm on the counter. "Did you know that Bella means beautiful?"

Dear Lord. "Yes, I know."

"Well, it certainly fits you." He licked his lips. "What time do you get off work?"

"Nine." As soon as the word left her mouth, she regretted it. She should have said, *None of your business.*

"How about a drink at Moore's?" He waggled his eyebrows as he handed her a limp five-dollar bill.

"Oh, um, thanks, but I don't think so." She began to retrieve his change from the register drawer.

"You got plans?" His eyes narrowed behind his glasses.

"No." *Why can't I just lie? What is wrong with me?* She looked at the coins in her palm and realized she had lost count.

"Come on, just one drink. I promise you'll have fun. I'm not leaving until you say yes." His gaze raked down her body, then returned to her boobs.

Flustered, she lost count again. "I'm sorry, could you please stop talking so I can count your change?"

"Sure thing, beautiful." He continued to stare.

Bella willed herself to concentrate and finally held out the coins. "Ninety-seven cents."

Todd brushed his fingers over hers as he accepted the change. "Let me pick you up tonight."

"I'm sorry. I can't." She looked over her shoulder, praying another customer would appear. No luck.

"Why not?" he asked sharply.

Bella's stomach churned. She hated rejecting men. No matter how gentle or graceful the excuse, they always seemed to take it badly. "You seem like a really nice guy, but I'm just not interested."

"Do you have a boyfriend or something?"

Bella opened her mouth to respond, but then another customer pulled up to her register with a cart full of gardening supplies. *Oh, thank God.* She turned to him with a grateful smile. "Hi there, did you find everything you need?"

Todd hovered until two more customers got in line, then he wandered out of the store.

An hour later, he was back. At first, he lurked a few yards away, pretending to study a display. Then he disappeared down an aisle, returning a few minutes later to stand in line at her register.

When it was his turn, he smacked a box of "gourmet" chocolates onto the counter. "I talked to Ashley. She said you don't have a boyfriend."

"Ashley doesn't know anything about my personal life." Bella scanned the chocolates. "$2.60."

He pulled cash out of his wallet. "So you do have a boyfriend?"

"No." As soon as the word left her mouth, she wished she'd just lied. She kept her eyes on the register drawer as she counted his change.

"So you're not taken. And you're not busy. You just don't want to go out with *me*."

Bella scraped a quarter, a nickel, and a dime into her hand, then dropped the coins and his receipt onto the counter, avoiding skin contact.

"The thing is," Todd said, "you don't even know me, but you're judging me—based on what? Looks? You want some manly jock named Chad?"

"I'm not judging you. I just—"

"You know, you're not perfect either." His voice was loaded with contempt. "You're overweight. You carry it well, I admit. You've got the hourglass thing going on. But you might want to rethink your standards. You're a chubby girl pushing thirty. And you work here, so I know you don't have money."

Bella cringed. There were grains of truth in Todd's cruel words.

"You should give me a chance." His abruptly shifted from cutting to cajoling. "I'm a nice guy, unlike the jerks you're probably banging."

Bella could have hugged the grandmotherly woman who interrupted by plunking a garish vase onto her checkout counter. "Thanks for shopping at Overstock Oasis," she said firmly to Todd before facing the new customer. In her peripheral vision, she saw him linger for a moment before slinking away.

A few minutes later, Nadine stopped by Bella's register. She scrutinized Bella's face for a second, then asked, "What's wrong?"

Bella leaned against the counter. "Oh, I'm fine. It's just… Remember the guy Ashley was telling me about? The one who works with her boyfriend? He came in here to ask me out."

"Ah. I take it that you weren't interested."

"Of course not." Then she remembered Nadine didn't know she was gay. This would be a good opportunity to segue onto the topic without making it a big deal.

"I'm guessing he didn't take it well."

"No. He got angry, and then he called me fat and old."

"Charming." Something sparked in Nadine's eyes. "If he bothers you again, tell me, okay?"

Bella wasn't sure what Nadine could do about it, but she liked the idea of Nadine looking out for her. "Okay, I will."

A new customer deposited two miniature gnomes onto the counter, ending the conversation. Nadine nodded a quick goodbye and disappeared into an aisle.

Bella resolved to tell Nadine about her sexual orientation another time. She wasn't ashamed; she just didn't talk about her sexuality at work. But all of her friends knew, and she had recently decided that she and Nadine were friends. She'd tell her soon. No big deal.

Chapter 9

When Nadine arrived for her shift, she found Ashley by herself, contending with a long line of impatient-looking customers.

Nadine caught her eye. "Where is everyone?"

"I don't know!" Ashley's face was flushed, beads of sweat on her forehead. "I know you're not allowed to work the register, but can you find someone else to come up here?"

A few customers shot curious glances at Nadine, probably wondering what she had done to get banned from the register. One man seemed to recognize her. Nadine hurried past the line before he could say anything.

Grady, Jason, Bella, and Kenny were standing around the table in the break room, all wearing tense expressions.

"What's going on?" Nadine asked.

"We got a report from corporate," Grady said. "This store was in the top ten percent for shrinkage last quarter."

Shoplifting, Bella mouthed to Nadine.

"This has *never* happened," Grady said. "We're almost always in the bottom quarter. Folks around here don't shoplift. This ain't that kind of town."

"Damn right," Jason muttered.

"Clearly, there's a new crew in Cheriville," Grady said dramatically. "And we're going to shut it down. Corporate sent us protocols for a high-shrinkage store, and we're going to follow them to the letter." He held up a page with Overstock Oasis letterhead.

"Number one, do not leave customers unattended. Ask if you can help them find something. If they say they don't need any help, talk to them about the merchandise. The bottom line is, keep an eye on them."

Nadine imagined employees dogging customers, refusing to leave them alone. *Sounds like a dreadful experience for everyone.* Bella and Kenny didn't look happy with the idea either.

"Number two, pay special attention to customers who carry large bags or purses. If anyone comes in the store with a purse bigger than this"—he held his hands a foot apart—"don't let them out of your sight."

Bella and Nadine exchanged glances. Older women with enormous handbags comprised at least half of their customers.

"Number three. Corporate is sending us a video-surveillance system. It should be here next week."

Great. When she'd first started, Nadine had been relieved to learn the store didn't have security cameras. Now there would be endless footage of her working there.

"Finally, antishoplifting signs. Corporate is sending over official signs, but until then, we'll use what Jason found on the Google." Grady held up a piece of paper that read *Shoplifters will be prosecuted!!* in blurry black-and-white text above a clip-art silhouette of a police officer wielding handcuffs. A fifth grader could have done better.

"Any questions?"

Kenny raised a hand tentatively. "Um, what do we do if we see someone shoplifting?"

Jason stepped forward. "Excellent question. Officially, we're not supposed to confront shoplifters, but I did some research on Virginia law. If y'all see someone conceal an item, we can legally detain the suspect for up to one hour while we call the police."

Bella frowned. "Wait. How do we detain them? Won't they just run away? I mean, I guess we could try to physically restrain them. But that sounds dangerous."

"Well—" Jason said.

Grady held up his hand. "Do not use physical force. Corporate policy forbids touching a customer for any reason. If they run, well, there ain't much we can do."

Jason tightened his mouth. He'd probably been fantasizing about tackling thieves like the linebacker he never got to be.

"All right." Grady pointed to the door. "Back to work. Remember, keep an eye on those customers."

They filed out of the break room, looking morose. Just as Nadine reached the doorway, a strong hand on her shoulder pulled her back. It was Jason.

She turned around. "What do you want?"

Jason stood close enough that she could smell his pungent breath. "Did you know that employee theft is a leading cause of shrinkage?"

The temptation to smack him was overwhelming. Instead, she lifted her chin and said, "Your point?"

"Is it a coincidence that the shoplifting started right after we hired a convicted criminal?"

She held his gaze but refused to respond.

Jason leaned even closer. "I wonder what would happen to your probation if you were caught stealing."

Her stomach twisted. *Fuck.* If she committed a crime—or faced a false accusation—on supervised release, she could face more prison time. Images of metal bars and sadistic guards flashed through her mind.

Jason grabbed her upper arms and squeezed, his fingers digging into her skin. Then, just as suddenly, he released her and stormed out.

Nadine trembled in rage. How dare he touch her? *Sanctimonious creep.* She looked down and saw red fingerprints on her arms. The marks were evidence of assault, not that she could do anything about it.

She turned to leave but instead whirled back around and punched a metal filing cabinet, bruising her knuckles. The cabinet was unaffected. She gave it a futile kick before she walked out onto the floor.

Nadine stayed in the stockroom her entire shift, slashing boxes and dumping merchandise into carts. She didn't trust herself to take anyone's shit without losing her composure, so the plan was to avoid human interaction for as long as possible.

She worked until the sunlight that streamed through the small window turned orange and faded to black, leaving her to work by the light of the single hanging bulb.

The metal doors swung open, disrupting her thoughts. Bella strode in. "There you are! Didn't you hear my announcement?"

Nadine brushed the dust from her pants. "What announcement?"

"We're closed. Everyone's gone. Well, except you and me. It's time to count the cash."

"Oh, right." Nadine had forgotten she was scheduled to close. She collected her water bottle and satchel and followed Bella.

"Rough day?" Bella asked as they walked to the front of the store.

"Mmm. Something like that." She'd decided not to tell Bella about Jason's aggression, fearing Bella would endanger her own job trying to do something about it.

"Me too." Bella sighed. "Grady and Jason are obsessed with shoplifting. They kept following customers and asking them weird, pointless questions. So by the time the customers came to check out, they were really pissed off. But of course I can't say anything."

They reached the checkout counter with the safe stored underneath. Directly overhead, the speaker played a peppy track that had tormented Nadine for weeks. She pinched the bridge of her nose. "God, that song is annoying. Makes me want to jam an ice pick in my ear."

"The worst." Mischief sparked in Bella's eyes. "You know, I know how to turn it off. And since no one else is here…"

She walked over to the stereo system and dug around in the nest of wires in the back. After a moment, she yanked one of the connectors. The music stopped.

"Bless you." Nadine exhaled as the beautiful silence soothed her soul. "The music here is awful."

"You know what we need?" Bella pulled out her phone and tapped the screen. "We need an antidote." She reached for the microphone that was used for in-store announcements, turned it on, and set it next to her phone. The opening chords of a rock song blared over the speakers.

"Wait." The song was familiar. "Is this—?"

"David Bowie!" Bella laughed, swinging her hips back and forth. Her hair bounced as she moved.

"Dance with me!" Bella reached for Nadine, shouting over the music. "Come on. No one's here."

Nadine pointed to the glass doors and windows that faced the parking lot. Anyone who walked by would have a clear view of them. "I don't think so."

Bella danced over to the wall and flipped a switch, killing the lights. The only light came from the floodlights in the parking lot. She said in a breathy voice, "Welcome to the Oasis after dark." Then she twirled and gyrated playfully against a shopping cart.

Nadine felt warmth rising up from her abdomen. *Shit.* Bella had no idea she was dancing for a gay woman who was enjoying it far too much. She told her body to cut it out.

Bella danced back to the checkout counter and motioned for Nadine to join in. "Come on. You need this. I can tell."

Nadine moved her head and hips slightly to the beat.

When the song ended, Bella flipped the lights back on. "Did that help?"

"Yes. Thank you. I did need that." She didn't think anything could have lifted her mood, but her anger was gone. Now she was busy feeling other things. Inappropriate things. But, God, she was only human.

For once, Bella's cash drawer matched the register's total exactly. "Register's good."

Nadine nodded. "Okay."

Bella appreciated Nadine's nonchalance. She didn't want to be praised like a first grader just because she counted correctly.

After they counted and bagged the remaining cash, Bella slung her purse over her shoulder. "Ready?"

Nadine started to follow, then abruptly stopped. "Sorry. I left my jacket in the break room. I'll meet you outside."

"Cool." Bella dug through the chaotic contents of her purse until she located the keys to the store. She stepped outside, breathing in the cool September night air.

Someone grabbed her from the side. She started to cry out, but a wet mouth covered hers, muffling her scream. A scratchy beard scraped her face.

Todd.

He wrapped his arms around her, pressing his large hands into her back, squeezing her tight against him. Bella struggled, but she was trapped. She could barely breathe through the overpowering stench of body odor and cologne.

Todd leaned forward, rocking against her, attempting to dip her backward. One hand released its grip to squeeze her ass.

When he shifted, Bella managed to free one of her arms. She pushed against his chest, trying to get away from his mouth so she could scream.

Someone's arm intervened and pushed Todd off her. Bella stumbled and looked up to see Nadine slamming him into the wall.

"You stay the fuck away from her," Nadine hissed.

"She wanted it! She was giving me mixed signals."

"Shut up!" Nadine shoved him again. His head thumped against the concrete. Nadine held him there with her forearm and her knee. "Bella, do you want to call the police?"

Bella tried to catch her breath. "Let me think for a second."

She knew what the county sheriffs were like in Cheriville, having encountered them before. They were old-school, unfailingly chivalrous, but also not inclined to believe women who made allegations against men. Especially white men.

Then she considered Nadine, the only witness. If she called the police, Nadine's name would be in the official report, and it would be only a matter of time before reporters learned of the incident. And what if Todd accused Nadine of assaulting him? It might affect her probation.

Bella couldn't let that happen. "No. No cops."

"Are you absolutely sure? This was sexual assault."

The selfless concern only made Bella more certain of her choice. "I'm sure."

Nadine leaned in close to Todd's face. "Listen to me, you disgusting little shit. I've been to prison once, and I'll happily go back if you touch her again. Do you understand me?"

Todd's head bobbed rapidly.

"Get the fuck out of here." She released her grip, and he scampered off into the parking lot. It was over.

Nadine turned to Bella. "Are you okay?"

"I'm—he—" Bella leaned over and spat on the pavement. Then she gagged and spat again. "I can still taste his mouth. And the smell... My Lord. I need to go home and boil my body."

"Here. Let's sit down." Nadine gestured to the nearby wooden bench.

They sat together, close enough that their thighs touched. Bella was still shaking, but the contact helped to soothe her.

"Do you know him?"

"Yeah. That was Todd, the guy who was hitting on me the other day. I probably should have been more direct. I mean, I told him no, but he kept arguing, and I didn't know what to say."

"Stop that," Nadine said sharply. "This wasn't your fault. You said no. And even if you hadn't, he had no right to assault you. What he did was a crime. You could have him arrested."

"I know." Bella wished Nadine would drop the idea of involving the police. It wasn't an option.

"Why didn't you want to call the cops?"

Bella bit her lip. "The sheriffs here are not that helpful. And I just— they would have asked your name. It would have been in the paper. I didn't want that."

"Oh, Bella." Nadine softened. "I appreciate the thought. I really do. But I can take care of myself. Look, it's not too late. We can still call."

Bella shook her head. "I don't think he'll bother me again. Not with you around."

"He better not." Nadine touched her hand to Bella's shoulder.

That was all it took. Bella leaned forward and collapsed into Nadine's arms.

Nadine held her close and stroked her back. For a long moment, they stayed like that, alone in the deserted parking lot. The only sounds were their breathing and the buzz of the fluorescent lights overhead.

Chapter 10

"How's the job?" Michaela's badge caught the light as she leaned back in her chair, her index fingers pointed in a steeple against her chin. She peered at Nadine across the desk.

Nadine shrugged. "It's fine. The same."

"Any more trouble with reporters?"

"Not lately. Some of the customers still make snide comments, and every so often someone tries to pick a fight with me."

Michaela frowned. "What do you do when that happens? You haven't been drawn into any altercations, have you?"

Nadine was about to shake her head, but then she flashed back to the scene in the parking lot two nights ago.

For one nauseating second, she had thought Bella was kissing Todd back. Jealousy had sliced through her like a jagged razor. When she had realized what was happening, she'd wanted to pound that slimy creep against the wall until he hemorrhaged blood and brains. If she hadn't stopped when she did, her probation would have been revoked for sure.

Michaela gave her a sharp look. "Did something happen?"

"No. I removed myself from the situation."

Michaela started to respond when a discordant jingle blared from her phone. "Just a second." She answered the call. "Schwartz. Yeah? When?" She pushed back from the desk. "Wait here," she said to Nadine before stepping into the hall.

Nadine glanced around Michaela's cluttered desk. She noticed a small picture frame on the side credenza. It was angled just enough for Nadine to see the photo of Michaela wearing a white suit and embracing a woman in a sparkly white dress.

Nadine had guessed her probation officer was most likely gay from the moment they met due to her butch haircut, bare face, and the men's shirts she wore on her broad frame. Still, she was surprised that Michaela displayed such a personal photo at work. Probably no one would dare to say anything, not when Michaela looked as if she could kick anyone's ass.

Michaela returned to the office and plopped back in her chair. "Where were we?"

"I was just saying that work is fine. But I'm very concerned about my housing."

Michaela scanned Nadine's paperwork. "When do you leave Renn House?"

"In just under two weeks. I asked again about an extension, and they said there's no way. Someone else is moving in the day I get released."

Michaela frowned. "That's not much time. Have you been looking? Did you call the landlords on the list I gave you?"

"I called them all, but they're either full or the rent is too high. My paycheck is pitiful, and I don't have savings anymore. My money is gone." Thanks to private security costs, legal fees, and fines imposed at sentencing, her finances were decimated. What little had remained in her bank account during prison had covered the last two months of food, transportation, and health expenses.

"What about renting a room? Perhaps from a friend?"

Nadine shook her head. "I've responded to ads for housemates, but they all back out when they find out I'm a felon or when I tell them my name. As for friends, I don't have anyone I can ask."

"Right." Michaela looked thoughtful. "You're in a unique situation."

"I can't be the only offender with this problem." Nadine thought of her suitemates at Renn House. Jodie had still been looking for work when her three months ended; she had moved in with family. Jenna would have to leave in about a month and still had nothing lined up.

"Oh, you're not. Lots of folks struggle with housing after prison. But the ones who end up on the street tend to be elderly sex offenders and chronic addicts—people who truly have nowhere to go. I didn't say your situation was *harder*. It's not. It's just different."

"Because I'm famous."

"Yes. But also because you don't have much of a support network. Most people like you—educated, professional—have friends and family with resources. They get back on their feet right away. But you always say you don't have anyone. Is that really true, or are you too proud to ask?"

"Um, I'm close with my sister, Patricia. But she lives in the Philippines with her husband. And I can't ask her for money. They're just getting by as it is, and she has a baby. It's the same with my other relatives. They all live in the Philippines, and they don't have much."

"What about your friends? And all the people you knew from politics?"

"I had plenty of colleagues and contacts but not many I would call friends. Most people resented my access to Alyssa. Plus, I was usually the bad guy who dealt with underperforming staffers or anyone who didn't have her best interests at heart. I was close to a few people at one time, but now...not so much."

Nadine shrugged like it wasn't a big deal, but in truth, those friendships were a real loss. The only people she had called friends were like her— fiercely loyal to Alyssa. But thanks to the scandal, those people hated her more than anyone.

"They blame me," Nadine said softly. "They blame me for Alyssa losing the election. Most of them hate me."

"Okay." Michaela jotted something on a notepad. "I'm going to make a few calls. In the meantime, keep applying for apartments and rooms. And really think about your network. I know they're angry with you, but I can't imagine that every last one of them would refuse to help. Would they really want you to be *homeless*?"

The word echoed in her brain. Were they really talking about this? "I'll think about who I can ask."

"Reach out to some people. Someone might have a connection in the area or be willing to loan you some money." Michaela paused. "Sometimes forgiveness comes from the person you least expect."

Nadine couldn't imagine that anyone would forgive what she had supposedly done, but there was one person she might ask, the one person aside from her sister who knew the truth.

Alyssa Jackson was the last person Nadine wanted to call, and yet it seemed she had no other options.

As Nadine broke down one box after another, she tried to think of a solution to her housing dilemma. Another day of emails and phone calls had gotten her nowhere.

She considered her options if she failed to find housing in the next week and a half. She had enough money for four, maybe five nights in a motel. After that, she could try homeless shelters or living in her car. She had no idea what else she could do. Where did people in her situation go at night?

During Chicago winters, homeless people often spent their nights on the L train, riding from Howard to 95th Street and back again, over and over. Nadine had seen them when she'd taken the train to Alyssa's downtown district office early in the morning. But the Richmond area barely had a functional bus system, let alone a train that ran all night.

Just call Alyssa. Nadine knew it was ridiculous to think about sleeping in her car when she knew someone with plenty of resources who could help—and who owed her everything. She just wished there were another way.

The metal doors swung open. Bella's long hair was loosely tied to one side, and her earthy eyeshadow made her brown eyes pop. *God.* She was stunning.

"What's wrong?" Bella asked.

How did Bella read her so well? "Nothing's wrong. Well, nothing here at the store. Just the usual ups and downs of life as a convicted felon."

Bella sat on a box. "Tell me."

Nadine sliced through another box as she decided how much to say. She was ashamed of her situation, but part of her wanted to tell someone. "I'm being discharged from the foundation soon, and I'm having trouble finding a place to live."

Bella's eyes widened. "You don't have anywhere to go?"

Nadine continued to break down boxes as she recounted her attempts to secure an apartment. When she finished, she finally looked at Bella.

Bella's face creased with worry. "Where will you go if you don't find anything?"

Nadine shrugged. "That's what I'm trying to figure out."

"You can stay with me," Bella said without a hint of uncertainty.

The offer was unexpected but not really surprising. Bella was a kind person with a big heart. Of course she would offer her home to someone in need. "Thank you, but I couldn't impose on you. It wouldn't be right."

"You wouldn't be imposing at all. I have a one-bedroom apartment, so there's plenty of room, if you don't mind sleeping on the couch. I should warn you, though: I'm a terrible slob. But I'm trying to get better about picking up after myself. Anyway, I'd enjoy the company. Really."

Bella seemed to be sincere. Still, Nadine couldn't accept, could she?

Moving in would disrupt Bella's life. She'd be too nice to say anything, but Nadine worried it wouldn't be long before she resented having someone else in her space.

At the same time, Nadine had to consider the ethics of sharing an apartment with a beautiful woman who didn't know she was gay, let alone attracted to her. There were so many reasons not to say yes. But faced with the alternative, Nadine didn't want to say no either.

"Let's see how the next few days go. I've left messages to follow up on my applications. A place could come through any day."

"Okay. But if you don't find something, you're coming to stay with me. No arguing. I won't let you live on the streets, for God's sake."

"I wouldn't be on the streets. I have my car."

"No!" Bella slapped her hand on a box. "Lord. You will not sleep in your car. I won't allow it. *Hell* no."

Nadine was used to sweet, accommodating Bella; she had rarely seen her so resolute about anything. But she couldn't—could she? "Let's just see."

Nadine paced her small bedroom, clutching her phone.

For about the tenth time that evening, she tapped *Contacts*, selected a number listed only as *AJ*, and stared at the call icon.

She hadn't spoken to Alyssa Jackson in over two years. Alyssa hadn't contacted her in prison, not even a letter. Nothing. She had no idea if her former boss even had the same phone number. But she was running out of options.

Nadine held her breath as it rang. At least the number hadn't been disconnected—that was a good sign. Then she heard the voicemail greeting, unchanged from years earlier. *Hi there. You've reached Alyssa's phone. You know what to do.*

Nadine couldn't speak on a recording, not about what she really had to say. She hung up and tossed the phone on the bed.

And then it rang.

Nadine's hand trembled as she answered the call. "Hello?"

"Nadine. It's really you." Alyssa's voice was exactly the same as she remembered—deep with a slight midwestern accent.

"Yes." Suddenly Nadine was at a loss for words. "It's me."

"I heard you got out. I'm happy for you."

That broke the spell. Alyssa was *happy* for her? Nadine nearly choked. A few years ago, she would have done anything just so Alyssa would smile at her. Now, ten seconds into a conversation, she wanted to slap her.

"We really shouldn't be speaking," Alyssa continued. "Still, I'm glad you called. It's nice to know that you're okay."

Nadine found her voice. "Okay? I'm not okay. I'm broke. I'm about to be homeless."

"Homeless?" Alyssa gasped. "How is that possible?"

"Because I don't have any fucking money, Alyssa. Because I blew up my life to protect you, and now I'm working for minimum wage. I can't afford an apartment. And no one wants me as a roommate, considering I'm a convicted felon and despised by the entire nation."

Alyssa was silent for several seconds. Then she asked, "Why did you call me?"

Nadine closed her eyes. "Because I need help. I need money."

"I wish I could help. I really do." Alyssa sighed. "But I've already done what I could."

Nadine's eyes popped open. "What? What did you do? You haven't done anything."

"How do you think you got into Renn House?" Alyssa's tone turned haughty. "Do you think they wanted the public scrutiny that came with offering you a bed when there aren't enough beds for offenders who really need them?"

Nadine's chest tightened. "You bribed them to take me?"

"I didn't *bribe* anyone." There was a dangerous edge to her voice. "I called in a favor. I knew the press would be all over it when you got out. I thought it would be better if you went somewhere secure, away from Washington, someplace that could keep the reporters away."

"So that's why I got in." Alyssa had helped, but only because it was in her own interest. Of course.

"Yes. I took a big risk to help you out." Alyssa waited as if expecting a thank-you.

Nadine had none to give her. "Can't you call in another favor? I need long-term housing. I need a better job." She hated that it sounded like whining. Maybe she could appeal to Alyssa's self-interest once more. "Imagine if someone spotted me sleeping in my car. The press would cover it, and you would be back in the news."

"Oh, Nadine. I can't do that. Someone might trace it back to me, and then everything would be thrown into question. I'm supposed to hate you, remember? We shouldn't even be talking. It's too risky."

"Too risky for you," Nadine said flatly. She had nothing left to risk.

"I'm going to run again. For president."

"I thought you might. You know that's going to be hell for me, right?" Another run meant another eighteen months of news coverage. The scandal would be rehashed, and Nadine's name would be back in the news every time Alyssa's opponents brought it up. *How can we trust you to lead when you didn't know your own senior advisor was accepting bribes in your name?*

"I can't do what we always dreamed about, all of the good things we wanted to do for the country, if I'm connected to you. It's not that I don't care for you. You know I do. But I need to put the country first."

Oh please. The noble patriot routine? Alyssa had a lot of nerve to play that card with the one person who knew the truth about her.

"I'll always care about you, and I'll always be thankful," Alyssa said, "but I need to keep you at a distance. Do you understand?"

Nadine understood all right. The woman who had once cried in her arms, begging for her political life, was discarding her like week-old fish. Just like everyone else. "I don't seem to have a choice."

"Please don't call me again."

The line went dead.

Chapter 11

Bella slid the purple candles into a neat row, then stacked an alternating pattern of blue, pink, and yellow candles on top. Organizing candles was one of the few opportunities to be artistic at her job, and she liked to take her time.

She heard footsteps and looked up to see Grady glaring at her.

"Forgetting something?" he asked.

"Huh?" Bella looked at the candles.

"Shrinkage. How long has she been standing there?" Grady jerked his head. A few yards away, a middle-aged Black woman was browsing the cookware.

"Oh, um, not long?" Bella really had no idea. In the first days after Grady's announcement, everyone had made a perfunctory effort to pay more attention to customers—with the exception of Nadine, who seemed to be exempt. But gradually, they had fallen back into their usual routines.

"Go talk to her. Make sure she's not stuffing things into her purse."

The woman examined the selection of slow cookers on the bottom shelf.

"I don't see how she could fit a slow cooker in her purse," Bella said.

Grady scowled. "Go."

Reluctantly, Bella approached the customer. "Hi there. Can I help you find something?"

The woman looked up. Her gold cross necklace glimmered under the florescent lights. "No, thank you." She turned back to the merchandise, moving down the aisle to the pressure cookers.

Mission accomplished? Bella turned back to see if Grady was still watching.

He was standing near the endcap, arms crossed over his chest. He pointed, indicating that Bella should follow her.

Ugh. Bella trailed after the woman, hovering a few feet away.

The woman shot her a questioning look.

"Um," Bella said, "did you know those pots are on sale?"

"I can see that." She pointed at the large red sign that said *SALE*.

"Oh, right." Bella felt like an idiot.

The woman continued down the aisle, then turned the corner. Bella attempted to act as if she happened to be headed in the same direction.

Halfway down the bath aisle, the woman spun around. "Are you following me?"

"What? Oh, no. I just—"

"Do you think I'm going to steal something? Because I'm Black?"

Bella's cheeks burned. "It's not just you. We're supposed to watch everyone."

"What about her?" She pointed to a white woman who was watching the scene with interest.

Shit. "I'm so sorry. I'm really not racist."

"Save it." Disgust blazed in her eyes. She turned and strode to the exit.

"See?" Grady appeared behind Bella. His voice was triumphant. "I was right. She was planning to steal something."

Bella threw up her hands. "I'm taking my break."

She marched to the back of the store and pushed open the stockroom doors.

Nadine sat on a box, sipping from a bottle of water. Her eyebrows lifted. "What happened?"

"I hate this shoplifting patrol. It's so stupid."

"Sit down." Nadine gestured to a short box on the floor. "Tell me what happened."

Bella recounted the exchange, her cheeks burning all over again as she remembered the pain in the customer's eyes. When she finished the story, she blew out a frustrated breath. "Ugh. I'm sorry. Here I am complaining to you when you get harassed every damn place you go."

"It's okay." Nadine waved her hand. "That's different."

"Maybe. But you're also, um… Did you ever get racially profiled before you were famous?" As soon as she said it, Bella worried it was rude to ask.

"On occasion." Nadine rested her chin on her hand. "When you have brown skin and an accent in this country, people say all kinds of things. I've been asked where I'm from more times than I can count—and they don't mean Illinois. I've lived in the States since I was ten, and nobody ever lets me forget that I'm not *from here.*"

"I'm so sorry." The thought of anyone judging Nadine by her race and immigration status made Bella feel even worse.

"They don't always say it explicitly. Sometimes I just *knew* someone was treating me differently because of my race. There'd be this element of suspicion or even hostility that was absent when the same person interacted with someone white. And when I brought it up to my white friends, they were often skeptical—like maybe I imagined it."

Bella winced. "I can't imagine how shitty that would feel."

"It doesn't feel great."

"I'm not going to do that again. I mean, Grady told me to do it, but that's not an excuse. Next time, I'm going to refuse. Asking someone if they need help is one thing, but I'm not going to follow someone around and make them feel like—like that." She caught herself before she said *like a criminal.*

"Good." Nadine nodded. "I'm glad."

Bella wanted Nadine to say something like, *I know you're not really racist.* But that wasn't the point. Racial profiling didn't hurt any less because the perpetrator was ordered to do it. She had to own her actions and do better.

"Sometimes I wish I could quit." Bella brushed her hair out of her face.

"Why don't you? You're not planning to stay here another ten years, right?"

Bella's shoulders slumped. "I know it's pathetic that I still work retail—"

Nadine cut her off. "There's nothing wrong with retail. It's hard work, and customer service is a skill like any other. But why do you stay *here*, at Overstock Oasis, with buffoons like Jason and Grady running the place? Wouldn't you rather work somewhere more pleasant? Perhaps a grocery store or a bookstore."

"Hmm. Maybe." Bella imagined herself working at Barnes and Noble, recommending novels to the customers. "I guess I could apply, but they probably have better candidates than me. You know, people with education and credentials and more relevant experience."

Nadine looked as though she wanted to argue but said nothing.

Bella pushed the hair out of her face again. "I forgot my hair tie today."

"Here. Let me." Nadine reached over and ran her long fingers through Bella's unruly strands, smoothing and combing her hair into submission. Then she pulled and crossed sections into the beginnings of a snug braid.

"Oh, thanks." Bella relaxed under Nadine's touch. "How are you? Did you find an apartment?"

Nadine's hands stopped moving briefly, then resumed their work. "No."

"How many days do you have?"

"Three." There was a slight catch in Nadine's voice, one Bella might have missed before getting to know her.

"Please stay with me. I'd never forgive myself if you—I mean, I'm not just saying it. I really want you there. Please, you have to say yes." *Stop babbling.* Bella didn't mean to sound desperate, but this was urgent.

"Maybe... just for a little while," Nadine said quietly.

"Really? You're saying yes? Oh, I'm so glad." Bella turned to face Nadine with a big smile. "You can stay as long as you want."

Nadine gently guided Bella's head back around and resumed braiding. "I insist on paying my share of the rent, plus, I'll do my share of the housework."

Relief washed through her. Nadine would be safe. "Okay, sure, we'll work it all out. When will you move in?"

"On Wednesday, if that's okay. I have to vacate by five."

Bella's heart jumped. Wednesday was just a couple of days away. "Okay. I'll get the apartment ready." She'd have to clean...everything...and get rid of some things to make space. But it would be worth it.

Ashley burst through the doors. "Oh, there you are," she said to Bella. "Grady wants you back on the floor."

"I'm still on my break. It hasn't been fifteen minutes yet."

Ashley shrugged. "Well, he told me to tell you that, and I did. So, bye!" She turned and left, the doors swinging shut behind her.

Bella groaned. "I wish I could hide back here with you all day."

"I wish you could too." Nadine finished the braid and draped it over Bella's shoulder. It tapered to a slim tail that held without a tie. Nadine rested her hand on Bella's shoulder briefly, then quickly withdrew it.

Bella struggled for composure after the unexpected contact. "Thank you for the braid. And I'm glad you said yes. You won't regret it."

Bella tore through her apartment, frantically collecting empty bottles and dirty dishes. Nadine would be there in less than an hour, and the apartment was still a disaster.

After living in chaos for years, clutter blended in with the furniture to the point where she no longer noticed it. In her first pass through the apartment, she had missed the bra slung over the sofa and the pile of unopened mail on the TV stand.

She was exhausted after a full day on her feet, but anxiety powered her last-minute spree. She wanted so badly for Nadine to feel comfortable living there, and she worried that Nadine would be irritated with her poor housekeeping skills—or worse, that she would get sick of Bella's company.

Bella stashed items in the closets, wiped down areas with visible dust, and attempted to bring order to crowded surfaces by setting the contents in rows. She was leaning against the kitchen counter, catching her breath, when there was a tentative knock on the door. She ran to open it.

Nadine stood on the porch with a large duffel slung around her back and another hanging at her side.

"You're here! Welcome."

"Thank you." Nadine stepped inside and looked around the small apartment, her expression unreadable. Her gaze landed on the coffee table, where a stray sock still rested.

Bella snatched it up. *Oops.* "I was about to get that."

Nadine set her bags down. "I really do appreciate this. Like I said, it's only temporary."

"Like I said, you can stay as long as you want. Do you need help unloading the car?"

"This is all I have." Nadine pointed to the two bags. "I got rid of most of my things before prison, and since then, I've learned the value of minimalism."

Bella was the exact opposite of a minimalist. She could never seem to get rid of anything—not because she valued everything she owned but because she loathed cleaning and organizing. She'd rather have a root canal than deal with her things. It was a relief to know she wouldn't have to cram even more stuff into her closets.

"Feel free to borrow anything you need. I have enough crap for five people, as you can tell. I tried to clean, but obviously it's not perfect."

Nadine turned to her. "Bella, I'm so grateful for your generosity, I can't even tell you. Otherwise, I don't know where I'd be sleeping tonight."

Bella almost choked up at the thought of Nadine having nowhere to go, but she composed herself. "Well, I should give you the grand tour. This, as you've probably guessed, is the living room, and that's the kitchen over there. I don't have room for a dining table, so I just eat on the couch. It's kind of...yeah."

She led the way to her bedroom, which had received far less attention in her hour of cleaning. "And this is my room. It's still a mess, as you can see."

Nadine's mouth twitched.

"What? Is something funny?"

"Oh, nothing. It's just very girly."

Nadine had a point. The bedspread was solid pink with a ruffled trim, and a curtain of glittery beads hung over the window. The walls were adorned with colorful images of flowers and women—Bella's own artwork.

Nadine studied a sketch of a unicorn hanging on the closet door. The mythical creature pranced in a lush meadow under a wide rainbow.

Bella felt heat seep into her cheeks. *Nadine must think I have the taste of a twelve-year-old.* "I don't draw unicorns anymore. I made that one in high school."

"You drew all of these?" Nadine stepped closer to examine the unicorn.

"Yeah." Bella twisted a strand of hair between her fingers.

"You told me about the commissions, but I didn't realize... These are really good. I mean it. You're talented." Nadine turned to look at a monochrome sketch of a woman hugging her knees.

"Thanks." Bella felt her face grow even hotter. She couldn't help it. Nadine's praise made her insides turn mushy. "Really, thank you so much."

"Have you ever thought about pursuing a career in the arts? Maybe graphic design?"

Bella looked away. She had planned to major in graphic design until she flunked out of college. "No." She turned to step out of the bedroom. "Anyway, the bathroom is over here."

Bella made tacos for dinner. It was nothing fancy—just ground beef, a packet of Tex-Mex seasoning, and shells—but she knew she could make it without screwing up, and that was her top priority. She wanted to be a good host on their first night as roommates.

When Bella emerged from the kitchen with a plate of food, Nadine was studying the bookshelves.

"You read a lot." Nadine pulled out a novel and turned it over to scan the back cover.

Bella froze as she recognized the book—a lesbian romance novel. In fact, the entire shelf was crammed with lesbian fiction, most with incriminating artwork on the covers.

Oh shit. Bella had been so worried about tidying up her mess that she'd completely forgotten about her books. She tried to read Nadine's reaction. If only she could go back in time and stash them under the bed, not that she planned to avoid the conversation forever, but—

"Are you gay?" Nadine's eyes were free of condemnation yet loaded, like the answer mattered.

Bella worried she might not have hidden her attraction as well as she had hoped. "Yes, I am. Is that okay?"

"Of course it's okay." Nadine sounded oddly stern. "There's nothing wrong with being gay." She returned the book to the shelf. "I'm just surprised I didn't already know."

"Oh." Bella tried to think of something to say but drew a blank. She set the food on the coffee table.

"So you're in the closet."

"What?" Bella shook her head. "No. I am not *in the closet.* My friends know. My mom knows. I'm just not friends with anyone at work. Kenny would try to save my soul, and Ashley's a blabbermouth. As for Grady and Jason, I'd rather drink gasoline than tell them about my personal life."

Bella realized what she had said. "I didn't mean that you're not my friend. You are. In fact, you're the only friend I have at the store right now. I just didn't tell you because..." Bella hesitated. How to explain without freaking her out?

"What?"

"Because I wanted us to be friends. And I didn't want you to think I was, you know, some predatory lesbian who would come on to you."

Nadine frowned. "*Predatory* is the last word I would associate with you."

"Thanks. Um, it's good we got that out of the way. Now I don't have to worry about you finding out."

"Well, good." Nadine looked at the food. "Thank you again for cooking."

"Oh, sure. What do you want to drink?" Bella strove for a casual tone. "I've got water, soda, beer, and just about every kind of liquor—but I should warn you it's not exactly top-shelf."

"Liquor?" Nadine perked up. "Do you have tequila?"

"I do. I've even got limes. Be right back." Bella was relieved to have a moment to herself as she processed coming out to Nadine.

It went fine. Still, Bella couldn't shake the feeling that Nadine was unsettled for some reason, despite her reassuring words. Maybe she was one of those liberals who said all the right things but had never really known a lesbian.

Sure, Nadine was attractive. What gay girl wouldn't be drawn to her strong and sexy body, her intense brown eyes, and her hair that was always slightly mussed? Plus, she was smart as hell and had once been a formidable player in national politics—as evidenced by the cable news clips Bella had watched more times than she cared to admit. So, yeah, the woman was hot. But that didn't mean Bella couldn't control herself.

She resolved to be as respectful as possible while they shared the apartment. No lingering stares or walking around in her underwear. She would show Nadine they could be friends and roommates without her sexual orientation becoming an issue.

Bella sliced the lime, grabbed the bottle and two shot glasses, and took everything into the living room.

Nadine examined the label. "I've had worse." She sat on the couch and poured them each a generous shot.

Bella sat next to her. She thought about asking if Nadine had ever made prison hooch, as she had seen on *Orange is the New Black*, but decided it wasn't the right time. She raised her glass. "To new roommates?"

"Roommates? That's a nice euphemism for my situation." Nadine's tone was bitter, but then she softened. "But, yes, I'll drink to that."

They clinked their glasses together. Nadine tilted her head and downed the shot in one swallow.

Bella took a sip and grimaced. She usually only drank tequila blended with margarita mix. Not wanting to lose the moment, though, she braced herself and swallowed the rest of the shot. Her throat stung.

"So what's it like to be gay in Cheriville?" Nadine asked after a few bites of her taco. "I can't imagine it's fun."

"Oh, it's not that bad. At least not anymore. Things changed really fast, and now most people don't think it's a big deal. Sometimes I got depressed in high school because a lot of my classmates were homophobic. But I kept my mouth shut, and no one ever guessed that I was gay. Just like no one ever guesses now."

"You're certainly not obvious. You're very—" Nadine drew circles in the air as she searched for the word.

"Femme? Lipstick lesbian? Yeah, I've always been girly. I can't help it. I had one short haircut in my life, and I hated it." She shuddered at the memory. "Sometimes I wish I looked more obvious so I could scare away the likes of Todd—but I have to be myself."

"It's important to be yourself. When you try to hide who you really are, there may be temporary advantages, but it can also be damaging." Nadine looked off into the distance, sadness passing over her face.

Bella said gently, "I bet you miss being a lawyer. And your old life. I mean, this isn't you at all."

"I do miss my old life. I certainly miss the money. But the person I used to be—well, that wasn't entirely me either."

"What do you mean?"

Nadine pressed her lips together. "Nothing. So you grew up in Cheriville?"

"Yeah." Bella finished off her taco. "My mom is a secretary at the elementary school. I grew up ten minutes from here, and I've never lived anywhere else. Well, except for my one year at Mary Washington."

"What was college like?" Nadine asked carefully.

Bella knew what she was really asking. *Why did you drop out?* "It was, you know, Fredericksburg, Virginia. A truck-stop-slash-college town. There wasn't much to do there except study and drink. I was in PRISM—that's the queer student organization—and they had parties every weekend. I had never been around so many gay people before. That's where I met my first girlfriend. We were together for most of freshman year, but then I had to leave school."

Bella took a deep breath, then said in a rush, "I didn't flunk out because I partied too much, if that's what you're thinking." It seemed important to clarify this fact. "I only went to parties on Fridays. And I didn't even drink that much. I just…" She searched for the right words. "It was like I had this mental block. I'd sit there with the book open, but I couldn't make myself read it. I procrastinated for hours and wrote my papers at the last minute."

"Do you think it was anxiety?" Nadine asked.

"I mean, that was definitely part of it." Bella looked down at her empty plate. "My teachers in high school were really supportive. They knew I was trying, and they accepted late work from me all the time. But in college, it's easy to get lost. Like, no one even makes you go to class. And when I got behind, I couldn't deal with it. I couldn't face my professors. I ended up withdrawing from half of my classes." Even a decade later, she couldn't talk about it without feeling ashamed.

"Anyway," Bella said, "I had to pass 70 percent of my classes to keep my financial aid. I didn't realize that withdrawing from classes counted against you. I got an academic progress warning after the first semester, and then, after the second semester, I lost my eligibility for aid."

Nadine nodded. "And that's why you never went back?"

"Yeah. Without financial aid, my mom couldn't afford tuition. She doesn't make much money, and my dad…couldn't help. So I started working at Overstock Oasis. The original plan was to save enough to pay for a semester out of pocket, get my grades up, and get back on financial aid. But it hasn't worked out yet."

"Because of the money?"

"Yeah, that's part of it. It's hard to save when I make so little. Something always happens, like my car breaks down, and I have to start over." Bella picked at the crumbs on her plate. "Selling my drawings helps, but even when I manage to save some money, part of me doesn't feel ready. Like, what if the same thing happens again?"

"Well—"

"Look, I know what you're going to say," Bella said. "It's not too late. Why not try again, finish the degree, get out of Cheriville. I'm wasting my life at Overstock Oasis. I know that. I just... I already know."

Nadine's lips curved. "You're right. I was going to say it's not too late." She paused. "But I won't."

"Thanks." Bella attempted a smile.

Nadine leaned back, her plate still on her lap. "I'm glad you told me. About college, about your, uh, preferences. I'm glad for the chance to get to know you better."

Bella couldn't help wondering why Nadine wanted to get to know someone like her, a college dropout who had never left Virginia. Maybe Nadine was merely being kind to the one person at the store who had befriended her.

But something in Nadine's eyes made it seem as if she genuinely cared. The thought made Bella feel warm and a little woozy. Or maybe that one shot of tequila was one too many.

Chapter 12

NADINE AWOKE TO THE SMELL of coffee and an unfamiliar pattern of light on the ceiling. It took her a moment to remember where she was and why.

She looked down at the baby-pink bedsheet borrowed from Bella the night before. The sofa was lumpy, but she had slept on worse. Groaning, she stretched her arms out and sat up as metal springs creaked beneath her.

As she massaged her neck and shoulders, she contemplated the revelations of the previous evening. Bella was gay. Sweet, shy, hopelessly girly Bella. She had assumed otherwise based on stereotypes, but the bookshelves were packed with evidence that she'd been wrong. For someone who hadn't done well in school, Bella clearly loved to read—at least when the topic was women loving women.

Guilt nagged at her for not reciprocating Bella's candor, especially when Bella had been so nervous about telling her. It would have been the perfect moment to squeeze her hand and say, *I understand because I'm gay too.*

But something had held her back. She wasn't afraid of a bad reaction, obviously. She was more afraid of what else Bella might see.

For one thing, Bella might figure out that her dedication to Alyssa had been more than professional loyalty. That would be humiliating, but she'd live. Her biggest fear was that Bella would sense her emotions in the present. What if she caught a lingering look and realized her new houseguest had feelings for her?

Nadine hated the idea of making Bella uncomfortable in her own home. She was determined to hide her inconvenient attraction, and the best way to do that was to keep her sexual orientation to herself.

Footsteps in the hallway interrupted her thoughts. Bella appeared in the living room wearing skintight purple pajama shorts that barely covered her bottom and a thin white T-shirt that said *RVA* in faded blue letters. Every curve was visible, including her large breasts. Her hair was swept into a messy bun on top of her head, and her face wore the stain of yesterday's mascara.

"Good morning." Bella smiled sleepily. "I made coffee."

"Sm—" Her voice was a raspy croak. She cleared her throat. "Smells wonderful."

"Did you sleep good? I know that couch isn't very comfortable."

Nadine stopped herself from comparing it to her prison mattress, fearing Bella might take offense. "Yes, I slept well."

It was true. Even on the worn-out, creaky sofa, she had slept better than she had in weeks. For once, she had gone to bed without a pressing problem weighing on her. She had a place to stay for the immediate future—as long as she didn't screw it up.

Nadine followed Bella into the small kitchen and helped herself to a generous cup of coffee.

"Sorry, it's just the grocery-store brand," Bella said.

Nadine inhaled the aroma and sipped the hot liquid. It tasted like actual coffee. "After two years in prison, trust me—this is heavenly."

Bella chuckled. "Oh my. Your standards are even lower than mine." She held up a box. "I'm having a Pop-Tart for breakfast. Do you want one?"

Nadine considered the frosted toaster pastries to be children's food, but given Bella's affinity for sugary, processed snacks, she doubted there was anything better in the cabinets. And she was in no position to be picky. "Sounds good."

When the toaster sprang up, Bella placed a pastry on a paper towel and handed it to Nadine, then retrieved one for herself. "Do you mind if your bed becomes a table again?"

"Not at all." Nadine returned to the couch, folded the bedsheet, and set it aside. Once again, they sat side by side.

Nadine bit into the Pop-Tart, expecting to taste preservatives and too much sugar, but to her surprise, it was delicious. The light and crispy exterior was filled with warm, gooey fruit, like strawberry pie. "Mmmmph. That's...hmm. That's actually good."

Bella laughed. "Is this your first Pop-Tart? Like ever? You didn't eat them growing up?"

Nadine shrugged. "I think they might have been sold in the Philippines, but other foods were more popular."

"Ooh, like what?" Bella took a bite of her own.

"Well, for breakfast we'd usually have rice and sausage."

Bella raised her eyebrows. "Rice for breakfast?"

"Oh yes. Rice with everything. We had sweet pastries too, but the filing was more likely to be coconut or ube." Her mouth watered at the memory. It had been years since she'd had a proper Filipino pastry.

"*Ube*? What's that?"

"It's a purple yam. We use it in ice cream, cake, all sorts of sweets. They sell it at Asian stores in the city. I should pick some up for you to try."

"That would be awesome. I would love to try Filipino food."

"I could cook for us sometimes, if that would be helpful. I want to do my share."

"You can cook? Oh my Lord, I already love having you here." Bella beamed at her, and their eyes locked.

Nadine shifted under Bella's gaze and looked away. She quickly swallowed the last bite of her Pop-Tart. "Could I use your shower?"

"Of course. You don't have to ask."

Nadine fished through her duffel for clean clothes and headed to the bathroom. She started to lift her shirt when a frantic voice interrupted.

"Stop! Stop!" Bella burst into the bathroom. "Oh, crap. I meant to clean all this up."

"What?" The bathroom was far from spotless, but there wasn't much visible clutter.

"Um, this." Sheepishly, Bella pulled back the paisley-print shower curtain.

The bathtub was full of shampoo bottles, hair products, makeup, and accessories. There were so many products, she could barely see the floor of the tub. "Oh my."

Bella's face flamed. "My bathroom counter was a disaster, so before you got here, I threw everything into the tub so it would look clean. I meant to put everything away after you went to sleep, but I forgot. I'm sorry. You must think I'm the biggest slob you ever met."

Nadine shook her head. "What I think is that someone needs to call Guinness World Records about the number of hair products you own."

"I know." Bella covered her face with her hands. "I have a problem." She peeked through her fingers. "Do you regret moving in?"

"Of course not." Nadine smiled reassuringly. "Here, let me help you."

They piled Bella's beauty products back onto the counter. "Well, sorry again," Bella said. "I'll let you shower."

Once Nadine had the bathroom to herself, she stripped off her pajamas and stepped into the tub. The sill at the bottom of the frosted window on the shower wall was packed with assorted bath products, nearly all fruit scented. Nadine sniffed the bottle of Suave Tropical Coconut body wash. It smelled like Bella.

She lathered her body and moaned with pleasure as she leaned into the scalding spray. Suds spilled down her skin and pooled at her feet as clouds of steam rose around her. It was heaven.

She imagined Bella in the shower, her long hair slicked down her back. Then she caught herself and banished the vision. Such thoughts would only lead to trouble, and she couldn't afford trouble right now.

Instead, she turned her thoughts to a theory she had been thinking about since she had arrived at the apartment. It would explain Bella's struggles with math, her inability to study an assigned text—though she devoured books in her favorite genre—and the clutter lurking in every corner of her home.

Bella had obviously tried to tidy the apartment before Nadine arrived, but she clearly tended toward disorganization and distraction. For example, Bella had absently left the Pop-Tart foil wrappers on the counter despite the trash can being two feet away.

Nadine suspected ADHD. If she was right, she was fairly certain Bella had never been diagnosed. The question was whether to even bring it up. Bella had abandoned the idea of college a long time ago; maybe Nadine should leave it alone.

Still, even in her current job, Bella struggled. She berated herself when she had to use a calculator, or when her cash drawer failed to match the register.

The last thing Nadine wanted was to make Bella uncomfortable. But she couldn't let Bella continue to suffer when she had some insight that might help. She had to say something. She just needed to figure out when and how.

Nadine fished for her car keys in her jacket pocket. "Well, I'll see you at work." She nodded at Bella.

"Wait." Bella tilted her head. "You don't want to carpool? We have the exact same shift."

"Yes, but someone might see us drive in together. Aren't you worried people will guess that I'm staying with you?"

"But you are staying with me." Bella frowned. "You don't want anyone to know?"

"No, it's not that. I assumed *you* wouldn't want people to know. I'm not exactly popular with the management, and I don't want Grady and Jason to give you any grief."

"Oh, they already have." Bella rolled her eyes. "Grady warned me to keep away from you, but I don't care. I'm not ashamed that you're staying with me, and I won't act like I am."

There it was again, the heat in Nadine's abdomen when Bella stood up for her.

Bella stepped into black flats dotted with rhinestones, then bent over to adjust the heels. "Besides, you need to update your address with the store. They'll probably make the connection."

While Nadine had dutifully informed Michaela of her new address, she hadn't thought about updating it with the store for a temporary arrangement. She wondered how long Bella expected her to stay. "Okay, let's carpool. Your car or mine?"

"Um, can we take yours? Mine is kind of messy."

ADHD. But this wasn't the time. "Of course."

As it turned out, no one even noticed when they walked in together because everyone was focused on the new security system. Jason balanced on a ladder, attaching a video camera to the ceiling while Grady, Ashley, and Kenny gawked from below.

"That's the wrong wire." Grady pointed. "You need to use the red one."

"Look, I know what I'm—fuck! My finger!" Jason shook out his hand. "You distracted me."

Ashley spotted Bella and Nadine. "Y'all, guess what? We're going to be on TV."

Bella glanced at the boxes on the counter. "I can see that. How many cameras are there?"

"Not enough, if you ask me," Grady said. "I wanted one for every aisle. But at least we'll have coverage in the front, back, and middle of the store."

Ashley sighed. "No more picking wedgies in the kitchen aisle. Unless it's an absolute emergency."

Nadine blinked. "I'll be in the stockroom."

For once, Grady and Jason were too distracted to comment.

"See you later, roomie," Bella said.

Kenny's eyebrows shot up, but no one else seemed to realize what Bella had said.

They would find out soon enough. Nadine hoped Bella didn't get harassed as punishment for her kindness.

Chapter 13

BELLA WRAPPED A STRAND OF hair around her curling iron and held it there until it sizzled, then released the clamp. The loose ringlet bounced like a spring.

Nadine rapped on the bathroom door. "Are you almost ready? It's time to go."

Bella checked the time on her phone. "Oh, crap." It was one thing for Bella to be late, but Nadine couldn't afford even one mistake. Grady and Jason still resented Nadine's presence, and while they weren't actively sabotaging her as much as they had at first, they would jump at any excuse to fire her. "Be right there!"

There was no time to fix her face, so she grabbed her makeup bag and shoved a few products into it. Since Nadine was driving, she could fix her face on the way.

She emerged from the bathroom to find Nadine standing at the door, her black hair still damp from the shower. Nadine never primped before work, or any other time—although old photographs indicated that she could pull off a glamorous look if she wanted.

"We have, like, no food," Bella said on the way to the car. "Maybe we should stop at the store on the way home."

"Hmm." Nadine opened the door and slid into the driver's seat. "Okay."

Bella settled into the passenger seat and flipped open the mirror on the sun visor.

When the car didn't immediately start, Bella turned to look at Nadine. "What? Is something wrong?"

"Nothing's wrong. I'm just... Would you mind if I cook tonight? I'm out of practice, and I don't know if I'll be able to find the right ingredients here. But I'd like to make some Filipino food."

Bella wasn't sure if she liked Filipino food, but it didn't matter. The idea of Nadine cooking for them brought Bella more pleasure than she cared to admit. "I'd love that. I've been in a food rut for, well, my entire adult life. Anything that isn't from a box sounds amazing."

"Good." Nadine turned her key in the ignition, and the car sputtered to a start.

Bella exchanged a little smile with her reflection. So far, she and Nadine were doing well as roommates. Nadine might have been thrown when Bella revealed her sexual orientation, but she had recovered quickly—and now she was comfortable enough to cook. It was a good sign.

Bella squeezed the eyelashes of her right eye with the curler and counted to ten. Then she carefully brushed the wand through her lashes, coating them with a thin layer of mascara. But when the car hit a bump, her hand wobbled, depositing a black gob under her eye.

"Oops." Bella tried to wipe it off with her thumb but only smeared it into a thick line. "Crap. I look like a football player." She'd have to use soap and water at the store.

Nadine glanced at her, then returned her attention to the road. "You put a lot of effort into your hair and makeup."

She thinks it's a waste of time. Nadine probably thought makeup was only worth wearing to an important job, like being a lawyer or an advisor to a presidential nominee.

"I know I don't have to wear makeup to work. It's just..." Bella tried to think of how to explain it. "It makes me feel better. Like, I'm stuck in this tiny town, dealing with Grady and Jason's degrading bullshit all day long. But at least I look pretty."

Bella cringed as she heard her own words. Nadine probably thought she was shallow and vain in addition to being a chronic underachiever. "Ugh. I know I'm pathetic."

"You're not pathetic." Nadine's voice had a hard edge. "I'd certainly never describe you that way, and if anyone else ever does, I want you to send them to me."

"Thanks." Bella parted her lips and swabbed on tinted lip gloss.

"And you always look nice," Nadine added softly.

Bella watched in the mirror as crimson flushed into her cheeks. Nadine's opinion mattered to her a great deal. She knew Nadine appreciated her sharing her home, but Bella wasn't sure what Nadine thought of her aside from that. How could she possibly measure up against the super-educated lawyers and politicians from Nadine's former life?

She didn't want Nadine to think she was some ignorant small-town fuckup. But she couldn't kid herself. Nadine never would have spent time with Bella before she went to prison. If Nadine could trade her friendship with Bella for her old life, she'd do it in a second.

But now, at least, she had two compliments to get her through the day. *Not pathetic. Looks nice.* She would hold those words close to her chest while she waited for work to be over.

Bella took a break from stocking and arranging merchandise to scroll through her Instagram feed. Nothing new since she'd last checked about two minutes ago.

God, I'm so bored.

Bella had been working on the floor for almost two hours. It felt more like ten. Few tasks were more boring than picking up after customers and organizing shelves, dealing with the same piles of cheap merchandise day after day. No wonder she never bothered to clean her apartment.

Her phone buzzed as a notification banner appeared. It was a text from Raelyn. *Drinks tonight? Maybe a late dinner??* A row of booze and food emojis followed.

Bella's thumbs hovered over her phone's keyboard. If things were different, she would invite Raelyn to join them for dinner, but Raelyn's opinion of Nadine hadn't changed. Mixing her two friends was a bad idea. She responded: *Sorry I have plans. Maybe later this week?*

Raelyn wrote back, *Oooh, plans??? Who is she?*

Bella groaned. If she evaded the question, Raelyn would only push harder. *Not a date. Nadine is cooking for us.*

Bella chewed her lip, watching bubbles appear, disappear, and reappear before the response finally came. *How nice of her. Another time.*

Like a true Southern woman, Raelyn knew how to wrap disapproval in a neat little package with a bow on top. But Nadine wasn't the monster Raelyn imagined. Yes, Nadine had done something bad in the past, but she could also be kind.

Besides, it wasn't as if Alyssa Jackson would magically become president if Bella refused to eat Nadine's cooking.

She shoved a stack of shower curtains onto the shelf. *I'm not doing anything wrong.*

Bella arrived at the time clock the second her shift ended. As she punched out, Nadine appeared behind her.

"Long-ass day." Bella slung her purse over her shoulder.

"Aren't they all?" Nadine's polo was dusty, and her face, like Bella's, was shiny with sweat and grime. "Let's get out of here."

Outside, they walked next door to the Food Lion.

"I hope Todd isn't working tonight," Bella said as they approached the entrance.

Nadine stopped. "I didn't even think of that. Do you want to go somewhere else?"

"No, it's okay. He's the one who assaulted me. I shouldn't have to go somewhere else. Besides, he won't mess with me when there are witnesses."

"Certainly not while I'm around, if he likes his limbs intact."

Pleasure flooded Bella's chest. Nadine had become protective of her in more ways than one, and she liked it.

She plunked her purse down in a metal shopping cart, but before she could begin pushing, Nadine grabbed both handles and steered it into the store.

Bella smiled to herself as she realized Nadine intended for them to share a cart. It made her feel as if they were friends, shopping for their shared household.

Nadine looked around warily before pushing her sunglasses up to her forehead. Bella prayed no one would recognize Nadine, but she would give sassy Southern-girl hell to anyone who bothered them.

"What are you going to make?" Bella asked.

"I thought we'd start simple." Nadine dropped two packs of chicken into the cart. "Chicken adobo with rice. Most Americans find it palatable. And the ingredients are cheap."

Bella grinned. "I *love* palatable food. And cheap is good." She scrimped on groceries whenever she could, sometimes surviving on ramen noodles to make it to payday. As a new employee, Nadine's budget must be even tighter.

They wandered through the store, picking up the ingredients Nadine needed, plus other essential items. When they reached the breakfast aisle, Bella stopped in front of the Pop-Tarts. "We're almost out of these, which is weird because I bought a big box of them last week."

Nadine looked sheepish. "I may have eaten a few. I admit they are…not terrible. Despite lacking nutritional value."

Bella laughed. "Well, since I've already corrupted you, let's pick some new flavors to try. How about s'mores? Oh, and they have strawberry milkshake." She held up a neon-pink box.

"Milkshake? Seriously? I see we're abandoning all pretense that it's anything but dessert."

"Hey, it's part of a complete breakfast." Bella tossed both boxes into the cart. "Here, I'll get some fruit-flavored ones too. For our health."

When they reached the checkout counter, Nadine pulled out her wallet.

"Hey, no. I've got it." Bella dug into her purse. She had decided beforehand that she would pay for the groceries since she obviously had more money.

"Absolutely not. It's the very least I can do." Nadine placed her hand on Bella's arm. "Please. I want to."

"Okay. But I'll pay next time."

"Fine." Nadine presented her card to the cashier, a bored-looking teenager with black hair, blonde roots, and a shark's-tooth necklace.

Bella held her breath, waiting to see if the woman recognized Nadine.

"Y'all are together?" There was no hint of recognition or judgment.

"Yes," Nadine said. "We're together."

Bella liked the sound of those words far too much.

Chapter 14

NADINE CLOSED HER EYES AND inhaled the rich aroma of adobo. *God, I've missed this.* After two years of prison food, then a regular diet of oatmeal and canned soup at Renn House, cooking in a real kitchen unexpectedly caused her to choke up.

She was glad Bella wasn't there to witness her tears. She didn't want to explain. Of course Bella knew she'd gone to prison, but lately the topic made Nadine more self-conscious than usual.

She dabbed her eyes with a paper towel. *I don't want her to see me as a felon.* The rest of the public could fuck off with their scorn and condemnation, but Bella's opinion mattered to her. And that opinion, inevitably, was shaped by the belief that Nadine had committed a terrible crime.

I could tell her the truth. The little voice sounded a lot like Patricia. If anyone in her strange new life might believe her, it was Bella.

But could she take that risk? What if she told the truth and Bella thought it was a desperate, cowardly lie? She couldn't stand to live there if Bella didn't believe her.

Nadine tossed the paper towel into the trash and watched it flutter to the bottom of the can. *It's too late to take it back.*

When the chicken was cooked through, she turned off the burner. A separate pot kept the rice warm. It wasn't as fluffy as the rice she'd once made in her old cooker, but it would be infinitely better than the soggy instant rice they'd served in prison.

Nadine stepped into the living room, where Bella was curled up on the couch, immersed in drawing on her iPad.

Walking up behind Bella, Nadine peered at the iPad. The image was of a young woman with dark hair, thin lips, and a pointy nose. "That's beautiful. Another commission?"

"Yep. It's full color and full body, so I'll make good money. It's based on this photo." Bella tapped the screen and switched to the original image. She had perfectly captured the woman's features and slight smile while smoothing her skin and accentuating her flowing hair.

"A remarkable likeness. And quite flattering."

Bella laughed. "Hey, it keeps the customers happy."

"So we don't have to eat now, but the food is ready."

"Oh, sweet." Bella closed the cover of her iPad. "I'm ready now, if that's okay. It smells awesome, and I'm really hungry."

They filled their plates in the kitchen and settled onto the couch to eat. Nadine tried not to watch as Bella sampled the dish, but then she snuck a sideways glance.

"Mmm!" Bella's eyebrows flew up. "You can really cook!"

Bella's reaction was so emphatic that Nadine worried it was an act. "You don't have to pretend—"

"I'm not faking. This is great. It tastes like the chicken samples at the food court. You know, the ones that entice you to buy more chicken. It's just a bit more...I'm not sure how to describe it." She twirled her fork. "Tangy, almost?"

"That's the vinegar. I used less than usual because most Americans aren't used to the flavor."

"Well, it's good. Seriously. Thank you so much for cooking." Bella loaded her fork and took another bite.

"Anytime. I've missed it." Nadine held up a spoonful of rice. "Especially the rice. I'm very picky about how it's made."

They ate in silence for a few minutes until Nadine noticed Bella watching her curiously.

"Why aren't you using a knife?" Bella asked.

Nadine looked down at the fork and spoon on her plate. "This is just what I'm used to."

"You weren't allowed knives in prison?"

Nadine tensed but decided that the question was asked without judgment. "No, that's not why. I grew up eating meals with a fork and spoon. It's just how Filipinos eat—where I'm from, anyway. I can't speak for the whole country."

Bella looked thoughtful. "Do you miss the Philippines?"

"Sometimes. I miss the food for sure. And my family." She thought of Patricia holding Miko. "Mostly I miss my sister."

"Your sister lives over there? I thought your whole family moved here when you were a kid."

"Patricia is my half-sister. We moved here because my mom got a work visa, but my dad... He didn't like America. He'd been an accountant in the Philippines, but his English wasn't great, so he could only get hired for manual labor. It was hard for him. He didn't like that my mom made more money. Anyway, he left when I was a kid and went back to the Philippines. We never had much of a relationship after that."

"I'm sorry. That really sucks."

"It's fine." Nadine lowered her gaze. She didn't want pity.

"My dad left too, so I understand. I mean, I don't know your exact experience, of course, but I know it hurts to feel like you're not wanted."

Nadine looked up, surprised. "When did your father leave?"

"When I was three. He left Cheriville after he lost his job, and we never heard from him again. Sometimes I'm not even sure if I remember him or if I'm just making up memories from photographs and from what I've been told." Bella shook her head. "Anyway, according to my mom, he's an addict and a piece of shit, so it's like, whatever. I don't even care." Her lopsided smile told a different story.

"Still, it's hard when a parent leaves. I'm sorry we both went through it." Nadine scooped rice with her spoon. "Did your mom remarry?"

"Nope. She never even dated after he left. She never said it exactly this way, but I think her marriage was so bad that she'd rather be lonely than deal with a man again."

"It was the same with my mom, except she passed away when I was in college." Nadine stared down at her plate. "It's funny. It's been almost two decades, but I still..."

"Oh God, Nadine."

"It's okay." Nadine held up her hand, not wanting to go down that road. It was too painful. She took a few breaths, collecting herself. "So we were both raised by single mothers. I didn't know we had that in common."

"Yep. We're both in the deadbeat dad club. Cheers. And screw them." Bella raised her glass. "But you said your sister has a different mom. Did your dad remarry?"

"Not legally. They don't have divorce over there, but he met someone new and had my sister."

"Wait. No divorce at all?" Bella's eyes widened. "Not for any reason?"

"Indeed. You can only get an annulment, and it's a long, expensive process. The Catholic Church has a great deal of influence on family law." Nadine smiled wryly. "But actual behavior is another story. People just split up and live with new partners."

"Wow. Is it, like, really conservative there?"

"Not as much as you might think. Filipino women can be very independent."

"Well, that's good. Still, if they're Catholic, they probably wouldn't like me." Bella pulled on her hair. "You know, because of the whole gay thing."

"Oh, I don't know about that. There are gay and trans celebrities, and a lot of Filipinos are fine with it." Nadine ran a considering gaze over Bella. "I think they'd like you quite a bit."

Bella blushed, and Nadine tore her gaze away. *Be careful.* She couldn't afford to look at Bella like that.

It was time to steer the conversation to safer territory. "I also miss Filipino food, the things you can't buy here."

"Oh yeah? Like what?"

"Tropical fruit. I grew up eating jackfruit, *lanzones*. We had a mango tree in our backyard, and when I was a kid, I would climb up there and pick one when I was hungry." She could almost feel the juice running down her chin.

"I've never heard of jackfruit. Or the other one. But we do have mangos."

"Mangos are different here. I remember when we first moved to the States, I didn't understand why American fruit wasn't as sweet as the fruit back home."

"I guess I don't know what I'm missing." Bella sounded sad. "I'll probably never find out. I've never been outside the country."

"You're still young. You still have time."

"Yeah, maybe." Bella took another bite. "They speak a different language there, right?"

"Yes, Filipino. There are many different languages, but that's the main one."

Curiosity glittered in Bella's eyes. "Can you still speak it?"

"I can, but not nearly as well as my sister. I came here with a ten-year-old's vocabulary, so there are a lot of words I don't know. Or maybe I just don't remember."

Bella grinned. "Can you teach me to say something?"

"What do you want to know?"

"I don't know. Anything. How about *hello*?"

"Hmm. For a greeting, it's most common to say *kumusta*. It means *how are you*?"

"Ka-moo-sta?" It sounded clunky in Bella's mouth.

"Kumusta," Nadine said again, emphasizing the smooth vowels.

"That's what I said, isn't it?" Bella giggled. "Sorry, I have the worst Southern accent. But I'll try to get better. Maybe you can teach me something every day. Just one word or phrase."

Nadine rubbed her chin. "I'm not sure you'd ever use it. Most Filipinos in the US speak English."

"But I'd be able to talk to you. Just think, we could talk shit about customers right in front of them."

"Sadly, I don't think that would be wise." With Nadine's terrible luck, someone would understand them and complain to Grady.

"Hmm. Maybe we could say nice things about them, and they would *think* we're talking shit. That's almost better." Bella winked, and for a moment Nadine forgot to breathe.

"Well." She scraped the last bite of food from her plate. "We'll have to work up to that."

"That's fair. But I want to learn one more word today." Bella looked around the room, then down at her empty plate. "I'd like to thank you for cooking. How would I say that?"

"*Salamat*. It means *thank you*."

"Salamat." Bella drew out the vowels with a Southern twang.

"Not bad." Bella's pronunciation was awful, but the effort was sincere.

"Kumusta! Salamat." Bella beamed. "I'm speaking Filipino!"

"Yes, you are." Nadine's mouth was dry, and once again heat stirred in her belly. Bella's proximity, her genuine enjoyment of Nadine's cooking, and her joy at learning Filipino were affecting Nadine in ways that were very wrong.

Dangerous ito. Be careful.

Chapter 15

BELLA CRAMMED HER CLEAN LAUNDRY into an overstuffed dresser drawer. Soon, the clothes would be riddled with wrinkles, but she'd worry about that later.

Nadine appeared in the doorway. "This really isn't necessary. There's no law against having a messy room."

"I know." Bella continued shoving clothes into the drawer. "I just want to make a good impression."

"Well, I appreciate that, but she's looking for drugs, firearms, stuff like that." Nadine leaned against the doorframe. "So, unless you've been leading a double life, I think my probation is safe."

Drugs. "Oh my gosh!" Bella jumped up. She pushed past Nadine, sprinted into the kitchen, and flung open a cabinet with a chaotic assortment of bottles and jars.

Nadine followed her. "What's wrong?"

Bella pushed through the spice jars and pulled out a jar of pills labeled in Japanese. "I went on this silly diet one time and bought this sketchy supplement on the internet. Shit, it was like five years ago. What if your probation officer thinks they're illegal steroids? What if they *are* illegal steroids?"

"Bella. Calm down. They're probably just sugar pills. You don't have anything illegal." Nadine sounded totally in control. And yet they both flinched when there was a sharp knock on the door.

Bella hovered in the living room while Nadine answered the door.

"Hello," Nadine said. "Please come in."

Nadine's probation officer strode into the living room and offered Bella her hand. "I'm Michaela Schwartz."

Bella's first reaction was *lesbian.* Michaela had short hair trimmed crisply at the sides and wore a black men's shirt over her stocky frame. The deep voice and firm handshake were additional evidence—but then again, Bella's gaydar had been wrong before.

"Hello. I'm Bella Clarke."

"Relax," Michaela said, apparently sensing Bella's nerves. "I'm just going to look around. Nothing too invasive."

"Okay. Great. Um, it's small and kind of messy. But there are absolutely no guns."

Michaela's eyes twinkled. "Good to know."

The inspection began in Bella's bedroom. Bella and Nadine watched from the doorway while Michaela glanced around. While far from perfect, the bedroom looked presentable enough…as long as the drawers stayed closed.

Michaela seemed more interested in the artwork on the walls than in searching for contraband. "These are great." She turned to Bella. "Did you draw these?"

"I did." Bella twirled a strand of hair. "I'm an amateur artist."

"She's a *professional* artist," Nadine said. "People pay for her work."

"I'm not surprised." Michaela smiled at Bella. "You're very talented."

The kitchen was next. Bella couldn't help squirming at the thought of her sketchy pills, but Michaela didn't even open the cabinets.

After a quick tour of the bathroom, Michaela returned to the living room. "You have a lot of books." She walked over to the shelves and scanned the titles.

Oh crap. My romance novels. Her damn books were going to out her again, this time to a federal probation officer. While many of the titles were ambiguous, Bella owned a couple of lesbian erotica anthologies with bold titles on the spines.

Michaela took a step back and turned to Bella with raised eyebrows.

I'm so busted. But given Michaela's probable membership in the same club, surely it wouldn't be a problem…right?

Michaela glanced between Nadine and Bella. "So you two met at work?"

"That's right," Nadine said.

"And you're friends?"

She thinks we're fucking. Bella's cheeks burned. "Um, yes. We've become friends."

Michaela's look said *don't bullshit me,* but she didn't comment. Finally, she asked Nadine, "Where do you sleep?"

"There, on the couch." Nadine pointed.

But it didn't look like anyone slept there. In her effort to create the illusion of a tidy living space, Bella had stashed Nadine's pillow and blanket in the hall closet.

"I see." Michaela studied Nadine. "I'm finished with the inspection. Nadine, could I speak with you outside for a moment?"

Bella swallowed nervously. Was Nadine in trouble because of her?

Michaela leaned against the porch railing and crossed her arms. "What is your actual relationship with Bella?"

"I'm not sure what you mean." Nadine's thoughts raced. Was this all about Bella's sapphic novels, or did Michaela have some other reason for suspecting they were more than friends?

"If you two are dating or involved, you can tell me. You won't get in trouble." Michaela studied her closely. "I'm gay. I have a wife. There's no need to be embarrassed."

Nadine swallowed. Was she giving off gay vibes? Sure, she had short hair, but only because she couldn't be bothered to style it. "We're just friends. And coworkers."

"Okay. But she likes women."

It wasn't a question. Nadine shifted her weight. "Yes, Bella is gay. But that doesn't mean we're sleeping together. Isn't it homophobic to assume we are?"

Michaela sighed. "I'm only asking because, in my experience, housing arrangements based on romance are unstable—especially when it's a new relationship. You might break up. Or you might want to break up but feel that you can't, and that's not good either." She paused. "Even if you're not interested, have you considered that Bella may have feelings for you?"

"She doesn't," Nadine said firmly. Gay or not, Bella would never be interested in someone with her history.

"Okay." Michaela seemed to relax. "Well, the apartment is fine. You certainly have my approval to stay here."

Nadine exhaled. "Thank you."

"Bella seems very nice. It's obvious that she cares about you. Maybe that's why I thought... Well, never mind. You're right. I shouldn't have made assumptions, and I apologize. Anyway, I'm glad you've made a friend."

"Thanks. Me too."

Michaela pulled out her phone. The screen was littered with notifications. "I'd better go. Text if you need anything, okay?"

Nadine took a moment to catch her breath before going back inside the apartment.

Bella was on the couch, her hands clasped over her knees. "What did she say?"

Nadine shrugged out of her jacket. "She said the apartment is fine."

"So we passed. Thank goodness." Bella smiled. "What else did she say? You guys were out there for a while."

Nadine hesitated. "Nothing important. She was asking about work, making sure everything is okay."

"Did she ask you if we were, um...?" Bella squirmed. "I know she saw my books, and it sort of seemed like she was implying..."

"Oh, yes." Nadine kept her voice light. "She asked about the nature of our relationship."

Bella winced. "Sorry. That must have been weird for you."

"It's fine. I told her we're just friends. She believed me, and that was it."

"Right. Friends." Bella nodded, but she was blushing as if she had been caught.

Michaela wasn't on to something, was she?

No. The idea Bella might want more than friendship was preposterous. Nadine was a charity case. She slept here because she had nowhere else to go, not because Bella wanted her around every day. In fact, given her past and what she had supposedly done, she was lucky Bella was willing to call her a friend.

Chapter 16

"I'm so sorry, but I'm not authorized to give you a discount." Bella made her sympathetic face.

"But it's damaged." The scowling white-haired man pointed again to a small dent on the box.

"Well, yes, the box has an...imperfection...but won't you be taking it out of the box anyway?"

"But I like to store my appliances in their original boxes." His voice had become a high-pitched whine.

Oh, give me a damn break. Bella wasn't in the mood for boomers acting like babies. "I understand. I really wish I could help."

He puffed out his lower lip in a full-on pout. "Walmart would give me a discount for this. They have better prices too."

"Well, maybe you should go to Walmart." Oops, too blunt. "I mean, I want you to get the best deal."

"Fine." He huffed. "You just lost a sale." He stomped away, leaving the blender on the counter.

"Salamat," Bella muttered.

She had started the day in a good mood, thanks to a Pop-Tart breakfast with Nadine, plus another Filipino language lesson—*kape* meant *coffee*— and a pleasant drive to work with the country music station blasting.

Then Jason had stuck her on register, and her morale had deteriorated, thanks to the parade of cranky customers that had plagued the store all morning.

She had just picked up a pen to doodle when a woman whisked through the automatic doors, carrying a large Overstock Oasis shopping bag. Gray hair bounced as she marched toward Bella's checkout counter.

Bella stifled a groan. All returns were awful because they took so much time to process, and her instincts told her this one would be extra annoying. The customer dropped the bag on the counter. "I'd like to return this."

"No problem. Let's take a look." Bella opened the bag and pulled out a down pillow. The tags had been cut off, and it was slightly yellow. "Um, do you have a receipt for this?"

The woman reached into her purse and produced a stack of receipts. "Let's see. Pillow. Ah, here." She handed Bella a wrinkled receipt.

The ink had faded to a shadow. Bella squinted at the date. "I'm so sorry, ma'am, but we only accept returns within sixty days. This pillow was purchased almost two years ago."

The customer puffed out her chest.

Here we go.

"Well, that's not enough time. Besides, this pillow is defective. It keeps losing feathers, and it's not fluffy anymore."

"You actually can't return used merchandise. And like I said, it's past the window anyway. I'm sorry, but we, uh…" Her attention was drawn to a man in a black baseball cap who was hovering a few feet away, scanning the store. "Sorry, what was I saying? Oh, we can't accept it. Please excuse me."

The woman opened her mouth to protest, but Bella hurried away from the counter.

"Hi there, can I help you?" Bella asked. The man wore square rimless glasses, and his mouth was drawn in a tight line.

He looked her up and down. "Yeah. Is Nadine Bayani here?"

Somehow, she had known he was looking for Nadine. Probably another so-called journalist who wanted to embarrass her on social media or some bitter rando seeking to vent his anger in person. Thankfully, Nadine had the day off. "She's not here."

"Well, when will she be back?"

Nice try. "We don't give out employee schedules. And if you're here to harass her, you should know that we don't tolerate it."

His eyes narrowed. "I just want to talk to her. That's all."

Oh, sure. Sounds very legit. "Well, I doubt she wants to talk to you. And she has already been through hell, so just leave her alone."

He looked her up and down as though a new idea had occurred to him. "Wait, are you two friends? Has she said anything to you about Alyssa Jackson?"

Bella raised her chin. "Yes, we are friends. But I'm not going to tell you anything. And, like I said, Nadine isn't here, so I'm afraid you've wasted a trip."

"If you say so." He walked away from Bella, muttering under his breath. But instead of leaving the store, he turned down one of the aisles. *Great. He's probably looking for someone else to pump for information.*

Bella returned to her register. The customer was still parked in front of the counter, having made no move to collect her pillow or her decrepit receipt. "Sorry about that. Is there anything else I can help you with today?"

"You can help me by giving me my refund. In cash." The woman pointed at the pillow. "I'm not taking this home."

"Again, I'm sorry, but that isn't possible. We can discard the item for you, but—"

"Didn't anyone teach you that the customer is *always* right?"

"Ma'am, the register literally will not accept this return. There's nothing I can do." The outdated registers weren't actually programmed to know the difference, but sometimes the lie worked.

The woman crossed her arms. "That's outrageous."

"Yeah, we don't have any flexibility. It's unfortunate because I really want to help. But I can't." Bella flicked a quick glance down the aisle where the man in the black baseball cap had disappeared. He was peering into the stockroom. *Ugh. He needs to leave.*

"You know, I could give you the address for the corporate office. You could write them a letter." Bella kept an index card with corporate's address next to the register for exactly this type of customer. She placed it on the counter.

"I absolutely will." The woman fished in her purse and pulled out a pen to copy the address.

"Okay, great. Let us know if you hear back. And again, I'm very sorry."

While the customer began to write, Bella took off in search of Nadine's stalker. On her way to the back of the store, she ran into Jason.

"Aren't you supposed to be on register?" Jason snapped.

Great, one of his moods. Bella thought fast. "I am, but I thought I saw a shoplifter."

Jason's eyes sparked. "Where?"

"There's a man in a black baseball cap skulking around, not buying anything. I also saw him looking into the stockroom."

Jason squared his jaw. "I'm on it. You go back to your register."

When Bella returned, there was no sign of the customer or the pillow. *Phew.* She perched on her stool and waited.

The man in the cap soon emerged from the far aisle with Jason at his heels.

"Get out," Jason said. "And don't come back."

The man glared at Bella as he exited the store.

Jason turned to Bella. "Nice work."

Bella saluted. As soon as Jason turned around, she rolled her eyes.

Her phone buzzed against her thigh. She slid it out of her pocket to see a text from Raelyn. *Hey lady. When do you get off tonight? Long-ass day and I need some chocolate.*

Bella tapped her response: *Six. Ice cream?? 6:15?*

Raelyn responded with a thumbs-up emoji. Bella returned the phone to her pocket, but it buzzed a few seconds later. This time, it was a news alert: *CNN exclusive: Senator Alyssa Jackson (D-IL) declares campaign for presidency.*

Interesting. The man looking for Nadine had said something about Jackson. Was he a reporter covering the campaign? It was possible, but he had a certain aura of sleaze that made her doubt his motives were journalistic. Still, the timing was curious.

Raelyn was already camped out at the ice cream parlor with a large fudge sundae. Judging from her crisp blouse and heavy eye makeup, she had come directly from the bank.

"Hey," Raelyn said through a mouthful of ice cream. "Sorry I didn't wait for you. It was an emergency."

Bella grinned. "I can tell. Hang on. I'm going to order."

She examined the tubs of ice cream through the glass. They were arranged like works of art, with candy and fruit displayed on top of each flavor.

"Good evening!" said the young woman behind the counter. "Thanks for coming in. Would you like to try anything?" Her brown hair was secured in a perky ponytail under her visor, and she wore a crisp pink shirt that said Susie's Ice Cream. Bella had been just like her when she first started working retail, nervous and eager to please.

"No, thanks. I've had them all, so I'd just be taking advantage."

"Oh wow. Every single one?"

"Yeah, I grew up here. I've been eating Susie's Ice Cream since I was a kid, and most of the flavors haven't changed."

The young woman wilted a bit.

Bella hastened to reassured her. "Oh, I don't mean that like it's bad. Don't mess with what's working, right?"

"Sure thing." Her ponytail bounced as she nodded. "Folks here like the classics."

Bella returned to the table with two scoops of chocolate raspberry swirl in a paper cup. As the first spoonful melted on her tongue, she sighed at the rich, tangy taste. "God, I love this place." She took another bite before asking, "So why was your day so long?"

"The damn customers. Like, I'm sorry your boss owes you money. That sucks. But ranting at me for ten minutes isn't gonna make the money appear." Raelyn plunged her spoon into a mountain of whipped cream. "Honest to God, I'd almost rather get robbed at gunpoint than deal with these toolbags for thirty seconds."

"I know exactly what you mean." Their jobs weren't all that different, really. The bank required a professional appearance and paid better than Overstock Oasis, but they both spent their days dealing with the public. *Maybe I'm more qualified for other jobs than I thought.* Bella considered Nadine's suggestion that she could get a job at a better store—but she couldn't leave Nadine at the store all alone.

Raelyn scooped out another spoonful. "What's new with you?"

"Not much. Pushy customers. Drawing portraits for cash. The usual." Bella licked her spoon clean and dug in for another bite.

"And how's your roommate?" Raelyn kept her tone neutral, but Bella knew how she really felt.

"Nadine has been great. Honestly. She even cooked for me last night. I mean, not *for me*." Bella hoped she wasn't blushing. "She made chicken adobo and shared it with me. It was really good."

Raelyn's intense green eyes seemed to see through her. "Wait a minute. You're not... Do you have a crush on Nadine Bayani?"

"No!" Bella shook her head vehemently. "We're just friends."

Raelyn sat back. "Friends, huh? I thought you just felt sorry for her."

Bella squirmed in her seat. "I do. But she's not a bad person. She cares about me."

Raelyn pressed her lips together but said nothing.

"That reminds me—some creepy guy was looking for her at the store today." Raelyn was unlikely to sympathize, but the incident still bothered Bella. "I don't know if he was a reporter or if he was there to harass her. We get both."

Raelyn wiped a smudge of chocolate from her chin. "He was probably a reporter. Nadine is back in the news after what Alyssa Jackson said today."

Bella frowned. "Did Alyssa say something about Nadine? All I heard is that she's running again."

Raelyn pulled out her phone. "She was talking about what happened in the last election, and she almost cried on camera. The clip went viral. Here, I'll find it." She tapped and scrolled, then pushed the phone across the table.

Bella pressed *play*. Alyssa appeared on the screen, sitting next to her square-jawed husband, Brice. Her chin-length blonde hair was straight and shiny, and she wore a sleek navy pantsuit that flattered her slim figure.

Across from them, the interviewer leaned in. "Three years ago, you were leading in the polls. Then you were accused of accepting fraudulent contributions from Atlas Health Source in exchange for dropping your plan to cap health insurance premiums. We know now that Nadine Bayani made that deal without your knowledge, but can you tell me what the experience was like for you?"

Alyssa closed her eyes. When she finally opened them, her eyes were shiny with tears. "You know, Melanie, it was very hard. Because I know who I am. I've been in politics for two decades, and I have never once compromised my integrity. Never."

Brice slung an arm around her shoulders.

Composing herself, Alyssa continued. "What Nadine did hurt me personally. It hurt my husband and my child. But you know who it hurt more? Working families. The men and women who struggle every day to keep a roof over their children's heads, put food on the table, and access affordable healthcare. These are the people Nadine hurt the most. The election wasn't about me, but when I lost, America lost. And that's what hurts more than anything."

Bella slid the phone back to Raelyn, her stomach unsettled. "Yeah, this could explain the guy who came in today. He was probably a reporter hoping for a comment."

"Alyssa is right, you know?" Raelyn set her spoon down and looked directly at Bella. "I love Alyssa Jackson, and I know you do too. But she wasn't the only victim. What Nadine did hurt more people than we could ever count. Rob Gunn cut food stamps, for God's sake. *Children* are going hungry, and Nadine has that on her hands."

"I know." Bella agreed with everything Raelyn was saying. So why didn't her feelings reflect those horrible truths?

"And don't even get me started on the Supreme Court."

"Yeah." Bella cringed at the reminder of Gunn's first appointment, a young, ultraconservative whose decisions would impact the country for decades.

"And it's not just the election. Do you ever think about what would have happened if Nadine hadn't been caught? If she had become White House chief of staff, she would have cut something really important from Alyssa's healthcare bill. Who knows what else she would have done? What other parts of Alyssa's agenda she would trade away? Chiefs of staff have a lot of power."

Bella stared down at her ice cream, now soupy. Raelyn's words stung because they were true. Nadine had confessed on national television.

Raelyn reached out to touch Bella's arm. "Look, I don't think it's right for her to be bullied or homeless. I just think you should be careful. She's not a good person."

Not a good person. The words clanged in Bella's ears. She didn't want to think of Nadine as a bad person. But would a good person do what Nadine had done?

"You're right. Sometimes I forget what she did. I guess I don't want to remember." Bella had ignored the truth to the point where she'd developed feelings for Nadine.

"You always see the best in people. It's one of the things I love about you. But don't let her suck you in with her charms because that's exactly what she did to Alyssa Jackson. Just keep your distance, okay?"

Raelyn was right—she was getting sucked in. But how could she keep her distance from Nadine when they worked and lived together? When her body buzzed every time Nadine was near?

Chapter 17

A CHIME ROUSED NADINE FROM her early evening nap. She fumbled for her phone and read the message on the screen through bleary eyes: *Alyssa is so evil!!*

Ah. Morning in the Philippines. Text balloons appeared in rapid succession as Patricia vented. *I can't believe she fucking cried. Why can't everyone see that she's faking?? It's so obvious. Aghhhhh. I hate her so much.*

The couch squeaked as Nadine lurched to a sitting position. The small apartment was dark, and there was no sign of Bella. She switched on the hot-pink lamp on the end table before responding. *I didn't watch the interview. The headline was enough.*

It's all going to start again. I hope you're ready. I wish people knew the truth. A series of sad and angry emojis followed.

I know the truth. You know. That has to be enough. Nadine put the phone down on the coffee table, then stood and stretched.

Bella was usually home by now, and Nadine couldn't help worrying. She knew it was silly. Bella was an adult, and she could be out doing any number of things—the things people do when they don't have to hide from the world.

Nadine should have been glad to have the apartment to herself. It was the only way she got true privacy. But as much as she cherished the alone time, after ten hours, she was ready for Bella to come home.

In the kitchen, she spooned leftover chicken adobo and rice into a bowl, leaving enough for Bella to eat when she got home. She smiled, recalling the morning's Filipino lesson. Bella's accent hadn't improved at all, but she had successfully memorized several words.

While the microwave warmed her dinner, she thought about which word to teach Bella next. Maybe the word for rice, kanin. After all, they'd be eating a lot more of it, now that she knew Bella liked her cooking.

The front door creaked open, followed by the sound of something heavy hitting the floor—Bella's massive purse.

Nadine stepped out of the kitchen. "Kumusta ka?"

The expression on Bella's face stopped her cold. Bella met Nadine's gaze, her eyes hard, then she glanced away, combing her fingers through her hair.

Nadine's protective instincts surged. "Are you okay?"

"Yes. Everything's fine." Her tone said the opposite.

"I'm heating leftover chicken for dinner. Would you like some?"

"No, thanks. I'm going to have something else." Bella took a step toward the kitchen, then abruptly spun in the other direction. "Actually, I'm going to take a shower." She disappeared into the bathroom.

Nadine sat on the couch with her dinner. Something had obviously happened. Bella could have had a bad day at the store—that place had a way of shredding one's sanity—but after her cold refusal of dinner, Nadine suspected that Bella's mood was directed at her.

Was this about Alyssa? Maybe Bella had seen the interview and bought into Alyssa's fake tears. Nadine ground her teeth at the thought.

Nearly half an hour passed before Bella emerged from her shower, wearing purple pajama pants and a snug black tank top that hugged every curve of her breasts. Her damp hair was piled on her head in a towel. Nadine looked away before she got caught staring, but Bella walked right past her and into the kitchen without even glancing in her direction.

She heard the freezer door open and close and the whir of the microwave. A few minutes later, Bella returned to the living room holding a beer and a small plastic tray, one of the freezer-burned prepared meals she ate when she was desperate. She hovered at the edge of the living room before she finally sat next to Nadine, placing the tray and the beer on the coffee table.

The couch had never felt so cramped, but there was nowhere else for Nadine to go in the small apartment. She stayed out of Bella's room by unspoken agreement, and she was not about to hide in the bathroom like a teenager. Or take extra-long showers like Bella.

The only thing left to do was break the silence. "Long day?"

"Yeah." Bella dipped her chin in a slight nod, then stuffed another forkful of food into her mouth.

Okay. Bella was angry with her. But why? They'd been laughing together that morning. *What changed?*

Nadine wanted to tell Bella to grow up and have a conversation about whatever was bothering her, but she was only too aware of her precarious position as a guest with no lease or formal agreement. If this arrangement fell through, she'd be screwed.

Instead, she asked cautiously, "Is something bothering you?"

Bella swallowed, then turned to face Nadine with troubled eyes. "I just...I've been thinking. Why did you do it?"

Nadine breathed in deeply and slowly exhaled. She knew what "it" meant. *Why did you sell out poor people to win an election?*

The urge to tell the truth clawed at her gut. Maybe Bella would believe her. Maybe it would be okay.

Still uncertain of what she'd end up saying, she eased into the story. "We came in third in Iowa." Nadine set her plate on the coffee table. "It's hard for a female candidate to get past the Iowa caucus. It always has been. We spent every penny we had and then some, and we had nothing to show for it." She could still see Alyssa's crumpled face, her tears—real tears for once—when the results came in.

Bella sat completely still, gaze on her lap.

"The problem with tanking in an early contest is the money dries up fast. Donors won't support a loser, and without money you can't compete in later states. Alyssa needed ad buys, ground troops. And she had to show the big donors that she could still raise money online. It was her only chance to stay in the race."

Bella looked up to meet Nadine's eyes. "What are you saying? That it was worth it? You promised to screw over *poor people* who can't afford health insurance."

"I..." Nadine clenched her jaw. "I didn't—"

"Did you know I'm one of those people? I pay three hundred dollars a month for my shitty Overstock Oasis health insurance that I can't even use because the deductible is so high. I can't afford to go to the damn doctor. Alyssa wanted to help people like me, and you were going to take that away."

Nadine's fingernails dug into her palms. She hadn't expected to face anger about the scandal here, not in the home that had become her only safe space, the only place where she wouldn't be judged or attacked.

"How were you going to pull it off?" Bella asked. "Were you going to tell Alyssa the truth after you made a dirty deal behind her back and hope she'd keep quiet to avoid a scandal? Or were you just going to trade away the premium cap and tell her she didn't have enough votes?"

"Look, I don't know what brought this on. But if you don't want me to stay here, I'll go."

"I didn't say that." Bella stabbed a piece of limp broccoli with her fork but didn't eat it.

"Then what do you want from me?"

"I want to know why you did it. Rob Gunn is president because of you, and people are hurting, literally dying, because of his horrible policies. I don't like to think about it, but it's true."

The words were like a punch to the stomach, taking her breath away.

"Sometimes I feel like I know you." Bella's voice caught. "But I clearly don't because I don't understand how you could have done what you did. Did the consequences even matter to you? Do you even feel guilty or...?" She made a frustrated gesture.

Nadine crossed her arms over her body like a shield. Bella would never believe she was innocent. Why should she? Why should anyone? "There's nothing I can say to you that would change your opinion."

"So you don't feel guilty."

"You have no idea how I feel." The words tasted like acid. In reality, she felt guilty all the time—guilty for lying, guilty for the heartbreak she'd caused her sister. The past two years had been such a mindfuck, she sometimes felt guilty of the crime.

Bella slumped her shoulders. "Okay. I thought maybe I was missing something. But I guess I'm not." She shook her head. "It's my fault. Since I've gotten to know you, I wanted to think...wanted to believe... I don't know. I guess I'm just in a weird mood." She picked up her tray and her beer. "I'm going to eat in my room."

Nadine watched as Bella walked away. The bedroom door clicked shut.

She sagged back against the couch. It had been a fantasy to think Bella might be different from the rest of the world. Bella would never harass and bully her like the others, but in the end, she saw what everyone else saw: a coldhearted criminal. Nadine never should have allowed herself to hope for anything different.

I shouldn't have moved in with her. This night, this conversation, never would have happened if she had simply lived in her car. She would be cold and hungry and alone, but at least she would still be numb.

A loud, obnoxious sound woke Bella from her dream. Fuck. It was her alarm. She groaned and rolled over on her side, twisting her legs in the sheets.

She grabbed her phone from the nightstand and silenced the alarm, then curled against a pillow while her brain emerged from the fog of heavy slumber.

Her shift started in two hours. Nadine's did too. Soon she'd have to leave her cozy bed and face her coworker-slash-roommate-slash-person who induced a confusing mess of feelings every time their eyes met.

Bella winced as she recalled the argument from the night before. *Oh Lord. Everything is fucked-up now.*

She'd had a rock in her stomach ever since the ice cream parlor. As much as she hated to admit it, Raelyn was right. Last night's train wreck conversation had only confirmed it.

It's my fault. Nadine had never lied to her. She had never claimed to be innocent or misunderstood. Even when she thought Bella might kick her out of the apartment, she hadn't groveled or feigned remorse. Instead, it was Bella who had been pretending.

As she pushed herself up in bed, Bella resolved to pull back from their deepening friendship. She wouldn't evict Nadine or treat her badly, but she would stop getting—as Raelyn put it—sucked in.

She would be professional at work and polite at home. But there would be no more oversharing, no more flirty Filipino language lessons. And no fantasizing about world-famous criminals who weren't even queer. Absolutely none of that.

Feeling determined, she kicked off the covers, slid out of bed, and opened her bedroom door.

Nadine sat cross-legged on the couch, nursing a cup of coffee. She looked up, her gaze guarded.

"Good morning." Bella walked past Nadine without waiting for a response.

In the kitchen, she toasted a Pop-Tart and made coffee. She returned to the living room with one in each hand. "I'm sorry for being weird last night. Everything is fine. Really."

"Okay…"

"Would you like to drive to work together?"

Nadine eyed her warily. "Sure."

"Cool." Bella nodded. "I'll be ready on time." She carried her breakfast into her bedroom.

That was good. She'd been pleasant but detached. She could do this.

Chapter 18

NADINE STABBED THROUGH PACKING TAPE, stomped on the box, and kicked it into the growing pile of cardboard that had borne her frustration all morning.

I have to move out. She didn't know where or how, but she couldn't remain in the small apartment with someone who made her feel like this.

Sure, Bella had been cordial on the drive to work, but losing the shared smiles and jokes, the moments that felt like real friendship, hurt more than any sneer from a stranger. She couldn't deal with it at work *and* at home, where she couldn't even retreat behind a bedroom door.

Money was still a barrier to finding her own place, and her record and reputation hadn't changed, but maybe there was a new listing in the area. She resolved to search Craigslist that evening when she could access Bella's Wi-Fi.

Nadine sliced the next box, dragging the boxcutter down the seam and—"Fuck!"—straight into her thumb. Blood trickled down to her palm.

The metal doors swung open. A man wearing a black baseball cap and rimless glasses strode in and stopped a few feet in front of her. Nadine opened her mouth to tell him customers weren't allowed in the stockroom, but when their eyes met, she knew he'd been looking for her.

"I was going to ask how you're adjusting to small-town retail, but I guess that's my answer." He gestured at her bloody thumb.

"Who are you?"

He held his hands up. "Hey, I'm not here to mess with you. I came to talk."

"Fine. Tell me your name." She held her hand away from her body but made no other move to address the blood.

"Ryan Mitchell. I work for Jeff Zaller. And I just want to ask you a few questions."

"Oh, I see. Zaller wants to challenge Rob Gunn, like every other Democratic senator under eighty years old, and you're doing opposition research on Alyssa for the primary. But why do you think I'd help you? Don't you think I've hurt Alyssa enough?"

"See, that's the thing." Ryan crossed his arms. "I don't think you did a damn thing to Alyssa Jackson except save her pretty ass from a well-deserved stint in prison."

"Oh, so you're a conspiracy theorist. How unfortunate for your boss. Does he know you're doing this?"

He scoffed. "I'm someone who sees through Alyssa's *earnest little patriot* act. I also know Atlas wasn't the first or the last time she traded promises for cash."

What was he talking about? Was Alyssa reckless enough to commit the same crime twice? And if there was evidence of another bribe, could it somehow lead to a reexamination of the Atlas deal?

"Look," Ryan said, "I'm not sure why you took the fall for her. But whatever the reason, it can't have been worth it." He glanced around the dingy stockroom. "Clearly, she didn't take care of you. You're alone, and everyone hates you."

The words stung because they were true. Even Bella thought she was evil.

And that was exactly why this was futile. There was no point in recanting and accusing Alyssa. The media frenzy might cast enough doubt to cost Alyssa the primary, but it wouldn't lead to the public actually believing Nadine.

Unless the truth came from Alyssa herself, Nadine would never recover her reputation. The best she could hope for was to be left alone, starting with Ryan.

"Tell me, Ryan, what exactly was your thought process here? You think I'm so loyal to Alyssa that I spent *two years* in prison for her. Yet you expected my loyalty would crumble when you pointed out that my life sucks?"

He cocked his head. "I thought you might be interested in talking to someone who doesn't believe you're Satan. Someone who wants to hear the real story, who has a professional interest in bringing that story to light."

"Well, you thought wrong." A fat drop of blood spilled off her hand and hit the floor. "I need to clean this up." She strode past him to the door.

"Wait." He caught up with her and thrust a business card into her uninjured hand. "Take this. Think about it. You can call me anytime."

She hadn't meant to take the card, but her fingers closed around it unconsciously. She stuffed it into her pocket and used her good hand to catch another drop of blood.

He looked at her with pity. "Whatever she promised you, whatever she has on you—this isn't worth it."

"Goodbye." She walked past him and pushed through the door to wash the blood from her hands.

"Attention, Overstock Oasis shoppers." Bella's voice crackled over the speakers. "The store is now closed. Please bring your items to the checkout counter."

That was her cue. They had spent most of the day avoiding each other, but tonight they were scheduled to close the store together.

Nadine hovered in the bath aisle while Bella checked out the last customer. When the transaction was finished, she approached the register. "Hi."

"Hello. Ready to close?" Bella sounded upbeat, but Nadine recognized her customer service voice. Polite. Distant.

"Yes, I'm ready." *Ready to get this over with.*

Bella opened the safe and placed three stacks of cash onto the counter. "How was your day?"

Well, I maimed myself with a box cutter, and a shady political operative tried to recruit me to take down my corrupt ex-boss. "It was fine, thanks."

Nadine counted the stacks of cash while Bella tallied the bills and coins from her register. She jotted down the total and looked up.

Bella was still counting, mouthing numbers to herself with a creased brow. Finally she said, "I'm short. More than five dollars." She smacked the counter. "Damn it."

"It happens. Don't be so hard on yourself."

"Yeah." She stuffed the cash into the plastic bag they would give to the bank.

When the bag was signed and sealed, Bella gave Nadine a self-conscious shrug. "Well, I have to get my purse. I'll be back."

While she was gone, Nadine considered whether to tell Bella what had been on her mind before things had changed between them. It seemed like the worst possible time to bring up Bella's academic struggles, and yet there might never be a good time.

Bella returned with her purse hanging from her shoulder.

They reached Nadine's car and climbed in. Both stared straight ahead as Nadine drove to the bank.

Nadine decided to say something. If Bella didn't want to listen, that was her choice, but she deserved to know what Nadine suspected. Anyway, with their friendship crumbling, there wasn't much left to lose.

When they stopped at a red light, she turned her head. "Bella?"

"Yeah?" She kept looking straight ahead.

Nadine searched for a way to broach the topic, then decided to be direct. "Have you ever considered that you might have ADHD?"

Bella turned to look at her. "What?"

"Attention deficit hyperactivity disorder."

"I know what it means." Bella wrinkled her forehead. "But I'm not… Why would you ask me that?"

"I've noticed some things since I met you. Certain behaviors and patterns. It could explain your academic difficulties. No one's ever mentioned it to you?"

"That's what little kids have when they can't sit still. They get put on Ritalin. You think I'm like that?"

Nadine shook her head. "No. You can have trouble paying attention without being hyperactive. In fact, it presents that way for a lot of girls. That's why so many are never diagnosed."

Bella frowned. "But I pay attention to things. Like my artwork. And my books."

The light turned green. Nadine turned down the street that led to the bank. "You pay attention when you're interested," she said, keeping her eyes on the road. "But people with ADHD struggle to focus when they're bored. It can make schoolwork extremely challenging."

"Is that why you think I have it?" Bella voice was small. "Because I flunked out of college?"

"That's one reason." Nadine pulled into the drive-through lane behind another car. She faced Bella again. "You also seem to struggle with organization and counting."

Bella's cheeks flushed. "I know I'm messy and bad at math. And I know I'm not smart like you. Believe me, you're not the first person to tell me that."

"You *are* smart." Nadine clenched her hands with anger at the people in Bella's life who had made her feel that way. She had only known Bella for a few weeks, but she could see that Bella had insight and intuition that others lacked, not to mention talent. "You're a lot smarter than you realize. But if I'm right, it means you never had a chance to adapt to the way your brain works."

Bella twisted the handle on her purse. "How do you even know about this?"

"I had a friend in law school who struggled with focus. She almost dropped out after her first year, but one of her professors suggested she get tested. She got help, and it changed her whole life."

"Help meaning Ritalin?"

"I think Katie took Adderall. But it wasn't just medication. She learned how to manage her ADHD so she wasn't constantly fighting her own brain. She stopped feeling overwhelmed all the time." Nadine would never forget the change in Katie after she had started treatment.

"So you think I need medication?"

"I don't know. I'm not a doctor, and I could be wrong. But I think you should read about ADHD. If what you read sounds familiar, consider seeing a professional who can tell you for sure."

Bella looked away. "No one ever said that to me. I don't know what to think."

"We don't have to talk about it anymore. You don't have to talk to me at all." Nadine sighed. "Look, I know I'm not your favorite person right now. But if there was any chance it could help, I had to say something."

The car in front of them drove off.

Nadine pulled up to the drop-off slot and lowered her car window. She waited for the bag, but Bella was still looking out the other window. "I need the cash."

"Huh? Oh, right." Bella retrieved the bag from her purse and handed it over.

Nadine dropped the bag in the receptacle, then looked back at Bella, who stared blankly through the windshield.

So much for two witnesses. They drove back to Bella's apartment in silence.

Nadine hoped she had done the right thing. She would always care for Bella, even if their friendship never recovered. If she had made Bella feel worse about herself without anything good coming out of it...well, she'd have one more thing to feel guilty about for the rest of her life.

Chapter 19

EASILY DISTRACTED...LOSES THINGS...DISORGANIZED LIVING SPACE...
Bella scrolled through the list, mentally checking off symptoms. It was the third quiz she had consulted that morning, and she didn't need to tally her score again to know the answer was the same: ADHD, predominantly inattentive.

Nadine had the morning off, so Bella—seeking space to think—had volunteered to work in the stockroom. But instead of opening boxes, she read one website after another about ADHD. Clinical criteria, quizzes, checklists, and personal essays. It was overwhelming, yet she couldn't stop. Could this really be the answer to the question she had never known to ask?

She was stunned by how much she related to what she was reading. She had spent her life feeling like an underachiever. Even her elementary school teachers had complained that she wasn't applying herself because she rushed through assignments with little concern for details. She had never understood why adults expected her to spend more time than necessary on boring assignments. Now she wondered if her sloppy schoolwork was a symptom.

Her high school years had been miserable, full of sleepless nights and stress that gnawed at her stomach. At times she had pretended to be sick so she could catch up on homework. Her teachers had been understanding, but no one had ever suggested she might have ADHD.

No one until Nadine. Bella felt more insecure around Nadine than she had felt in a long time. Sure, they both worked at the same crappy store, but Nadine had a law degree. She only worked at Overstock Oasis because she could no longer practice law. Meanwhile, Bella's position as Grady's third key was her greatest professional achievement.

But Nadine believed she was capable of more.

She kept hearing Nadine's words: *If there was any chance it could help, I had to say something.* The concern had been selfless and genuine. Bella had been a jerk to Nadine for two days, but Nadine still cared enough to take a risk.

The doors swung open.

Bella startled and dropped her phone into her lap.

Ashley strutted in wearing black leather boots and denim jeggings. Her hair was tied up in twin poofy buns that adorned her head like mouse ears. "Hey. Some crabby-ass dude doesn't believe we don't have any more toasters. He thinks we have more in the back. So I'm pretending to look." She rolled her eyes.

"Ah, one of those." Customers imagined the stockroom to be an expansive warehouse with rows of extra inventory, but the stockroom at Overstock Oasis contained only unopened boxes of merchandise and a lot of dust. So when a customer demanded an employee check for a sold-out product, it was a nice opportunity for a five-minute break.

Ashley plopped down on a box and pulled out her phone.

Bella picked up her own phone and scrolled through her Instagram feed. Nothing new. She looked up. "Hey, Ashley?"

"Yeah?"

"Um, please don't take this the wrong way, but do you know how to buy drugs?"

Ashley guffawed. "Oh my God."

"I'm sorry, just forget—"

"Of course I know how. You don't?" Ashley shook her head. "Man, you are so innocent. It's adorable."

"Hey, I'm not that innocent. I've tried weed before."

"Uh-huh." Ashley looked skeptical. "Is that what you're looking for? Weed?"

"No." Bella chewed the inside of her cheek. "I was wondering if you knew where I could get some Adderall."

"Oh, gotcha." Ashley nodded, bobbing her hair poofs.

"It's not for fun," Bella said quickly. "I'm testing a theory about how my brain works. I know I should go to a doctor, but my deductible—"

"Hey, I get it. Our insurance sucks. I don't go to the doctor unless I'm barfing blood. But, yeah, I can score you some addys. No problem. Tino has a hookup for every pill you can imagine. Well, every pill that's fun. Might take me a day or two, though. Is that okay?"

"Of course. It's not urgent."

"Cool." Ashley checked her phone. "Welp, time to deliver the bad news."

Just as Ashley stood up, Bella noticed a cube-shaped box in a cart behind her. "Wait…isn't that a toaster?"

Ashley spun around, revealing that her jeggings said *yummy* in metallic script across the ass. "I'll be damned! We really did have one in the back." She pocketed her phone and picked it up. "Anyway, I'll text you the price. Then you can tell me how many pills you want."

"Maybe we shouldn't discuss crimes over text. I only need a couple— let's say two or three pills—and I can pay anything under a hundred dollars." She couldn't risk taking a bottle of illegally purchased pills back to the apartment, not when it might jeopardize Nadine's probation. But she figured she could hide one or two pills in the store. Or maybe she would just take them all at once, swallowing the evidence.

Ashley snorted. "It's not gonna be a hundred dollars. Probably more like five bucks a pop." She laughed. "You're lucky I'm so honest."

"Oh, okay. Thanks for that. And thanks for not judging me."

"Hey, anytime." Ashley grinned and left the stockroom.

Well, that was easy, almost disturbingly so. In as little as a day, she'd be able to experiment with ADHD medication. She wondered if she would experience the calm that some people described, or if she'd get wound up and hyper?

Not that a self-assessment meant much. She should really consult a professional, but her shitty health insurance had a five-thousand-dollar deductible, and she couldn't afford to pay for a specialist. She only went to the doctor if it was a true emergency. For now, she was on her own.

Bella drove past acres of soybean fields to the quiet, residential street where she had grown up. She stopped at the corner gas station for a sweet tea slushie, a staple of her high school years, then drove to the modest brick house where her mom still lived.

She let herself in with the same key she had used since middle school. As she pushed through the door, the familiar smells of her childhood home surrounded her.

"Mom? It's me."

"In here!" her mom yelled from the kitchen.

Bella dropped her purse in the entryway, slipped off her shoes, and walked to the kitchen with her drink.

Her mom was at the kitchen counter, drying a plate with a gingham dish towel. Her long, blonde hair was swept into a loose ponytail. She put down the dish and greeted Bella with a hug. "So glad to see you. Can I get you anything? Oh, you already have a drink."

"Yep, I'm good." Bella sat at the kitchen table.

Her mom picked up her coffee mug and sat across from her. "How's work? And how's your famous coworker?"

Bella hesitated. Her mom still didn't know Nadine was staying with her. After Raelyn's disapproving reaction, Bella had omitted that detail the last time they spoke by phone.

"Actually, she's crashing on my couch for a while."

"What?" Her eyes bugged. "Since when?"

Bella fiddled with her straw. "Almost a month ago. She didn't have anywhere else to go, and I felt bad. I guess we've become... Crap, I don't even know anymore."

"You two are friends? I thought you hated her."

"Yeah, I used to hate her before I met her. But she's not what I expected. She's tough, but she has been kind to me. She even, um, helped me once." Bella stopped herself from mentioning the incident with Todd, knowing it would upset her mom. "I don't know. Raelyn thinks she's manipulating me."

"What do you think?"

Good question. "I honestly don't know. I want to trust her, but I don't know how to reconcile my personal experience with what she did in the past."

Resting her hand in her chin, her mom asked, "Well, have you ever asked her about what happened? Why she did it?"

"Yeah, I have, but I didn't get anywhere. When I think about the person I've come to know, I can't imagine her selling out vulnerable people. But she admitted that she did. It doesn't make any sense."

"You've always had good instincts about people. If she were manipulating you, I think you'd know it. Maybe prison changed her. Or maybe there's more to the story."

"Maybe." Bella sucked down the last of the slushie. "Mom, have you ever...did you ever think I might have ADHD?"

"ADHD? Like the hyper children?"

"Yeah. I mean—no. Not everyone gets hyper. Some people just have a hard time focusing. It's called inattentive type." She took a breath. "I think I might have it."

Her mom frowned. "What makes you think that?"

"Because I've been reading about it, and the symptoms sound exactly like me. Remember how I always procrastinated and then rushed through my homework? How I could read novels for hours, but I couldn't make myself study a textbook? How my desk and my room were always a mess?"

"Sweetie, everyone thinks school is boring. Is this about what happened in college?"

Bella flinched. They rarely talked about Bella's freshman year flameout. After a summer of arguments and tears, they had an unspoken agreement to leave it in the past.

"Mom, I really did try." Bella's voice shook. "I know you think I didn't work hard enough, but I wasn't blowing it off. I wanted to do well, and I felt horrible all the time. And now I can't help but wonder—what if I'd gotten help? Maybe college would have been different."

Flustered, her mom said, "I never heard of inattentive-type ADHD. None of your teachers ever thought you had a problem. Maybe I should've gotten you evaluated, but I didn't know anything about that." She blew out a breath. "It wasn't easy, you know, raising you on my own, working forty hours a week, never having enough time or money. But I did my best."

Bella grasped her mother's hand. "Hey. I'm not blaming you, Mom. I'm really not. I don't even know if it's ADHD. Maybe it's anxiety or a learning disability or something else. But it's something. I don't think it's normal to struggle so much to write a paper or clean a room."

Her mother squeezed back. "Okay. Maybe you should see someone and try to figure it out. And then if you ever go back to school…"

"Yeah. It would be good to know." Bella stared at the table. They both knew she wasn't going back to college.

Nadine was loading a cart with squirrel statues when Jason stomped into the stockroom.

"Kenny went home sick." He said it as though it was her fault.

"And you've come to ask for my thoughts and prayers?"

He huffed. "I need you to close. There's no one else."

"Fine." They glared at each other until Jason spun around and stomped out.

Great. Nadine was exhausted after a long, punishing afternoon that had included unloading a truck by herself. The last thing she needed was one-on-one time with the douchebag assistant manager.

At least by staying late she could delay returning to the apartment. Bella would probably be locked in her room with another frozen dinner. After two years of rejection, Nadine had thought she couldn't feel pain like this anymore—but she wasn't as numb as she'd believed.

When it was time to close, Nadine made her way to the front of the store. Jason greeted her with a sour expression, then turned to the safe, grumbling under his breath about criminals handling cash.

He counted the money first. Then, he watched Nadine count it with narrow eyes, scrutinizing her every movement.

Unperturbed, Nadine recited the total.

Her composure seemed to agitate him even more. "Yeah, thanks." He snatched the cash and bagged it, scrawling his name on the outside. Then he pushed it toward Nadine for her signature.

After sealing the bag, Jason looked her in the eye. "You haven't fucked up."

"Excuse me?"

"Here at the store. I thought you'd be out on your ass by now, but you've been a model employee. Which means we can't get rid of you. So how does it feel to know that this is your life? You were Miss Big Shot Attorney, and now you're a low-level, minimum-wage grunt. And that's all you're gonna be until you die."

Nadine stared back, refusing him the satisfaction of even a slight reaction.

Jason shook his head and scooped up the bag of cash. "Well, you know the drill. I make the deposit, and you're the witness." He sneered. "Like your word counts for anything."

Nadine fumbled with her keys, then realized the front door was already unlocked. When she entered, the apartment was dark except for a dim light coming from the living room. She walked toward it, blinking rapidly as her eyes adjusted.

Bella sat on the couch bathed in pink light from her table lamp. She was still and silent, clutching a glass tumbler in her hand as she stared blankly ahead.

"Hi." Nadine stood in front of her.

Bella looked up. The lamplight reflected streaks of tears on her face. Her puffy eyes were ringed with smeared mascara. "Hi."

"What happened?" Nadine sat on the couch and faced her. In that instant, she no longer cared what had happened between them or that Bella might not want her there. If someone had hurt Bella, she needed to know.

"Nothing happened." Bella's voice was hoarse. The potent smell of rum wafted from her glass. Or was it her breath? "Nothing ever happens because I haven't done jack shit for ten fucking years."

Nadine tensed. "Is this because of what I said yesterday about ADHD? Because I didn't mean—"

"No. I'm glad you said it. I've spent the whole day reading and remembering, and I think you're right. I think I finally understand what's wrong, what has always been wrong with me. And it's like…in some ways, it's a huge relief, but…" Bella swiped at her eyes. "But I'm also really fucking sad. Because if it's true, if I have a disorder that's treatable, then I wasted my whole adult life because I didn't know." Fresh tears leaked down her cheeks.

"Oh, Bella." Nadine placed a tentative hand on her shoulder. When Bella didn't pull away, she rubbed her back. "I'm sorry. I'm so sorry it feels that way. But it's not too late."

"Yeah, sure. Like I can be a freshman at thirty when I can't even afford the tuition." Bella took a deep breath, regaining some composure. "I'm sorry. I just feel so embarrassed. Especially around you."

Nadine pulled her hand back. "You don't have to be embarrassed around me. God, I'm not in a position to look down on anyone. And even if I were, I wouldn't look down on you." She sighed. "I know you hate what I did as much as anyone, but you treat me like a human being. You're sensitive, kind, talented—and you're a good person. You should be proud of yourself. I really mean that."

"Thank you," Bella whispered. She shifted to face Nadine, eyes shiny with tears. Then she flung herself forward, smashed her lips against Nadine's, and pulled her close.

Nadine froze at first but then quickly surrendered, losing herself in the hot, wet mouth that tasted of rum and salt and *Bella*.

Then she remembered—*I can't*. She broke the kiss, tearing her swollen lips away as she pressed her palms to Bella's shoulders and pushed. The loss of contact made her chest ache.

Bella's eyes were wide and horrified. "Oh my God."

"Bella, it's... I..." Nadine fumbled for words, any words that would fix what had just happened.

Bella staggered to her feet. "I can't believe I just... Oh Lord." She ran into the bathroom and slammed the door.

Nadine sank back on the couch, shaky and aching with desire. Fuck.

Why had she kissed back? She should have pulled away, should have stopped before anything happened, before Bella realized her feelings. But it was too late.

Bella knows now. Fuck. She knows.

Maybe, somehow, it would be okay. Bella could blame the rum, and Nadine could blame exhaustion. They could both forget it ever happened.

Unless.

That fiery kiss left no doubt about their mutual attraction. They were both single. If they both wanted it...

Nadine shook her head, banishing the thought. Bella had been drunk and sad, reaching for any warm body. When she sobered up, she would remember that Nadine was a criminal who had betrayed the country and made Alyssa cry. That's who Nadine was to Bella and who she would always be to the world. Bella deserved better.

Nadine looked over at the bathroom door. What was Bella doing? Crying again? Puking her guts out?

Then the shower started. Nadine had lived there long enough to know Bella would stay until the hot water ran out.

Nadine stretched out on the sofa and hugged her knees to her chest. On top of fucking everything, she had to pee.

Bella huddled on the floor of the bathtub as hot water poured down on her like heavy rain. Her limbs were loose from the rum and the steamy shower, but her mind was clear.

I kissed Nadine. Not just kissed—attacked. She had thrown herself at the woman and smothered her with sloppy desperation.

Her cheeks burned. She had forced an unwanted kiss on a straight woman, and, worse, it had turned her on. For a second, she'd thought Nadine was kissing her too, until hands pushed her away.

I'm as bad as Todd. How ironic that she'd spent days judging Nadine, who had never once harmed her personally, only to behave like this.

Bella sat under the spray until the water turned lukewarm, then cool. She dragged herself to her feet and lathered her hair as the temperature turned even colder. Icy water shocked her skin as she rinsed the suds from her hair. By the time she hugged her body with a towel, her teeth chattered.

She couldn't face Nadine tonight. Not like this. When she was dry enough, she opened the bathroom door and slipped into her bedroom, quickly closing the door behind her. Then she pulled on pajamas and crawled into bed, dragging the covers over her head.

Tomorrow, she would apologize. She would blame the booze, say that it didn't mean anything. She'd say whatever it took to make it okay. Tomorrow.

Chapter 20

BELLA STOOD BEFORE THE BATHROOM mirror, assessing the wreckage. Her swollen eyelids were like a neon *I've been crying* sign. Her hair was frizzy and tangled from sleeping on it wet.

She washed her face and combed her hair, resulting in a marginal improvement. *Well, I look as pathetic as I feel.*

It was time to face Nadine. Her stomach lurched as she peeked out from behind the bathroom door.

Nadine was reclining on the couch, studying her phone. A mug and a half-eaten Pop-Tart sat on the nearby coffee table.

Bella stepped out. "Hi."

Nadine's head shot up as her phone fell into her lap. "Hello. Good morning." She swung around to a sitting position. "How are you doing?"

"I'm okay." Bella searched Nadine's face for a sign of disgust but saw only worry, which was almost worse. *She's afraid I'm going to try to kiss her again.* "Can I talk to you for a minute?"

Nadine gestured to the space next to her. "Of course."

Bella hesitated, reluctant to be so close. But the only alternative was hovering over her. She sat.

Afraid to meet Nadine's eyes, Bella looked down at her chipped nail polish. "I'm really, really sorry for what I did last night. I know how it feels to be grabbed and kissed against your will, and I feel awful that I did that to you." She took a breath. "I'm not going to blame the alcohol or my mood. I don't want to make excuses. But I swear I will never do anything like that again." She looked up, expecting to see judgment.

Instead, Nadine looked confused. As if she didn't know what Bella was talking about. But obviously she knew—she'd been there. She was probably baffled that Bella's apology was so inadequate.

Bella babbled on. "I know I can't fix it by saying I'm sorry. I can't imagine how uncomfortable it must be to share an apartment with me. If you want, I could stay at my mom's house for a few days to give you some space. I mean, we'd still have to work together, but—"

"Bella." Nadine's voice broke through. "Stop. Stop talking." She closed her eyes, and when she opened them, they were full of turmoil. "You weren't the only one. I kissed you back. I kissed you too."

"You... What?" Bella flashed back to the crush of lips and tongue, Nadine's mouth moving against hers as she tried to escape, or....she had been kissing back? "But I thought you were straight."

Nadine twisted her T-shirt. "No."

"No? You're bisexual?"

Nadine glanced away. "No."

Bella's heart thumped. "Are you saying...?"

Nadine turned back to meet her gaze. "I'm gay."

What the hell? "I don't understand. Why didn't you tell me?" She thought back to Nadine's first night in her apartment when she'd discovered the lesbian romance novels. Bella had worried Nadine would be uncomfortable with *her* sexuality. Now she felt foolish—and hurt.

Nadine rubbed her temples. "Because I don't tell anyone. I've always been private. Now that I'm the least dateable person in America, there's no point in coming out as gay or anything else. And I didn't want to make you uncomfortable."

Bella grabbed a fistful of her own hair and pulled on it. "I can't believe this. I can't believe you're a lesbian too." She paused. "Sorry, is that word okay? Lesbian? I don't know how you—"

"It's fine," Nadine said, although her face said nothing was fine. "It's accurate."

Lesbian. Gay. Nadine was like her. The revelation sloshed around in her brain. Then she heard the rest of Nadine's words. *I didn't want to make you uncomfortable.*

It didn't make sense. Bella was obviously not a homophobe. Why would Nadine's sexuality make Bella uncomfortable? Unless...

Her head was spinning. "Do you...do you like me like that? I mean, have you been wanting to kiss me too?"

Nadine straightened her back. "I behaved impulsively. Just like you. We both know it shouldn't happen again."

"Oh. Right. Yeah, of course." She tried to think of something to say. *Keep it together. Act natural.* "Should we drive together? For work, I mean." They were both scheduled to start at eleven.

"Sure. We can take my car."

That was a given; Bella still hadn't gotten around to cleaning hers out.

"Okay, good. Well, I need some coffee. Oh, and another shower, I think." She stood, still a little unsteady, then turned to look at Nadine. "Thanks for telling me. I'm glad things are back to normal."

Nadine nodded, giving her a tight smile.

Hooray for complete bullshit. Nothing was normal anymore. Not even close.

The box was small but seemed to contain an anvil. Nadine grunted as she hoisted it to the top of the stack on the handcart. After checking the alignment, she wheeled the boxes down the ramp and into the stockroom.

Her muscles stretched and throbbed as she arranged the boxes into the neat stacks she had created. *Just another day at the gym.*

It helped to think of the punishing labor as a free fitness opportunity. Her endurance had increased; she didn't need as many breaks as she had a few weeks ago. The hard work was a great way to relieve stress and frustration, and these days she had an abundance of both.

When she finished dragging the last box into the stockroom, Nadine sat on the floor and leaned against a large box to catch her breath. It was a cool day in November, but her shirt was soaked with sweat.

She pulled out her phone and saw a message from Bella. *Text me when you're done with the truck. :)*

The message meant Bella would bring her a drink and a snack. Nadine texted back: *Just finished.*

It was another sign that Bella was no longer angry, that things were back to normal. Well, almost normal.

Within seconds of Nadine's response, Bella pushed through the doors, bearing a sandwich from the deli and a diet cola. "Special delivery." She sat next to Nadine on the floor.

"God. Thank you." Nadine twisted open the soda. She had guzzled the last of her water half an hour earlier. She tilted her head back and drank deeply, taking several gulps before she paused to breathe.

Bella was staring at Nadine's damp shirt, which clung to her breasts, revealing the outline of her skimpy sports bra and her nipples. When their eyes met, Bella flinched and looked away, pretending to glance around the stockroom.

And there was the difference.

"Um," Bella said, "you emptied that truck really fast."

"Yeah. This truck wasn't too bad. There were some heavy boxes but also a lot of light ones."

"Still, a whole truck in a such a short time. You've gotten really strong." Bella gazed admiringly at her arms, and Nadine felt it again—the heat between them. While Nadine had decades of practice at keeping her feelings to herself, Bella couldn't hide hers to save her life.

Bella shifted on the hard floor, curling her legs. "How do you say *sandwich* in Filipino?"

"We just say *sandwich*. I can't think of another word."

"Oh." Bella licked her lips. "Hmm. What about the word for food?"

"*Pagkain.*"

"Pag-ka-in." Bella pointed at the sandwich. "Pagkain." Her pronunciation was hopeless, but the word was comprehensible.

Nadine nodded. "Correct."

"Salamat." Bella smiled playfully, fluttering her lashes. "Maybe you can teach me another word tonight."

"Sure. I'm planning to cook."

"Oh, sweet. I can't wait." Bella pushed herself to her feet. "Well, I'd better get back on register."

"Okay. Thanks again for lunch."

Bella beamed. "Walang anuman."

Nadine watched as Bella walked away, hair swishing against her back. Her black jeans hugged and accentuated every curve.

God, it was getting harder.

Nadine set the burner to simmer and inhaled the heavenly aroma of Filipino chicken stew.

Bella walked in, wearing pajama shorts and an oversized T-shirt. "Mmm. That pagkain smells good."

"Thank you." At Bella's expectant face, she added, "Salamat. But it won't be ready for an hour."

"That's fine." Bella leaned against the counter. "Your cooking is worth the wait."

Nadine's phone chimed. *Patricia.* "It's my sister. I'm going to step outside. Would you mind turning the burner off if it starts to boil over?"

"Of course. Tell her I said hi." Bella started to leave the kitchen, then turned around. "I mean, kumusta."

"I will." Nadine grabbed her jacket and walked out the door, then down the steps. She sat on the curb and answered the call. "Hello, Pati."

"Hi, ate." Her sister sat on the floral-print loveseat, bouncing Miko in her lap. "Say hi to Auntie Nadine." The baby waved hesitantly.

"Hi, sweetheart. I hope you're being good for your mommy."

Miko reached for the screen and hung up.

Patricia called right back. "Sorry about that. I put him on the floor with his cars." She settled back on the loveseat. "How are you?"

It was a simple question that Nadine had no idea how to answer. "I'm okay." Then she remembered. "Oh, and Bella says hi. Actually she says kumusta."

"You're teaching your roommate Filipino?"

Nadine shrugged. "She wants to learn."

"Sounds like she's becoming a good friend. I'm happy for you." Patricia looked intently through the screen at Nadine. "What? What's wrong?"

Nadine winced. Patricia knew her too well. She glanced around the parking lot. "We kissed."

Patricia sat up, leaning in toward the screen. "What? She's gay too?"

"Yes." It felt good to tell someone what had happened, despite the interrogation she knew would follow. "She told me a while ago, but she didn't know, you know, about me."

"Eek, I can't believe it. Wow. Is she your girlfriend now?" Patricia bounced with excitement.

"No." Nadine shook her head vehemently. "Look, it was a mistake. She was sad, and I was lonely. But obviously, nothing like that can ever happen again."

Patricia furrowed her brow. "Why not?"

Her sister didn't get it. "You know why not. Because of who I am. My situation."

"Does she know the truth?"

"No."

"Why the h-e-l-l not?"

Nadine sighed. "At first, I didn't think she would believe me, but now…I think maybe she would."

"Hmm. I like her already. Perhaps she can talk some sense into you."

Nadine pinched the bridge of her nose. "As much as we both adore having this fight, can we skip it tonight?"

"Fine." Patricia sat back. "So she thinks you're evil, but she kissed you anyway. Why can't you two be together?"

A jacked-up pickup truck pulled into the parking lot. Nadine recognized Bella's frat boy neighbors, who had never paid attention to her. Still, she lowered her voice. "You don't know what it's like for me here. I'm a pariah. I'm not going to drag her into this existence. She already gets shit at work for being my friend."

The baby fussed off screen. Patricia leaned over and whispered to him in rapid Filipino, then sat back up. "So what are you going to do?"

"The plan hasn't changed. I'm saving up to rent my own place. Bella and I are just friends."

"So you move into a small apartment and hide there until you die? Meanwhile, Alyssa Jackson gets to be president of the United States. Am I missing something, or is that the entire plan?" As Patricia spoke, Miko's fussing intensified.

"I guess so. I thought we weren't going to talk about this."

But Patricia had dropped the iPad to soothe Miko, leaving Nadine with a view of the ceiling.

Nadine looked across the parking lot into the dark, open field across the street. The stars were bright and clear. She was still getting used to the quiet of the country, but she didn't mind the view.

Patricia reappeared, clutching Miko. "Ate, I'd better go."

"Okay. Kiss him for me." She waved her fingers at her red-faced nephew.

"I will. And you kiss Bella for me." She made a kissy face.

Nadine rolled her eyes. "Goodbye, Pati."

She set her phone down and rested her chin on her knees. The concrete curb was cold on her ass, but she wasn't ready to get up.

In prison, everything had been so simple. She had lost her career, her reputation, and her life, but she didn't deserve those things anyway. Out in the world, making choices was harder. She didn't know what to do.

Chapter 21

BELLA ARRIVED FOR WORK FIFTEEN minutes before the store opened, exactly on time. As she walked to the break room to clock in, she heard excited voices coming from Grady's office.

She swiped her badge, then peeked into the office to see what was happening. Grady, Jason, Ashley, and Kenny were crowded around Grady's desk, watching something on the computer monitor.

"What's going on?"

"The cameras recorded a shoplifter." Grady pointed triumphantly at the screen.

Bella squeezed between Ashley and Kenny to see. On the monitor, a woman hovered in front of the shelves that held angel figurines.

"Watch this." Jason hit the spacebar, and the grainy image came to life. The woman glanced to her right and then her left before pocketing a figurine in a quick, smooth motion.

"The suspect is Caucasian, between five and six feet tall," Jason said seriously.

"So case closed?" Bella said.

Ashley giggled.

"This isn't funny," Jason snapped.

Grady turned to Bella. "Do you recognize her?"

"Um." Bella didn't see how anyone could recognize the woman, given the poor quality of the video. "I can't make out the face."

"Damn it!" Jason smacked a filing cabinet. "These cameras are garbage. They don't even have sound."

"Wouldn't that be illegal?" Bella asked. "I think you need consent—"

"*Shoplifting* is fucking illegal."

Kenny flinched.

"Sorry, Kenny." Jason scowled at the monitor. "I'm just pissed off."

Grady held up his hand. "All right. If any of you see someone fitting this description, call for help right away. And don't let her out of your sight. I also want someone to keep an eye on the statues."

Bella couldn't think of anything more boring and demoralizing than babysitting ugly statues all day or, worse, making small talk with customers who were interested in said statues. *Not me, not me, not me...*

Grady scanned their faces. "Kenny, I'm assigning this to you."

"Yes, sir," Kenny said brightly. "I'll be the angels' guardian angel. Get it?"

No one laughed. Grady cleared his throat. "It's almost nine. Let's get to work."

As they filed out of the office, Ashley nudged Bella. "Hey. I got it."

Bella looked at her in confusion, then she remembered. Adderall. "Oh wow."

"Come into the break room for a sec."

Bella followed, and Ashley closed the door behind them.

Ashley pulled a small white cardboard box from her purse, the type of box that usually signaled inexpensive jewelry. "You said you only wanted a couple, so I got you five. It's thirty bucks even."

Bella stared at the box. "That's not bad." She retrieved her own purse from its cubby, opened her wallet, and counted the bills. "Here you go."

Ashley gave her the box. "Just let me know if you want more. Addys are pretty easy to get."

"Thanks. I will." But Bella wasn't planning to become a regular customer. She only wanted answers.

"Oh, and be careful around Nadine. I heard y'all are living together. She's on probation, right?"

"Yeah, it's called supervised release. Don't worry, I'm not going to take them home."

Ashley nodded. "Okay, but I wouldn't leave them here either. Grady and Jason will blame her if they find pills."

Shit. "Good point. I'll be careful."

"Cool." Ashley stuffed her purse back into a cubby and started toward the door.

"Hey, Ashley?" Bella stopped her.

"Yeah?" She turned around.

Bella took a breath. "What do you think of Nadine?"

"What do you mean?"

"I mean, she did some bad things. But you must not hate her if you care enough to not want her to go back to prison."

"Lord, no. I don't hate Nadine. She's a decent person, if you ask me. Not too friendly, but I don't blame her, the way people are always coming in here trying to start shit with her."

Bella wondered how much Ashley understood about Nadine's crimes. "You don't hold it against her that she—"

"That she was gonna fuck over poor people in exchange for campaign money?"

Okay, maybe she did understand. "Yeah."

"Tino did time." She looked down at her zebra-print flats. "He, um, stole a car. It was just for fun, and he was gonna give it back, but I guess it was considered grand theft auto." She made air quotes with her fingers.

"I didn't know that."

"Yeah, it was a long time ago, but people still hold it against him. Like, he's been trying to get a better job, but no one wants to hire him, so he's stuck bagging groceries." Ashley looked up to meet Bella's eyes. "He's a good guy, you know? He did something stupid, but he shouldn't have to pay for it his whole life."

Bella nodded. "Yeah. I agree. He's lucky to have you."

Ashley smiled. "Thanks. I love that goofball." She checked her phone. "Well, I gotta get on register before Jason has a fit."

Bella slipped the small box into her pocket and walked down the hall to the single-stall restroom. She locked the door and opened the box. Five blue ovals sat on a square bed of gauze.

She wished for the thousandth time that she had decent health insurance. It was ridiculous to buy medication this way, and as Ashley had reminded her, it was against the law.

Bella placed a pill on her tongue, then turned on the faucet. Cupping her hands, she placed them under the water until she'd collected enough. Then she slurped the water and swallowed the pill along with it. *Done.*

Her reflection stared back in the scratched-up bathroom mirror. Would she feel any different, any better? And would that mean she had ADHD?

She looked at the other four pills in the box. Ashley was right. She couldn't leave them at the apartment or the store without putting Nadine at risk.

The chances of getting caught were small, but she wasn't going to fuck around with something as important as Nadine's probation. Bella would never forgive herself if Nadine got sent back to prison because of something she did.

There's no other choice. She poured the pills into the toilet bowl and flushed.

Bella was sorting through candles and applying discount stickers when she realized something was different. She felt calm, almost subdued. Instead of fidgeting, checking her phone, and losing track of what she was doing every three seconds, she'd been focused on her task.

Usually when she worked on markdowns, she had to check the price multiple times because by the time she reached for the stickers, she'd forgotten which discount to apply.

Since taking the pill, she was able to check the tag, hold the number in her brain, apply the appropriate sticker, and move on to the next candle. It was effortless.

Was this how normal people felt? Present in the moment, their thoughts deliberate instead of flitting around like a moth in a jar? No wonder other kids had been able to pay attention in class while she doodled and twitched and obsessively checked the time.

She finished the candles, then moved to the next aisle, where Kenny was pacing in front of the angel figurines.

Poor guy. She nodded at the shelf. "Any trouble?"

"Not yet." He looked disappointed. "No one has even looked at them all morning."

Maybe because you're freaking people out. "Well, since you have to be here anyway, would you mind marking the statues that are going on clearance?" She held out the sheet of stickers.

"Okay."

Bella wanted to try something else. She walked to the front of the store. Ashley was ringing up a customer while another person waited impatiently.

Bella moved to a vacant register. "Sir, I can help you over here."

He rushed over, as she'd known he would. Men hated waiting in line to an almost comical degree.

For the next hour, she tried to determine if working the register was any different on Adderall. She felt more mellow, without her usual restless anxiety. Counting change seemed to be easier; she didn't lose track and start over as much. Or was she paying more attention because of some placebo effect? It was hard to say.

A young woman with curly red hair stepped up to the counter with a vanilla-scented candle, one of the items Bella had just marked 30 percent off. But when she scanned the tag, it came up full price.

"Oops, sorry about that. There should be a discount." Bella considered the math problem: 6.99 times 0.7. Seven times nine was sixty-three...

"It should be four eighty-nine." The customer held up her phone, which displayed the answer on a calculator app.

"Oh, right. Thanks." Okay, Adderall didn't make her an instant math genius. But it was a hard problem to do in your head. Even the customer had resorted to technology.

Bella stayed on register for another thirty minutes. By the time she went on break, she was certain the effect was real. The drug had improved her concentration—a lot—and it calmed her down in a way that she had never experienced.

She wanted to tell someone, but Nadine wasn't scheduled to work until later in the afternoon. Anyway, she probably wouldn't approve of Bella popping a pill she had purchased from Ashley. So she texted Raelyn: *Are you busy tonight? Want to come over?*

Remembering her friend's animosity toward Nadine, she added: *It would just be us.*

Three thumbs-up emojis appeared in response.

Bella threw a frozen pizza into the oven. While it cooked, she loaded the blender with limeade, tequila, triple sec, and ice. Just as she was about to switch it on, there was a knock at the door.

"It's open!" She pressed *liquify*, and the machine whirred to life, turning the ingredients into a frothy green cyclone.

Raelyn walked into the kitchen, clapping her hands when she saw the margarita mix in the blender. "Oh my God. Bless you."

"I still don't have margarita glasses." Bella opened the cabinet. "Your options are a wine glass, a coffee mug, or a plastic cup."

"Wine glass. I'm feeling fancy."

"You got it." Bella poured the drinks. "I like your hair. You look like Ruby Rose."

"Thanks, lady." Raelyn spun around to show off the new style, coiffed on top with a buzzed undercut. "That was the idea. Cheers."

They clinked their glasses and sipped.

"I hope it's not too strong," Bella said. "I know you have to drive."

"Nah, it's perfect. And I'll only have one."

Bella led the way to the living room, then realized Nadine's pillow and blanket were still on the couch where she left them each morning. She picked them up and set them on the edge of the table.

"How's *that* going?" Raelyn asked, scrutinizing Bella as they plopped down.

Where to begin? There was so much to tell—the kiss, Nadine's sexuality—but she wasn't sure she was ready for Raelyn's reaction. Instead she said, "Nadine thinks I have ADHD."

"Hmm, really?" Raelyn sipped her drink.

"You don't sound surprised."

"Bell, you've always had your head in the clouds. I never thought ADHD specifically, but it makes sense." She chuckled. "Remember how messy your locker was in high school? You couldn't even open it without half your stuff spilling out."

"Yeah. And my room and my car and everything." Bella sloshed her margarita around in her glass. "I took an Adderall today."

"Wait, you already saw a doctor?"

"No." This was the embarrassing part. "I bought some pills from my coworker's boyfriend's friend."

Raelyn's mouth fell open. "Jesus. You gotta be careful with that shit. You could be buying anything." She gestured to Bella's glass. "And now you're mixing it with alcohol?"

"Oops." Bella's glass was already half empty.

"Buying prescription drugs off the street is probably a felony. I didn't think you'd be so reckless."

"No way. A few pills can't be a felony."

"Let's look it up." Raelyn pulled out her phone and tapped the screen. She held it up. "See? Unless you have a prescription, Adderall possession is a Class 5 felony in Virginia."

"Oh, shit. I didn't think it was that serious." *I committed a felony. Just like Nadine.* She'd never imagined the words *felon* or *criminal* applying to her, but if she had somehow been caught...

"Where are the other pills?"

"Gone." Thank goodness she hadn't saved any. "I flushed them at work."

"Okay. Well, what's done is done. Just don't do it again." Raelyn sighed. "So what was it like?"

"Honestly, it was amazing. I was calm and focused all day. I think if I'd been on medication in college, I might not have flunked out."

"Maybe you should see a doctor," Raelyn said gently. "You know, get a professional opinion."

"I want to, but my health insurance sucks. I'd have to pay out of pocket."

"It might be worth it. I don't want to minimize the hardship of paying for something like that, but a friend can't diagnose you. Neither can the internet. If you really think you have ADHD, there's only one way to be sure."

"Yeah. I've been doing a lot of reading, and it just—it's like everything finally made sense. Why I'm like this, why things always felt so hard." Bella picked up her drink, then thought better of it. "I know I should see a doctor, but it's just so much money. And what's the point of spending hundreds of dollars on treatment if all I'm doing is working at Overstock Oasis?"

"Are you still thinking about going back to college someday?"

Someday. Because she had no actual plan. "Yeah. I'm saving money. But now that I know I might have, like, a brain disorder, I don't know. Maybe school just isn't for me."

Raelyn tilted her head. "What do you mean? If you do have ADHD, you can get treatment. Wouldn't that make college easier?"

"Yeah, it might. But I've been an underachiever for so long, I don't know if it's enough. I can never get those years back. There's so much I never really learned because I faked my way through high school. Lord, I can barely add and subtract." Bella picked up her margarita again—*screw it*—and emptied the glass.

"Hey." Raelyn touched her arm. "You graduated high school just like everyone else. And you did it despite having untreated ADHD or some other disorder. That's even more evidence of your intelligence."

"I suppose." The oven timer chirped. "Oh, that's the pizza."

An hour later, they slouched on the couch, empty plates and glasses spread out on the coffee table. Bella had downed two margaritas, and she was thoroughly buzzed. She stretched her arms above her head. "You know, I thought about what you said. About Nadine not being a good person."

"Oh yeah?"

"You made a fair point. She did something really bad, and I'm not discounting that. But I feel like she's suffered enough, you know? She served her time."

Raelyn scoffed. "She only served two years. Most people think it should have been ten."

"You say that like it was nothing. But imagine if someone told you that you had to spend *two years* in prison, no freedom or privacy, separated from your friends and family. It would be devastating."

"Yes, but—"

"And now she's on probation with all these conditions restricting her life. She lost everything. She's stuck here working for Grady and Jason. And everyone hates her, so she can't go anywhere else."

"Well, yeah. I'm sure that's hard."

"It's like she's free, but she's still in prison." Bella burped. "Whoa, that's deep."

At the sound of the front door opening, they both turned their heads.

Nadine walked in with slumped posture and mussed hair. She froze when she saw Raelyn.

Bella sat up straight. "Oh, hi. This is my friend Raelyn. Um, Raelyn, this is Nadine."

Raelyn smiled politely. "Hi, it's nice to meet you."

"Hello." Nadine's feet remained planted in the entryway.

"There's pizza and margaritas in the kitchen," Bella said. "You can join us." She glanced at Raelyn. "Here, we'll make room."

Bella and Raelyn scooted over, clearing a space.

Nadine looked as if she would rather turn around and go back to work than sit next to Raelyn. "No, thank you. I need a few things from the store. I'll give you time to catch up with your *friend*." She spun around and walked out, the door banging shut behind her.

"I'm sorry," Bella said. "She's not usually... I'm not saying she's friendly to people she doesn't know, but she's not usually hostile."

Raelyn studied her. "If I didn't know better..."

"What?"

"I'd think she was jealous."

Bella squirmed. "Why would you think that?"

"Number one"—Raelyn pointed at her head—"my Ruby Rose haircut. I look like a sexy butch, so she probably guessed I'm queer. Then there's the way she said your *friend*."

Could it be true? Nadine had been rude for sure, but was jealousy the reason?

"Reason number three," Raelyn said, "is the way you're looking at me with total panic right now and also fluttering your eyelashes like you hope I'm right."

Busted. Raelyn knew her too well. "We kissed."

"Holy shit." Raelyn sat back. "When?"

"A few days ago. She's gay."

"Whoa! I can't believe it." Raelyn shook her head. "Well, I can believe she's gay, but that detail was never in the news."

"She's a private person."

"Are you two...together?" Raelyn's wary tone made no secret of how she would feel about that.

"No." Bella looked down at her pink fingernails. "After I kissed her, I was afraid I really messed up. I thought she felt violated. But when I tried to apologize the next day, she told me she enjoyed it—and told me she's gay. But then she said it shouldn't happen again."

Raelyn blew out a breath. "Okay. Did she say why not?"

"No. I mean, I'm guessing it's because she's not interested. What other explanation could there be?"

"Impossible. Anyone would be interested in you."

"Oh, right, because I have so much to offer. I'm thirty, no education, working at Overstock Oasis, and living ten minutes from my mom's house. Nadine is… Well, her life is a mess right now, but she was a lawyer. She's brilliant. She'd never get serious about someone like me."

"Bella, *she* doesn't deserve *you*. You're an honest person, and she's Nadine Bayani."

"Nadine is an honest person." Bella held up her hand before Raelyn could object. "It's true, okay? She could have let me think the kiss was all my fault, but she *came out to me* just so I wouldn't feel bad." Bella heard her own words. "Oh, crap. I don't think I was supposed to tell anyone that she's gay."

"I won't tell anyone. Not even my mom."

Bella exhaled. "Thank you. Maybe we can tell Kathy one day, but I'd rather keep her secret for now. She's been through so much, and I want to do whatever I can to support her."

"Blerg, you're smitten. I can tell. Look, I'm not going to lecture you." Raelyn paused as though considering whether she should take that back and go for it. "Just don't forget who she is and what she did, okay?"

"I won't." Bella brushed her hair out of her face. "Not that it matters. She made it clear the kiss was a mistake."

"I know jealousy when I see it. And she was jealous of me." Raelyn laughed. "Hell, we're like sisters. Tell her that when she gets back, okay? I don't want her to start plotting my demise."

"Okay, I'll tell her." *Maybe.* Part of Bella liked the idea of Nadine being a little jealous.

"In fact, I should get out of here before she comes back. It's getting late anyway." Raelyn stood. "Thanks for the drink and the pizza. And keep me posted, okay? Whatever happens."

"I will. But nothing is going to happen."

Raelyn shook her head, resignation in her eyes. "Something already did."

Chapter 22

NADINE DROVE AIMLESSLY ON WINDING country backroads until she happened upon Route 33. Two turns later, she was headed back to Bella's apartment with nothing to show for her hour away but a pack of peanuts and a Diet Coke.

Not that she needed an excuse to decline socializing with Bella's *friend*. If she preferred to spend her evening at a gas station convenience store, that was her business.

Really, Nadine had every reason to be peeved. First of all, Bella hadn't mentioned her plans to have company over. It was rude to spring an unexpected guest on one's roommate, particularly when that roommate was unable to retreat to a private bedroom.

Second, Raelyn had been sprawled on the couch as if she owned the thing—the couch where Nadine slept every night. It was where she and Bella ate breakfast and dinner together and where, just a week ago, Bella had thrown her arms around Nadine, and…well.

Raelyn's behavior was unacceptable. The couch did not belong to her.

Not that she was jealous. The kiss had been a drunken mistake, nothing more. Bella was free to socialize with other young, attractive queer women. She'd just hoped that Bella would have the courtesy to keep her dating life away from their shared living space.

After all, Nadine wasn't just a guest. She paid two hundred dollars a month in rent—a point she would be making when she got back to the apartment, assuming *Raelyn* was no longer there.

As she walked from her car to the front door, she grew even more tense. Had she stayed away long enough?

She pushed through the door. The couch was empty, her pillow and blanket back in their rightful place. But where was Bella?

Had she gone with Raelyn back to her place? Or—oh God—what if they were in the bedroom together? The thought made her blood run cold.

Bella walked out of her bedroom, wearing loose gray sweatpants and a floppy navy T-shirt that said *INDORSEY*. Her eyes fell to the single plastic bag in Nadine's hand. "You're back."

"Yes." Nadine strode past Bella. She shoved the Diet Coke into the refrigerator, set the peanuts onto the counter, and tossed the empty bag. "I'm sorry I interrupted your evening."

Bella leaned against the wall, watching her. "You didn't interrupt anything."

"If you say so." Nadine walked past her again and sat on the couch. She knew, deep down, that she'd snapped at Bella for no reason. But she couldn't seem to relax.

Bella followed her into the living room. "Really, you didn't. And you live here too. You could have stayed."

"I told you. I had to run an errand."

"You seemed upset that Raelyn was here."

Nadine raised her chin. "I was *not* upset."

"Okay." Bella tugged on her hair. "But, um, Raelyn thought…I mean, she sort of observed that you might be jealous."

"Jealous?" Nadine stiffened.

"Of her. Because she looks gay. She's bi, actually, but with her new haircut—"

"That's preposterous. I didn't even notice her hair, let alone make assumptions about her sexuality. Raelyn thinks too much of herself."

"Okay. But just so you know, Raelyn has been my best friend since I was five. She's like my sister."

Friend. Just a friend. Nadine took a deep breath.

"You know, it's okay if you're jealous. I don't mind. I mean, when we kissed, it affected me too, and, um, I would be jealous if I thought you were on a date." Her face flushed bright red.

Bella's admission that she had also been *affected* by the kiss warmed Nadine in dangerous places. *This is wrong.* She had to deny it, and she had to be convincing. "Trust me, I was not *jealous*. That's the last thing I would feel about you."

Bella's face fell.

Fuck. Too far. She opened her mouth to take it back.

Before she could speak, Bella choked out, "Oh, okay. Sorry. Good night." She quickly retreated to the bedroom, slamming the door behind her.

Damn it. Bella hadn't done a thing except have a friend over, and Nadine had been an asshole about it for no reason. The irritation she had nursed for the past hour was gone. Now she just felt ashamed.

Bella woke up hungover, craving coffee and Pop-Tarts—specifically, the s'mores kind. But that meant going to the kitchen. Which meant walking through the living room. Which meant facing Nadine. Instead, she crept from her bedroom into the bathroom without making a sound.

In the shower, she twisted the metal knob until the water was scalding hot, enveloping her body in clouds of steam. She closed her eyes and tilted her head. The spray poured down her face, stinging her skin.

Nadine's words echoed in her brain. *That's the last thing I would feel about you.*

Bella wrapped her arms around herself. *God, I'm so dumb.* Raelyn had gotten her hopes up, but clearly Bella was the only one struggling with feelings. And now she had made it awkward, just when they'd been getting back to something resembling a friendship.

After her shower, Bella went to her bedroom to put on her hideous company polo and a pair of plain pants. When the steam had dissipated, she returned to the bathroom and locked herself in again. She curled her hair into springy ringlets instead of her natural, haphazard waves. Then she dusted her eyelids with four different shades of eyeshadow, blending them into a smooth gradient. She finished with a thick coat of mascara and rosy lip gloss.

So there. Nothing else was going right, but at least she would look good for the five-second walk from the bathroom to the front door.

It was Nadine's day off, but she was already awake. She sat cross-legged on the couch, a paperback book open in front of her.

"Good morning," Bella said as she walked past the couch.

Nadine looked up, her face blank. "Good morning." She looked as though she wanted to say something else, but instead she pressed her lips together.

Bella stepped into her black flats, tugged on her coat, and hauled her purse off the floor. "Have a good day."

Nadine mumbled something in response, but Bella didn't ask her to repeat it. It was probably something like "you too" or "same to you."

Whatever it was, it didn't matter. She didn't look back.

"And here's your change." Bella dropped a five-dollar bill, two quarters, and two pennies into the customer's outstretched hand. "Have a great day." She moved to pick up her phone.

"Hang on. This isn't right."

Bella turned back to the customer, a middle-aged white guy with a thick neck and a bald, shiny head that gleamed under the florescent lights. "I'm sorry?"

"I gave you a twenty." He showed her the change in his hand. "You owe me ten more dollars."

Bella was certain he'd paid with a ten. "I'm sorry, but you gave me a ten."

"No way. It was a twenty." He squared his broad shoulders. "I'm *one hundred* percent sure."

"Sir, I'm afraid you're mistaken. This is the bill you gave me, right here." She pointed to the ten-dollar bill in her drawer. Normally, she doubted her memory and attention, but this time she knew she was right. She had a vivid recollection of holding the bill in her hand.

"I know the difference between a ten and twenty." He rolled his eyes. "Look, I have a master's degree and you"—he jabbed a finger at her—"well, you work *here*."

Bella clenched her jaw. *Fuck. You.* The words cut deep, but she refused to take the bait. "Sir, I remember it clearly. You gave me a ten."

"You're wrong. And I'm not leaving without my money." He crossed his arms, refusing to move. The young woman in line behind him glanced nervously between them, then joined the line at Kenny's register.

"Sir, I assure you—"

"I want to speak to your manager."

As if on cue, Jason appeared, behind them, wearing his usual dour expression. "What's going on?"

Bella opened her mouth to explain, but the customer jumped in first. "Your cashier stole ten dollars from me."

"Excuse me?"

He pointed at Bella. "I gave her a twenty, and she claims I gave her a ten. But I *know* it was a twenty."

Bella gripped the edge of the counter. "Sir, I gave you the correct change." She turned to Jason. "Why don't we count the drawer?"

Jason waved her off. "We don't have time for that. Just give him the money."

"But—"

"I'm sorry, sir, but sometimes our girls get confused, this one, in particular."

"I'm right here." Bella's face grew hot as she pulled a ten from the drawer—the exact ten he had given her—and handed it to him.

The customer snatched it from her hand. "Thank you." He snickered as he marched off.

Bella glared at Jason.

He shrugged. "He seemed sure."

She slammed the cash drawer shut. "I'm going on my break."

Sure enough, when Bella counted her register at closing, the total was exactly ten dollars short. "Fuck!" She smacked the counter. "Oh, sorry, Kenny."

Poor Kenny was stuck closing with her. He watched her with round, nervous eyes, as if she were liable to lose her shit at any moment.

Bella had been stewing over that condescending customer all afternoon, and the confirmation that she'd been right only made her feel worse. She rubbed her eyes. "I'm sorry for being cranky. It's just this damn customer who cheated me and tried to make me look stupid. Like, okay, I'm not a neurosurgeon. I'm not the smartest person ever. But I know what ten dollars looks like. And it doesn't matter because all he saw was a dumb girl."

"I know what you mean," Kenny said quietly. "People think I'm stupid because I didn't go to a real school. But it's not that I didn't learn. I just learned different things."

"I don't think you're stupid, Kenny," Bella said kindly.

"Thanks, Bella. I don't think you're stupid either."

Bella counted the cash from the safe, confirmed Kenny's total, and signed the bag. "Let's get the heck out of here."

She drove to the bank with Kenny trailing in his car. There was one car ahead of her in line.

As she waited, Bella flashed back to the night Nadine suggested she might have ADHD. Bella had been a mess of contradictory emotions ever since. She was relieved that it might not be her fault but also angry that no one had ever suggested professional help. Most of all, she grieved a past that she couldn't change.

On top of those emotions, she had to contend with her feelings for Nadine. It all made her want to curl up and hide from the world, but with Nadine sleeping on her sofa, there was nowhere to hide. How much more could she take?

Bella deposited the cash, then waved to Kenny and headed home. Her empty stomach churned as she pulled into the parking lot. *This shit is not sustainable.*

They had to talk.

After several minutes of digging through her purse, Bella finally found her house keys, which had somehow burrowed into a hole in the lining. It was time to face Nadine.

Inside, a rich aroma filled the apartment. Bella dropped her purse, kicked off her shoes, and walked toward the sound of clattering dishes and running water.

Nadine was at the sink, her back to Bella. Her white tank top exposed her muscular shoulders, and clingy lounge pants showed off her firm ass.

She was washing up after what looked like a major culinary production involving measuring cups, several knives, and a cutting board. A large pot simmered on the stove, the lid slightly ajar with steam spilling out.

"That smells good," Bella said.

Nadine spun around.

Bella's gaze dropped to Nadine's breasts and the shadows of brown nipples under the fabric. *Crap. Stop staring.* She forced herself to meet Nadine's eyes.

Nadine self-consciously crossed her arms in front of her chest, then nodded at the pot. "I made stew with beef and plantains. You're welcome to have some."

"Okay. Thanks." *Here goes.* "Listen, I'm sorry for running away last night. And I'm sorry for avoiding you this morning. What you said hurt my feelings, but I should have been more mature about it."

"Bella." Nadine took a step toward her.

Bella held up her hand. "Please let me finish. It's my fault. I've been making things weird. I wanted you to be jealous because I wanted to believe you had feelings for me. But I was just being delusional. I mean, I'm this ditzy, small-town cashier. I know I'm not the kind of person you'd ever want to be with. That might sound self-pitying or whatever, but we both know it's true."

Nadine took another step forward. "You are not ditzy. And you're not delusional. Stop denigrating yourself, because I won't tolerate it."

Not delusional. "Are you saying…?"

Nadine sighed. "I admit I don't like the idea of you dating another woman. But I don't have any claim on you. And it's my own failings that make a relationship between us impossible." She closed the distance and brushed a strand of hair from Bella's face. "You don't even know how special you are. I am attracted to you. I always have been. But you deserve more."

Trembling, Bella caught Nadine's hand in her own. "You like me too? As more than friends?"

Nadine pulled back. "It doesn't matter."

"Of course it matters." Her whole body ached for Nadine. "If you like me too, then why don't you…? I mean, why can't we—?"

"Because of who I am. Because I'm trapped in hell, and I refuse to drag you there with me. I can't go out in public without people gawking and sneering. I'll never make real money again. And if you and I were together, this would be your life too. I won't let that happen."

Bella couldn't believe what she was hearing. Nadine liked her, wanted her. Nothing else mattered. "I don't care what people say. I don't care about money." Bella reached out to touch her shoulder.

Nadine shrugged away. "That's easy to say. But I've lived with the hate for years now, and it wears at you in ways you can't imagine. I won't subject you to it. Not even by association. Besides, it wasn't so long ago that you demanded to know how I could have committed such evil acts. Eventually, when the lust wears off, you're going to remember what kind of person you think I am, and you won't want a life with me either."

It was the last thing Bella wanted to admit when her heart told her to throw her arms around Nadine and never let go. But it was true. She still couldn't accept her past actions.

"Maybe if you explained it to me." Bella hated how desperate she sounded, begging for something to make it okay. "My instincts tell me you're not a bad person, that there must have been some other reason. Please help me understand. If you won't talk about it, what am I supposed to think?"

"I already told you that it's not—it doesn't matter. Talking won't change things."

"Yeah. I guess not." What good was talking if it only brought her confusion and heartache?

"You should take a shower," Nadine said gently. "The food will be ready soon."

"Okay." But she needed to know one more thing. "If we can't be together, can we at least stay friends?"

Nadine nodded. "Always."

"Good. Okay. Friends." Bella attempted a smile, then retreated to the bathroom.

She stripped off her work clothes and looked in the mirror. Nadine Bayani liked her, wanted her. It was surreal.

But they couldn't—because Nadine wouldn't—and so she stepped into yet another shower to keep her warm until the water turned cold.

Chapter 23

NADINE RIPPED OPEN A LARGE box, revealing Christmas-themed dinner plates featuring Rudolph, Santa Claus, and a snowman with a creepy smile. *Hideous.*

As she loaded the first batch into a cart, Jason charged into the stockroom. Barely glancing at Nadine, he strode past her to the circuit panel at the back of the room. He popped open the cover, studied the switches, and flipped one.

The lights went out.

"Damn it!" There was a thud, then a click, and the lights buzzed back on.

"What are you trying to do?" Nadine asked.

"I'm installing security cameras." He didn't look up from the panel.

"Didn't you already do that?"

"Yeah, I installed those piece-of-shit cameras from corporate with fuzzy pictures and no audio." He toggled another switch. "These are *my* cameras. Shoplifters won't be able to hide from these babies."

Oh, for God's sake. His obsession was out of control. "It's illegal to record audio on surveillance cameras."

"Oh yeah? Where did you hear that?"

"I'm a lawyer. It's illegal to record private conversations without consent."

"Correction. You *were* a lawyer." Jason smirked. "Maybe you just don't want me to record you. I bet a lot of people would pay for footage of you mopping the floors."

She sighed. "Fine. Commit a felony."

Jason rolled his eyes and walked out, leaving her alone with the plates—and her thoughts.

As usual, her thoughts returned to Bella. She could still hear the tremor in her voice, see the hurt in her eyes.

Nadine needed a distraction. She switched on the boom box she had discovered in the back corner a few days ago. It was already tuned to NPR. She returned to her work as monotone voices droned in the background.

At the top of the hour, an announcer read the headlines. Nadine froze when she heard Alyssa's name.

...Jackson is facing pressure from opponents to release the names of individuals who attended her private fundraisers. Today, Jackson refused, citing privacy concerns...

Ah. The private fundraisers. She remembered them well. *The names are a secret because her top bundlers represent industries she's supposedly planning to regulate.*

It was bold of Alyssa to repeat the same practice she had used before the scandal. But, then, Alyssa always did have boundless confidence, an instinctive belief that nothing could ever truly touch her. She had almost been right.

Nadine thought back to Ryan Mitchell's words. *She's doing it again.* Doing what?

She unlocked her phone and scrolled to the image of the blood-stained business card Ryan Mitchell had given her. Something had compelled her to snap a photo before she threw it away. Before she could stop herself, she typed in the number and sent a text: *What were you trying to tell me about Alyssa Jackson?*

The reply was immediate: *Is this Nadine?*

She wrote back, "Yes." Within seconds, the phone rang.

No way. Not on an unsecured line. She declined the call and typed: *I'm not talking to you on the phone.*

Again, the response was immediate: *I can meet you tomorrow.*

Nadine's stomach clenched. This was a bad idea. Ryan wasn't interested in proving her innocence. He just wanted to use her to beat Alyssa, to raise the same doubts that had cost her voters last time. Never mind the fallout for Nadine, who would once again be front-page news with half the country calling her a liar in addition to a crook—and Alyssa wouldn't hesitate to go nuclear if she even sniffed a threat to her presidential ambitions.

Truth wasn't magic. She couldn't call a press conference and fix everything like her sister thought she could. Patricia had never been the subject of a national witch hunt. She didn't know what it was like to be the target of death threats for months and then spend two years in a cage thinking about it. To be so fucked-up from the trauma that she couldn't trust the one person who might believe her.

She sliced an angry gash in the next box and opened it to find even more garish Christmas-themed housewares. As she dumped the merchandise into a cart, her phone buzzed. She pulled it out of her pocket to see a string of messages from Ryan. She skimmed through, barely reading them, and then typed back: *Don't contact me again.*

Pointless. Utterly pointless.

Bella frowned at the sketch of a woman in a superhero costume on her iPad. She had captured her client's curly brown hair, porcelain skin, and oval face so that it closely resembled the photo. But something was off—the gaze was too soft.

In the photo, the woman regarded the camera with penetrating eyes, reminding her of Nadine. Bella raised the height of the eyebrows and gave them sharper peaks. She zoomed out to study the results. Perfect.

Her work complete, she dropped her stylus, stretched, and flopped over in bed. It was her first day off in a week, and she had spent the entire morning surrounded by pillows, catching up on commissions.

After scrolling through her phone, Bella tumbled out of bed and headed to the kitchen for lunch. The fridge contained a large container of Nadine's beef and plantain stew from two nights ago, but the smell would remind her of their painful conversation that night. However, the only edible alternatives were Pop-Tarts and frozen waffles, so she took out the container and spooned some into a bowl.

Just as Bella removed the steaming stew from the microwave, there was a knock on the door. She glanced down at her yoga pants and oversized T-shirt. Presentable enough, especially to greet someone who was probably selling magazine subscriptions.

She opened the door and found herself facing the man in the black ballcap who had skulked around the store a few weeks ago, looking for Nadine. Despite her racing pulse, she attempted to project the confidence of someone with a threatening husband or brother in the next room. "What do you want?"

He blinked at her, then pointed his finger. "Wait…I remember you. You work at the store. You told your manager I was shoplifting."

"Again, what do you want?"

"I'm looking for Nadine."

How does he know where she lives? "She isn't here."

He craned his head to look past her as if he expected to see Nadine hovering in the background. "What are you doing here? Are you her roommate?"

Bella brushed her hair behind her shoulder. "That's none of your business." She didn't know who this man was or what he wanted from Nadine, but she wasn't going to give him a thing.

"Look." He stepped back, relaxing his aggressive posture. "My name is Ryan Mitchell. Nadine contacted me herself. Here, I'll prove it." Ryan slid his phone out of his pocket, tapped the screen, and showed her.

Bella studied the message. *What were you trying to tell me about Alyssa Jackson?*

It could have been from anyone. Bella pulled her phone from her pocket and compared the number to the one she had stored for Nadine. They matched. "How do you know her?"

He stuffed the phone back into his pocket. "I work for another candidate for president. A Democrat."

"Jeff Zaller?"

"Yes." Ryan seemed surprised; he'd probably assumed that a blonde register girl wouldn't know anything about politics. "Nadine has information that would be useful to his campaign. That's why I need to talk to her."

"Well, I doubt she wants to talk to you." Nadine felt bad enough about the last election; she would never help one of Alyssa's opponents.

Ryan squinted at her. "What has she told you?"

Bella crossed her arms defiantly. "She told me everything."

"Then why won't she talk to the press? Is she still obsessed with Jackson? Three years later?"

Obsessed? What the hell was he talking about? "What do you mean?"

Ryan narrowed his eyes. "She hasn't told you a damn thing, has she?"

"She tells me plenty. I just don't know what specific thing you're referring to because you're being so cryptic."

"Uh-huh. Sure." He pulled out his phone and checked the screen. "Just tell me where I can find her. Is she at work?"

Crap. She had to keep him talking. He knew something, some secret Nadine hadn't shared. "I'll tell you, but only if you tell me what you're talking about."

"She's probably at work. They told me she wasn't there, but I bet they were lying. I'll go back." He turned away.

"Wait! Did Alyssa know about the Atlas deal? Was she in on it?"

Ryan turned back, his chapped lips curved into a crooked smile. Then he shook his head and went back to his car.

Bella shut the door. Her arms were cold from the chilly outside air, and she still hadn't eaten—as her gurgling stomach reminded her. She returned to the kitchen to retrieve her stew, then sat on the couch to eat—and to try to figure out what the hell had just happened.

Alyssa was guilty of something. At least that's what Ryan thought, but he could be wrong. After all, it was his job to gather dirt on opponents. He wanted it to be true.

Bella had always sensed that there was more to Nadine's story. The woman she knew was resilient, a fighter willing to do whatever it took, but she also didn't seem like the type of person who would sell out others for personal gain.

On the other hand, Nadine was fiercely loyal. The night Todd had shoved his slimy tongue into Bella's mouth, Nadine had pushed him against the wall with a fury she'd never seen. She had defended Bella without hesitation, even though a police investigation could have cost her everything.

Had Nadine felt a similar impulse to defend Alyssa? Was she so loyal that she would lie about the senator's involvement in the scandal?

Many people had speculated that Nadine would incriminate Alyssa in exchange for a lighter sentence. After all, with her own career in shambles, Nadine had nothing to lose by turning on her former boss. But when she didn't, most people concluded that Alyssa was truly innocent. But what if that wasn't the reason?

Ryan's words rang in her brain: *obsessed with Jackson*. What did that mean?

Bella considered everything she knew while she ate the leftover stew. As she slurped the last of the broth, she concluded that the only thing she knew for sure was that she was missing something.

She retrieved her laptop, determined to figure it out. She started with Wikipedia, reviewing the details of the scandal.

Nadine's crime wasn't some convoluted conspiracy that required a chaotic bulletin board to map out. It was actually straightforward. Nadine had promised Jack Ritter, CEO of Atlas Health Source, that Alyssa's proposed cap on premiums would be dropped from her healthcare bill. In return, Atlas used the names and addresses of the company's subscribers to make thousands of fraudulent donations to the Alyssa Jackson campaign. Alyssa won the nomination.

The testimony was consistent on all sides, so none of those facts were in dispute. But that didn't mean the picture was complete. There could be other facts that were in play, facts that changed the meaning of events.

Bella scrolled through news articles, timelines, and opinion pieces, searching for some clue that suggested Alyssa had orchestrated the deal or at least knew about it. Plenty of people had speculated that Alyssa was involved—creating enough suspicion that she lost the general election—but there was zero actual proof.

Next, Bella tried YouTube, scrolling through videos of Alyssa from the last presidential campaign. She clicked on her speech following the Democratic primary in New Hampshire—her big comeback after a poor performance in Iowa.

In the video, Alyssa, wearing a plum-colored pantsuit, addressed a crowd of roaring supporters. Each time she started to speak, a new round of cheers drowned her out.

Bella scrutinized Alyssa's face for some sign of guilt or anxiety but saw only elation.

Alyssa basked in the applause. When she finally spoke, she glowed as she thanked the voters, the volunteers, and her staff. "And thanks to Nadine Bayani, my lawyer, my advisor, and so much more."

The camera panned to Nadine, who beamed and clapped hard. Her eyes shone with pride, relief, and...something else. Adoration. She looked at Alyssa as if she...they...

Holy shit.

No wonder Nadine was so private about her sexual orientation that she wouldn't even tell Bella. There was no rational reason for her to be so guarded with someone who was guaranteed to be accepting. Unless the reason was that she didn't want Bella to guess about Alyssa.

Bella began to piece together a whole new story: Alyssa was having an affair with Nadine. They cooked up the scheme together, and when they got caught, Nadine took the blame. She wouldn't implicate Alyssa, not because Alyssa was innocent but because Nadine was in love with her.

It finally made sense. Alyssa was a smart, athletic, powerful senator. Bella could never compete with someone like that. She remembered Nadine telling her they couldn't have a relationship because it would be unfair to Bella. *Yeah, right.* She felt like an idiot for believing those words were sincere. Now she knew it was because she would never be good enough, would never be anything like Alyssa, the woman Nadine really wanted. Her heart ached.

But she still had questions. What was Nadine's relationship with Alyssa now? They didn't seem to be in contact. Then again, Nadine knew how to keep a secret.

Bella knew for sure that Alyssa wasn't giving Nadine money. She had watched her at the grocery store, comparing food items and choosing the cheapest. Nadine was broke.

Besides, she wouldn't be sleeping on Bella's couch if she had the money to rent her own place. And she certainly wouldn't work at Overstock Oasis.

Maybe it was over between Nadine and Alyssa. Or maybe they had agreed to cut all contact for a while and then reunite in secret. The idea was romantic in a nauseating sort of way.

Her mind was running wild with assumptions and theories. She closed her laptop and sat back. She was onto something—she knew it—but she didn't have evidence or details.

Really, it was none of her business. If she was just Nadine's roommate, if they would never be anything more, did she really need to know? She should stay out of it.

Fuck that. Of course she needed to know. Her heart rate hadn't slowed a tick since she'd watched the video. There was no way she could let it go.

It might not be her business or make any practical difference, but she knew she'd obsess until she had answers. She had to talk to Nadine. Now. Tonight.

Chapter 24

Nadine knew something was wrong as soon as she stepped into the apartment.

Bella was curled up on the couch, clutching a throw pillow to her stomach and staring at her phone.

Nadine pulled off her shoes and went to sit next to Bella. "What's wrong?"

Bella sat up and set her phone on the coffee table. "Nothing. But I need to talk to you."

"Okay. What is it?"

"No, I mean—get settled first. Take off your jacket, get food, whatever." Bella fiddled with the fringe on the pillow. "I just want to talk sometime tonight."

Nadine removed her jacket and slung it over the arm of the couch. "I'm settled. Tell me."

Bella took a breath. "A man named Ryan Mitchell came to the apartment today."

"Ryan came here? I'm sorry—he shouldn't have done that. He works for Jeff Zaller's campaign, and he's been trying to get me to talk to him about Alyssa. I told him I have nothing to say, but he's persistent." She gave Bella a reassuring smile. "But he's not dangerous, just annoying."

Bella continued to worry the fringe on the pillow. "He said some things about you and Alyssa Jackson."

Nadine stiffened. What the fuck was Ryan trying to do? "I haven't told him anything. Whatever he said, he was making it up."

"Okay, fine. Forget about Ryan. I need to ask you something." Bella turned to face Nadine, still hugging the pillow. "Did you have an affair with Alyssa?"

"No!" *What the hell did Ryan tell Bella?* "No, we didn't have an affair. Not really." Shit, why did she add the last part?

"But it was something. Is Alyssa gay too? Or bi?"

"She's not gay. She might be bi. I don't know." The words spilled out before she could stop them. This was happening too fast. She wasn't ready for this conversation.

Five minutes ago, she'd been driving home, half-listening to NPR and trying to remember if she had enough cooked rice left for dinner. Now she was cornered with no time to figure out what she was willing to tell.

"But you were involved?" Bella searched her eyes. "I know I don't have any right to know, but could you tell me? Please?"

Nadine took a shaky breath. "I developed feelings for Alyssa. Feelings I'd never had for men, not even the men I dated."

"Oh wow." Bella leaned forward. "And before that you didn't know you were gay?"

Nadine looked down at her lap. "I think on some level I always knew I wasn't straight. I didn't care about boys growing up. Everyone assumed it was because I was too focused on school."

"Yeah, I know what you mean. Your friends are swooning over boys, and you're just, like, what am I missing?"

Still avoiding eye contact, Nadine traced circles on her knees as she spoke. "Yes, it was something like that. I dated men, even had a few boyfriends in college and law school. But I always broke up with them with some flimsy reason. Eventually I stopped trying and resigned myself to the single, workaholic life. Until I met Alyssa."

"You fell in love with her."

"I don't know if it was love." She had thought so once, but didn't love mean reciprocation? Otherwise it was all longing and heartache, lonely nights and hungover mornings. "I wanted Alyssa more than anything. I craved her, physically, emotionally. I lived and died for her approval, for every second of connection. I didn't care about anything else."

"Is that when you realized you were gay?"

Nadine shook her head. "Alyssa figured it out before I did. She always saw right through me. One night, we were up late working together, and she told me she knew how I felt about her."

Shuddering, she thought back to that strange and awful night when her last delusions shattered around her like glass. "I replayed my whole life that night, realizing what I should have known the whole time: I was gay. I was a lesbian obsessed with my boss—a senator with a husband and a child. It was a relief, and it was a nightmare."

"So... nothing ever happened between you two?"

"Not at first." Nadine continued to stare at her hands. "Alyssa told me it was okay, that she had feelings for me too. But she said we couldn't act on our feelings because she was married."

"Oh. Well, I guess that's noble."

Nadine laughed bitterly. "Except Alyssa never denied herself anything she wanted, certainly not for moral considerations. But at the time, I believed her. I wanted to believe her."

"You think she never really liked you that way?"

Finally, Nadine looked up. "Alyssa needed me. She needed my loyalty. The night of the Iowa caucus, when she came in third—that was the only time we ever kissed." Nadine could still see Alyssa's heart-shaped face, stained with streaks of mascara. Her lips were shiny with gloss, thin and soft. "It was the first time I ever kissed a woman. The way my body reacted...God." Any lingering doubts about her sexuality had evaporated when their lips had touched. "After that kiss, I would have done anything for her. I suppose that's why she did it."

"Wait, are you saying...?" Bella gasped. "Oh my God. Alyssa asked you to make the deal. The fake campaign contributions. She—"

"I didn't say that," Nadine said quickly. "She didn't ask me anything that night." *What am I doing?* She had no plan, had made no decisions about what to share. With every sentence, she inched closer to the truth, but was she ready for Bella's reaction?

Nadine took a breath. "She didn't ask me that night, but I think on some level, she knew she would need my absolute loyalty in the near future."

"Did Alyssa know about the deal? Was she involved? Please just tell me." Bella's voice cracked. "Please."

It was like standing on a ledge, overwhelmed by how easy it would be to fall. To just say the words.

"Alyssa knew."

Bella clapped her hand to her mouth. "Holy fucking crap. I knew it. Did you tell her what you were planning? Or was it her idea?"

"It was Alyssa's idea."

"Jesus. She's just as guilty as you." Bella sat back. "Why didn't you tell the feds? You could have gotten a lighter sentence, maybe even immunity."

Immunity. The media had speculated for weeks about whether Nadine would seek immunity. "To get a deal like that, I would have had to testify against Alyssa. She would have been finished."

"But you could have stayed out of prison." Bella stared at her in disbelief. "She was guilty, and you never turned on her because you were in love with her?"

"No. That wasn't the reason. My feelings...they made it easier. But I took the blame because I didn't want a white supremacist to be president. I'm sure you remember Rob Gunn's rallies during the campaign." Crowds of angry white men had chanted hateful slogans, while wearing rifles and waving Confederate flags. Instead of condemning them, Gunn had defended and encouraged their behavior.

"I remember. I've never been so angry and scared about an election."

Nadine nodded. "I knew that if he won, poor people would suffer. Immigrants would be deported, families torn apart. Hate groups would be emboldened. People would die. Plus, his Supreme Court appointments would undo generations of progress. He was that bad."

"And that's exactly what's happening."

"Yes." The first two years of Gunn's term had been every bit as horrific as expected. "If the scandal had come out during the primary, another candidate would have won the nomination. But by the time prosecutors figured it out, Alyssa was already the nominee. The general election was only three months away, and I thought..." Nadine rubbed her forehead with her palm.

"You thought what?" Bella asked.

How to explain it? "This may sound silly or arrogant, but at the time I thought I was the only one who could stop Gunn from winning the election. That's why I told them Alyssa had nothing to do with it."

Bella stared at her. "That's...amazing."

"But it didn't work." Even though prosecutors never charged Alyssa, the scandal tainted her candidacy—enough to flip the swing states to Gunn. "People believed she knew about it."

"Well, they were right."

"Yes, but..." Nadine paused. "Have you ever heard of Edwin Edwards?"

Bella frowned. "I don't think so."

"He was the governor of Louisiana in the 1980s, but he lost his reelection bid after he got indicted on corruption charges. Four years later, he ran for governor again, and his opponent was David Duke, the KKK leader."

"Whoa. The actual Ku Klux Klan?"

Nadine nodded. "The election was between a crook and a literal Klansman. But Edwards won, and Duke never became governor. That election year, all over the state, people had bumper stickers that said, *Vote for the crook. It's important.*"

Bella laughed. "That's great."

"It is, isn't it? Anyway, Alyssa winning the election—it was important." Nadine sighed. "I love this damn country. It hasn't been kind to me, but I really do. I would have done anything to spare it from Rob Gunn."

"That's really incredible," Bella said. "I mean it. Not many people would give up their freedom to try to protect people they don't even know."

"Thank you." It was a relief to feel even a little understood.

"But after Alyssa lost, why didn't you tell the truth?" Bella asked. "Maybe they would have reduced your sentence."

"No one would have believed me. I was the most despised woman in America, and I had every reason to lie. And even if people did believe me, they wouldn't have let me out of prison just for implicating Alyssa." Nadine hoped Bella would accept this, unlike Patricia. She didn't need two people hounding her to *just tell the truth* like it would solve everything.

"Did your lawyer tell you that?"

"I am a lawyer."

"Oh. Right." Bella frowned. "So is Alyssa helping you at all now? I mean, she owes you for taking all the blame."

"Yes, you'd think that would count for something. But Alyssa can't risk her career by associating with me. After all, she told everyone that I betrayed her. I'm sure you saw her crying on national television recently."

"Oh my gosh, that interview." Bella groaned. "Now that I know the truth, it's disgusting. Man, she's a good actress."

"Oscar-worthy," Nadine agreed.

"When she kissed you, do you think she was acting? Is she even queer? Or was she just faking so she could use you?"

Another good question, one Nadine had asked herself many times during her two years in prison. "I don't know. I'm not sure I'll ever know."

They sat quietly. Then Bella said, "I should let you get settled for real. I'm sure you're hungry. I had some of your stew for dinner, and I was thinking of having a little more. Want some?"

"God, yes." Warm comfort food was exactly what Nadine needed. Along with a stiff drink.

Bella got up and headed toward the kitchen. Then she turned back. "Nadine? I'm really glad you told me the truth. Thank you for trusting me."

"You're welcome." A guilty voice in her head reminded her that she hadn't trusted Bella with the whole truth—that she wasn't involved in the deal at all.

Bella would believe me. Nadine was sure of that now. But what would the consequences be?

Bella was loyal and tenacious. If she knew the whole truth, she'd be incapable of letting it go. She would want Nadine to do something about it—like telling the whole world. She might even do something reckless on her own.

But accusing Alyssa would only bring Nadine more hatred and trauma. She would rather live with the lies than go through it all again.

Anyway, telling the truth about the money wouldn't absolve her of the lies she had already told. It wouldn't make her worthy of someone like Bella.

Chapter 25

Bella finished organizing cookware, then turned the corner to find the bath aisle in shambles. Packages of shower curtains spilled onto the floor, and the bath rugs she had stacked an hour ago were in complete disarray.

Damn customers. As she crouched to pick up the shower curtains, her phone buzzed in her pocket. She slid it out and found a text from Raelyn.

Just donated $20 to Alyssa Jackson. It was followed by a grinning emoji and a screenshot of the website's *Thank you for donating!* page, featuring Alyssa's sparkling smile.

Bella stared at the text message. What could she even say? "Cool. You just gave twenty dollars to Nadine Bayani's criminal co-conspirator."

Raelyn would never believe her. Nadine was right—few people would trust a confessed criminal suddenly changing her story.

Besides, Bella wasn't about to betray Nadine's confidence when she had just learned the truth herself. Nadine hadn't explicitly told her not to tell anyone about Alyssa's involvement, but considering that it took months to pry it out of Nadine, Bella figured it was implied. But how was she supposed to talk about Alyssa as if she didn't know anything?

Bella had spent three days thinking about everything Nadine had told her, and she had come to an unshakable conclusion: Alyssa Jackson was scum.

It was one thing for Alyssa to allow Nadine to take the fall "for the good of the country." Yes, Alyssa would have been a better president than Rob Gunn. Fine.

But after she lost the election anyway, Alyssa should have helped Nadine. Instead, Nadine had languished in prison for two years while Alyssa, who was just as guilty, remained a US senator and sympathetic figure.

If anything, what Alyssa did was worse because she had manipulated Nadine into participating. Nadine never would have agreed to execute the scheme if it weren't for her feelings for Alyssa. Bella was certain of this.

The woman she knew would never make a corrupt deal for a candidate on her own. Nadine must have done it because she was in love—a love so intense and consuming that she had cast aside her morals to make Alyssa's dream come true.

The thought of Nadine having strong feelings for Alyssa made Bella sick. Sure, she was jealous—Bella would give anything to be loved by Nadine—but she was also certain that Alyssa was a sociopath who had never felt a thing for Nadine. It was all about her selfish quest for power.

What could Bella possibly say about Raelyn's twenty-dollar donation to a woman who deserved twenty months in a medium-security prison?

After typing and deleting several responses, she finally sent a thumbs-up emoji. Even that made her want to take a shower.

"Nadine? What was prison like?" The question slipped out before Bella could stop it. She knew Nadine didn't like to talk about prison, but after an evening of Chinese food and chardonnay, her mouth was ahead of her brain.

Nadine took a slow, pensive sip of wine.

"I'm sorry. I shouldn't have asked. You probably don't like thinking about it."

"It's fine. I don't blame you for wondering." Nadine set her glass down. "You sleep in a cage and wake up in a cage. My cell was six by eight feet, and I shared it with another prisoner. There's no privacy, no dignity. Just endless manual labor."

"Labor?" Bella pictured an old-fashioned chain gang. Those were still a thing?

"Mmm-hmm. People think prisoners sit around all day, but the entire system runs on inmate labor. You work all day for pennies per hour. Cleaning, cooking, laundry, yard work, maintenance. Things like that."

Bella nodded. "Oh yeah, I remember that from *Orange is the New Black*. The prisoners had different work assignments."

"Yes. But the guards knew who I was, and they liked to give me the most unpleasant jobs they could find. Scrubbing toilets, that sort of thing. One time a guard made me follow him into the bathroom. He pissed all over the floor right in front of me. Then he made me clean it up while he watched."

"Oh Lord. That's horrible." Bella cringed as she imagined the scene. Then she remembered Jason pouring coffee all over the floor and ordering Nadine to mop up the spill. He'd probably triggered a traumatic flashback, yet somehow Nadine had kept her cool.

Bella asked gently, "Did the guards single you out because they were mad about the scandal?"

"Most of them probably didn't give a damn about politics." Nadine's voice sounded far away. "Of course, they all thought I was guilty. But it was more than that. I was a brown woman with power, and then I was nothing. Certain men—who seem to be overrepresented in the prison guard profession—take pleasure in tormenting someone like me."

Bella opened her mouth to offer comforting words, but her mind snagged on something Nadine had said. "Wait. What did you mean just then? You said they *thought* you were guilty."

Nadine's head jerked up. "I didn't—that's not what I meant. They knew I was guilty."

"But that's not what you said. You said it like they were mistaken."

"I misspoke." Nadine looked away.

Holy shit. Could Nadine be innocent? Like, *completely* innocent?

Bella tried to remember exactly what Nadine had said when she'd told her about Alyssa's involvement. *It was her idea.* Bella had assumed Alyssa directed Nadine to make the deal with Atlas. But Nadine had never said that explicitly.

"Nadine, who made the deal with Atlas?"

Nadine sat back and crossed her arms. "You're twisting my words."

"Forget your words. I am asking you—"

"Bella, stop." Nadine's voice was sharp. "Please stop. I know you want to think of me as a good person, but I'm not. Okay?"

Bella couldn't accept this. Not anymore. "Listen to me. You *are* a good person. You took the fall to save this country from a monster. Just because it didn't work doesn't make it any less noble. If you did all of that when you weren't even involved in the crime, that makes it even more incredible. And you know what? If you were involved, then you made a terrible mistake, but you're still not a bad person."

Nadine's shoulders sagged. She looked small and vulnerable.

Bella slid closer on the couch and grasped her hand. "You have been caring and loyal and kind ever since I met you. That's who you are to me. If you did make the deal with Atlas, then I forgive you. I really do. You served your time. You've suffered enough, and I forgive you."

With her other hand, Bella touched the side of Nadine's face. "I know I'm not the sort of person you ever thought you'd be with. I know I'm nothing like Alyssa. But I care about you. I wish you would let me."

Nadine pulled her hand away.

Hurt flooded Bella's chest. *She doesn't want me.*

Then Nadine wrapped an arm around Bella's shoulders and pulled her in, capturing her mouth.

The kiss was intense—possessive. Nadine claimed her with every taste and suck and clash of tongues.

Bella merely responded, allowing her mouth to be consumed. Warmth pooled in her belly as she slid forward to return the embrace.

Nadine gripped Bella's shoulders, and for an awful moment Bella feared she was about to push her away. Instead, Nadine guided her backward until she lay flat on the couch.

Bella's heart raced as she gazed up at Nadine's dilated pupils and swollen lips.

Nadine descended on her, graceful yet pulsing with power. Her hard body molded to Bella's soft curves, and with only their shirts between them—neither bothered with bras at home—Nadine's erect nipples pushed into Bella's breasts, causing her own to harden.

Bella whimpered as Nadine trailed soft, potent kisses down her jawline. Heat crept up her neck, and she tensed her thighs to stop her legs from squirming.

Nadine tugged on Bella's shirt. "Get rid of this." She said it as if the shirt's existence was an affront.

It's happening. After slamming into one wall after another, Bella had broken through. But she didn't want their first time to be on the cramped sofa, with her ass wedged between cushions and their heads bumping the arm. "Wait," she croaked.

Nadine drew back, eyes wide and alarmed.

"Not here." Bella pushed herself up. "Come to my bed."

Nadine didn't want to think. Not about Bella's questions or the answers that were eating her alive. Certainly not about what they were doing, what a bad idea it was, and what it would all mean tomorrow. Instead, she sank into Bella's bed with its pile of mismatched pillows and rumpled sheets patterned with roses.

Bella lifted her T-shirt over her head and fell into bed beside her.

"Oh." Nadine lost herself in the vision of Bella's heavy breasts, soft belly, and full hips.

Bella shyly covered her stomach with her arm.

Nadine nudged it away. "Stop that. You're beautiful." It was true. Lying on her side, Bella was like a goddess from a painting, her blonde hair cascading in loose waves that moved with her body. Her brown eyes were dark with lust, and only a hint of lipstick remained on her parted lips.

Nadine traced Bella's collarbone, then trailed a finger into the valley of her cleavage. She cupped a creamy breast with the slightest squeeze, eliciting a gasp from Bella. She desperately wanted to kiss it—and she was amazed to realize she could. After months of pretending not to notice Bella's sumptuous breasts, she had permission to touch and taste and worship them.

"Lie on your back." Nadine tapped Bella's shoulder. She wanted access to every inch. When Bella complied, Nadine straddled her. She lowered her lips to Bella's breast, planting one kiss and then another on the delicate skin. When her tongue reached the hard, pink nipple, Bella's little gasps became a throaty groan.

As she continued to lick and tease, Nadine reached down to stroke Bella's belly. She followed the slope down to her shorts and kept going over the fabric, indulging in the slow exploration of Bella's generous hips and ass.

God, I'm gay. Gay, gay, gay. She had accepted as much in recent years, but the throbbing need between her legs was unlike anything she had ever felt with a man. This was how it was supposed to feel, why people risked marriage, money, careers.

Bella clawed at her back, pulling Nadine's shirt upward. "Please. I want to feel you. I need your skin on mine."

Nadine stripped the shirt from her body and flung it somewhere on the floor. Her breasts hovered over Bella, and now it was her turn to feel self-conscious. While Bella had luscious, womanly curves, Nadine was short with slim hips and humble breasts.

"Oh wow." Bella took in her body with greedy eyes. "You're so hot."

Nadine's breath caught at the naked adoration reflected back at her. *Bella would never reject me.* This simple truth overwhelmed her. No matter what it cost her, Bella would never push her away. But she couldn't think about that now, not if she wanted to keep feeling like this.

Instead, Nadine pressed their bodies together, savoring the feel of Bella's naked breasts against hers. The heat was rising in the room, and a drop of perspiration trickled into Bella's cleavage. When Nadine kissed Bella's other breast—the one she'd neglected—it tasted faintly of salt.

Nadine wanted more. She yanked on Bella's pajama shorts. "Off."

Bella raised her hips and pushed the shorts past her bottom, revealing lavender bikini panties with lace trim and a visible dark spot where arousal had soaked through.

Nadine's mouth went dry at the irrefutable evidence that Bella's desire was more than affection, friendship, concern. *Bella wants me.* She lowered her head to the panties, inhaling the heady aroma of sweat and sex. When she kissed the satiny fabric, Bella cried out and gripped the mattress with both hands.

As Nadine reached for the lacy waistband, sudden hesitation gripped her. With her head between Bella's thighs, it sank in that she was having sex with a woman for the first time, at age forty, without any knowledge of what Bella liked in bed.

Nadine had kissed Bella in an explosion of pent-up emotion. She knew that her sweet, generous Bella would let her continue without complaint. But she wanted it to be good for both of them. "Tell me what you want me to do."

"Anything." Her voice was raspy. "Do whatever you want."

Nadine traced circles on the panties. "I want to do what you like."

Bella propped herself up with her elbow and met Nadine's eyes. "I like it when you, um, have your way. You doing what you want to me is the hottest thing I could imagine, and I'm going to scream if you don't get back to doing it." She flopped back onto the bed. "Touch me, taste me, fuck me. Anything. Please."

"O-okay." Her heart pounded as she slid the panties down Bella's legs, revealing brown curls. "God. Bella." She kissed the curls, then dipped lower as wetness coated her chin. Tracing her tongue along the edges, she explored with light pressure.

Bella bucked her hips, urging her deeper. "Yes, yes, yes."

Nadine ventured into the slippery center until she found the unmistakable swell of Bella's clit. She circled and brushed it, reveling in taste and sensation. Arousal coursed through her, drenching her own panties as her hips moved up and down of their own volition.

She didn't know what to do, and yet she did. Bella was vocal and responsive, making no secret of what she liked and where.

"Yes. Just like that. Oh God." Bella grabbed Nadine's shoulders as her moans increased in volume and pitch. Then, all at once, she tensed and clenched, closing her legs as she shuddered hard.

Nadine lifted her head and watched in wonder as Bella's face contorted and then melted into a dreamy smile. *I made Bella come.*

"Oh. My. God." Bella's breasts heaved as she gasped for breath.

Nadine wiped her mouth, then moved to lie beside Bella so she could wrap an arm around her waist.

Bella stared at the ceiling, still breathing hard. Finally, her head lolled to the side as she met Nadine's eyes. "Thank you."

Nadine brushed a strand of hair from Bella's face. "Thank you for letting me."

Their lips met in a tender kiss. Nadine wondered if Bella could taste herself, a thought that made her own center throb.

As they kissed, Bella's fingers roamed over Nadine's back and shoulders, then moved to her collarbone and down to her breasts.

Nadine stilled her hand. "You don't have to." She didn't want Bella to feel obligated, no matter how badly Nadine craved her touch.

"I want to. I've wanted to for so long. Please let me."

Her thighs quivered. *God, yes.* "Okay."

Bella wrapped her arms around Nadine, holding her close as she placed reverent kisses on her cheek and chin. Without warning, she nipped Nadine's earlobe.

Nadine hissed and clenched her abs. "Oh—oh, I like that."

"Good." Bella's breath warmed her neck as she teased the outer ear with little bites and flicks of her tongue, making her shiver.

The light touch was glorious torture. Nadine dug her heels into the bed, unable to lie still.

When she was done with the ear, Bella slid downward and kissed her way to Nadine's breasts. "You're so gorgeous," she whispered. "I love your boobs and your shoulders and your skin."

Nadine twitched involuntarily as Bella lowered her mouth to one nipple. She had never enjoyed men licking her there, somehow finding it too stimulating and not sensual enough all at once.

But this. This, like a kiss, was completely different with a woman. She barely felt Bella's tongue, only glorious sensation.

When Bella peeled off her pants, Nadine remembered her cotton briefs. Not sexy, but at least they were solid black.

Bella barely looked at them—she just pulled them off and kicked them aside.

With no clothes between them, Bella curled up next to Nadine and caressed her slick curls with her whole hand, palm to fingertips. "You're so wet."

"Because of you. Everything about you turns me on." She was hot and swollen beneath Bella's touch.

Bella switched to a single finger and probed deeper. "You feel so good." She touched Nadine with skill and care, adapting the pressure and speed in response to the sounds Nadine couldn't stop making.

When Bella grazed her clit, Nadine sucked in a breath. "Holy hell." She reached backward and grabbed her own hair, needing something to squeeze as her body jerked forward.

Bella circled a few times, then trailed her finger downward to Nadine's opening. "Can I go inside? Do you like that, or...?"

Already out of breath, Nadine choked out, "Yes."

Bella slid a finger inside her and then another, thrusting into her. She started slow, then increased the speed.

Unable to lie still, Nadine bucked and groaned. The loss of control was foreign and frightening and better than she could have dreamed.

She was panting and desperate, grinding into Bella's fingers to drive them even deeper. When Bella's thumb brushed her clit, there was no going back. "I'm going to… Don't stop… There, right there…" Pleasure surged through her, then relief, then trembling aftershocks.

"God, that was hot." Bella slid up the bed and lay next to Nadine. "You know, I was going to do more than that." Mischief played on Bella's lips. "I still can. Perk of being a woman."

"Mmm." It was hard to speak. "I'm good. So good." She closed her eyes, then opened them again to look at Bella. "I'm gay. A lesbian."

"You told me that weeks ago." Bella's eyes widened. "Wait, this wasn't…? Was this your first time?"

"No." Heat rushed to her cheeks. "It wasn't my first time having sex. Just… my first time with a woman."

"Oh my gosh. I wish you had told me so I could have made it really special."

"You did." Nadine pulled Bella close and curled up against her. "You're special, and you were amazing."

Bella sighed and turned, fitting her back against Nadine's front so that they were spooning.

Nadine wrapped her arms around Bella. Tears stung her eyes but didn't fall. For years, she had fantasized that her first experience with a woman would be with Alyssa. She had hoped that someday she'd leave her husband and they would share more than a kiss.

Even in her fantasies, she had imagined her boss as a selfish lover. Still, she had thought that just touching her, pleasing her, would be everything.

Now she knew how lucky she was to share her first experience with Bella, who had shown with every touch that she genuinely cared for Nadine. Even knowing her flaws and thinking the worst about her past, Bella still believed she was a good person who deserved to feel good.

Bella reached for the sheet and pulled it over them, wrapping their naked bodies in tiny roses.

Nadine breathed into Bella's neck and held her tight.

"I love you," Bella said softly.

Nadine tensed. *No, no, no.*

Bella couldn't love her. It was wrong. Nadine would not fuck up Bella's future, no matter how much she... No. She could not.

"Bella..." Her voice broke. "You're a wonderful person, probably the best person I've ever known."

Bella stiffened in her arms. "Oh. Um, it's okay. You don't have to say it back."

"Sharing this night with you was amazing. I'll never forget it. But I can't be in a relationship with you. Not when it would cause you so much harm."

"Right. You said that before." Bella pushed herself out of Nadine's arms and rolled out of bed. She grabbed a towel that was hanging over her desk chair and, still facing the wall, wrapped it tightly around her body.

Nadine tried to think of what to say, anything to stop what was happening and how it was ripping her apart. But she had no words. Instead, she watched Bella rush past her. The bathroom door slammed. Soon after that, the shower started.

Cool air raised bumps on her skin as she slid out of bed and searched the floor for her clothes. She dressed quickly and fled to the couch...the couch that was all of four yards away from the bedroom. There was no escape.

Nadine huddled there in her borrowed bedsheet, listening to the shower. She couldn't get warm.

Fuck. Fuck. Fuck. How did she fuck it up so badly?

They had fallen into bed in a rush of lust and abandon. Surely Bella's declaration was in the same spirit? It was like three a.m. in Las Vegas. *What the hell, let's get married.* Anything to prolong the high.

Nadine should have said something polite and noncommittal so they could enjoy the fantasy a little longer. But no. Instead she had dragged them back to her miserable reality with Bella still naked in her arms.

She lay on the couch for a long time, eyes closed but not sleeping.

Finally, the bathroom door opened. Seconds later, the bedroom door closed. Then silence.

She sat up and switched on the lamp. The coffee table was littered with dishes, chopsticks, restaurant napkins, and half-empty food cartons. Bella's rosy lip prints adorned her glass of unfinished wine.

Nadine dragged herself off the couch and began to clean up the mess. She loaded the dishwasher, washed the wine glasses, and collected the trash. When she picked up the bag the food had arrived in, she found four fortune cookies inside, along with several packets of soy sauce.

She reached in the bag for a plastic-wrapped cookie and turned it over in her hand, trying to remember the last time she'd had one. It had been a few years—before she went to prison.

Fortune cookies didn't contain real fortunes anyway, just benign little sayings or cheery predictions of wealth and romantic success. Americans wouldn't stand for anything ominous. They didn't want to hear that they would end up poor or they'd never find love—or, worse, that they'd find it and lose it because they were too broken to reciprocate.

Nadine threw the cookies away. She knew her future already.

Chapter 26

A MELODIC CHORD PROGRESSION PIERCED Bella's slumber. Her alarm. She fumbled for her phone, silenced the alarm, and burrowed deeper under the covers. *Like hell.*

Sometime later, a knock on the bedroom door once again roused her from blissful oblivion.

"Bella? It's time to leave." Nadine jiggled the door handle.

Time to leave. The words floated around her brain like a screen saver.

Another knock. "Look, I know you don't want to talk to me, but can you just tell me if you want a ride? Otherwise, I'm leaving without you."

With a heavy sigh, Bella reached for her phone and typed a text to Nadine: *Leave without me.*

Then she texted Grady's cell phone number: *I'm sick. Stomach flu. Can't work today.*

Finally, she heard footsteps retreating from the door. She pulled the covers back over her head and closed her eyes.

Bella sat on the couch in her pajamas, inhaling steam from her coffee mug. She had spent the morning in bed, drifting in and out of sleep, emerging from her cocoon only when her bladder reached its breaking point.

The only two places to sit in her small apartment—the bed and the couch—were also the locations of last night's horrible decisions. She'd changed the sheets before sleeping, but she could still smell Nadine everywhere.

Why couldn't the sex have been bad? At least then Bella could console herself by concluding they just didn't have chemistry.

But no. It was everything she could have wanted. Powerful, raw, and deeply emotional. And when Nadine confessed it was her first time with a woman, Bella's heart had swelled with gratitude…only to be smashed a moment later. All because of Nadine's martyr complex that was now messing up two lives.

What the hell was her deal? How could Nadine still believe that Bella was better off without her?

Unless it was just an excuse. Truthfully, it did sound like bullshit. *I'm rejecting you because you deserve better.*

Maybe she really wasn't smart enough for someone like Nadine. Or maybe Nadine just didn't want to be with someone who still lived in the same zip code as her elementary school. After all, they were only friends in the first place because of Nadine's unlikely stint at Overstock Oasis—and Bella's willingness to overlook her crime.

Crime. Bella sat up straight, remembering the conversation from the previous night. After Nadine's rejection, she had almost forgotten. *They all thought I was guilty.*

Maybe it was a clumsy choice of words. But Nadine's reaction when called on it—the rapid blinking, the refusal to discuss it—told Bella otherwise.

Bella didn't understand Nadine's reluctance to confide in her. She didn't work for CNN. She was nobody, for God's sake. Who could she even tell? Raelyn? Ashley? Kenny?

Well, there was Ryan Mitchell. He might be interested in Nadine's slip of the tongue. She didn't have his number, but she imagined she could reach him through the Zaller campaign.

Bella fantasized about calling Ryan and sharing her suspicions. Maybe he could investigate and find out for sure. Then again, it seemed unlikely that he would succeed where prosecutors and reporters had failed.

If Nadine really was innocent, only a handful of people knew it. The CEO of Atlas had met with either Nadine or Alyssa that day—he knew which one. And, of course, Alyssa knew the truth.

Great. I'll just call up Senator Jackson and ask if she's guilty of campaign-finance fraud, accepting bribes, and perjury.

Bella unlocked her phone and scrolled through the latest news about Alyssa's campaign. She was making appearances in Iowa, New Hampshire, and South Carolina, holding town halls and choking down local delicacies in mom-and-pop diners.

Bella clicked on a video titled "Jackson Spars with New Hampshire Voter over Marijuana Flip-Flop."

In the clip, a man with dreads down to his elbows stepped up to the mic. "Hi, Senator. You support the legalization of marijuana now that it's popular. So what do you say to the countless Americans who were arrested for weed over the past two decades while you were too chickenshit to stand up for them?"

Alyssa's fake smile widened. "First of all, sir, you have mischaracterized both my past and present positions…"

The clip played on, but Bella wasn't listening. She was thinking. A random nobody got to confront Alyssa with a hostile question just because he lived in New Hampshire. Maybe an audience with the great Senator Jackson wasn't impossible.

Unfortunately, Virginia didn't hold an early primary. Bella would vote on Super Tuesday, more than two months after the Iowa caucus. Still, Virginia was close to DC, and Jackson was a senator. Maybe something was on the schedule.

Bella navigated to Jackson's campaign website—a flashy monstrosity that looked as if someone had barfed American flags all over the home page—and clicked on *Events*. At the top was an engagement scheduled for that very evening in Sumter, South Carolina: "Community Town Hall with Alyssa Jackson."

Interesting. South Carolina was about five hours away. It was almost noon, and the event was at seven.

She couldn't, right? What were the chances she would get into the town hall, let alone get a chance to talk to Alyssa? It was a ridiculous idea, certain to flop.

On the other hand, what the hell else did she have to do with her fake sick day? Stay home and wallow on the couch where they'd kissed, then go to sleep in her bed where they… No. She needed to do something. Even something foolish and doomed would be better than sitting around reliving last night.

Bella jumped off the couch and ran to her room. She flung a change of clothes and a few hair products into her only piece of luggage, a roller suitcase with a rainbow butterfly print. It would have to do.

Next, she searched her closet for something to wear that said "upstanding citizen" and "likely voter." She shoved aside one outfit after another, finally opting for black slacks and a flowy teal blouse with an empire waist. Smoky eyeshadow concealed that she'd been crying, and pink lip gloss completed the look.

She stocked her purse with power bars and canned soda, then turned off all the lights and hauled the suitcase to her car.

The air was cool, but the sun was out. Gauzy white clouds streaked the sky. It was a good day for a road trip. A good day to get the hell out of town.

When Nadine got home, she was filthy and sticky with sweat thanks to the afternoon spent unloading a massive truck—by herself, as usual, only this time there was no one to bring her a cold drink and carbs afterward.

Her stomach was in knots as she unlocked the door. *I have to fix this.*

Nadine was prepared to grovel—for sleeping with Bella, then ruining the night—and if she couldn't make it okay, she would move out. By now, she had enough cash for a week in a cheap motel. After that, she'd figure something out.

She pushed open the door, prepared to find Bella curled in a fetal position on the couch or buried under the covers in her bed. Instead, the apartment was dark and silent. She flipped on the light and looked around. There was no sign of her.

The bedroom door was ajar, the only light from the late afternoon sun. Nadine knocked, then pushed the door open and turned on the light.

The bed was unmade, but the sheets had been changed. The rose-patterned ones were crumpled in a pile on the floor.

Clothes were strewn across the bed. Nice clothes. Blouses and a dress, as though Bella had been trying on outfits to prepare for...what? A job interview? A date?

She's probably just visiting Raelyn. Nadine imagined the two women sipping cocktails while Bella told her friend all the embarrassing details, like the fact that Nadine had never been with a woman before. Nadine hated the thought of a stranger knowing her secrets, but Bella deserved to confide in someone.

Nadine showered and changed into sweats, then microwaved an ice-encrusted frozen dinner and settled onto the couch to wait. After a while, she turned on the television and watched a local news broadcast from start to finish. When she looked up again, it was dark outside.

She turned off the television and texted Bella: *Are you coming home tonight? If you want me to leave, just tell me and I will.*

No response.

Bella was a compulsive phone checker; she always texted back right away. This must be the silent treatment. The thought of Bella refusing to speak to her was like a weight on her chest.

Nadine opened Skype and messaged her sister. *I fucked up, Pati.*

Right away, Patricia initiated a video call. She was still in her nightgown—it was morning there—and cradling Miko, who sucked on a bottle of milk. "What's wrong, ate?"

No turning back now. "I slept with Bella."

Patricia's jaw dropped. "What? Omigod! When?"

"Last night."

"Wow. You finally had s-e-x with a woman. Did you like it?"

Nadine shifted uncomfortably. She never talked about sex with anyone, especially not her sister.

Before she could answer, Patricia said, "Wait. How did you mess up?"

Nadine sighed. "Bella told me she loves me. Right after we—you know. I told her we can't be in a relationship, and she got very upset. She called in sick to work, and now she's gone and not answering my texts."

"Oh no, ate. That's so bad."

"I know. I never should have slept with her. But she said these things to me. She said she forgives me, and it just filled me. I didn't realize how badly I needed to hear that from her."

Patricia scrutinized her from the other side of the world. "You need to tell her the truth. You should tell everyone—you know my opinion on that—but at least start with Bella. She deserves to know."

For once, Nadine didn't argue. Patricia was right. She had always been right, about the whole damn thing—the folly of falling on the sword, the futility of trying to build a new life on a pile of lies.

"Do you want Bella to be your girlfriend?" Patricia stroked Miko's head.

"What I want doesn't matter. You know what it would be like for her. I won't let my mistakes ruin her life."

Patricia scoffed. "There you go again. You think you know what's best for everybody, and it always turns out to be *you suffering*. Bella doesn't need you to protect her. She needs the truth. She's an adult who can make her own choices."

She couldn't help remembering that Bella had said something similar last night. "Maybe I should trust her."

"It's not about trust. It's about respect."

"You're wise, little sister. Sometimes it's like you're my ate."

Nadine's phone chirped with a notification. It was a text from Bella. "I have to go. Bella just got back to me, and I need—"

"You need to talk to her. We'll talk another time. Tell me what happens, okay?"

"I promise." Nadine ended the call and tapped the message icon.

Something came up. I'm not coming home tonight.

After a few seconds, another message followed: *I don't want you to leave.*

Nadine took a deep breath. She still had a place to live. That was something. But what could have "come up" coincidentally on the day Bella had called in sick to avoid her?

Maybe it was code for getting drunk with Raelyn or staying at her mom's. Or maybe it had nothing to do with her at all. Maybe something else was going on—on top of everything happening between them.

Nadine texted back: *Are you okay? Is there anything I can do?*

The response came a few minutes later. *I'm fine.*

"Well, that clears it up." Nadine threw her phone to the other side of the couch.

Chapter 27

BELLA ARRIVED IN SUMTER AN hour before the town hall, relying on her GPS app to navigate the unfamiliar streets. After a few missed turns, she found the event site—a Baptist church—with thirty minutes to spare.

A massive brick building loomed over her, indicating there would be plenty of room for a large audience. Bella relaxed as she revised the odds that she'd get into the event.

She joined the line, which extended down the sidewalk and snaked around the courtyard. While she waited, she reviewed her game plan. She would try for a seat near an aisle with a direct path to the stage. She wouldn't speak during the town hall—what she had to say wasn't for public consumption—but when the event was over, she would join the supporters mobbing the candidate for selfies.

When she reached Alyssa, she would hold out her phone—set to record video—lean in close, and ask her question. She didn't expect an honest answer, of course, but she hoped Alyssa's reaction would tell her what she wanted to know. And she'd have the whole thing on video.

As she got closer to the double doors at the front of the church, Bella saw they were checking IDs and searching purses. Her own purse contained a bottle of cola and a bag of gummy bears. She stuffed the gummy bears in a zipper pocket, hoping they wouldn't look too closely. If they objected to the cola, she'd just chuck it.

When she reached the checkpoint, a grouchy-looking security officer with massive triceps looked her up and down. "ID?"

Bella presented her driver's license and opened her purse.

But instead of looking inside, the officer returned her license and said, "The event is for South Carolina residents only."

"What? You can't be serious. I drove five hours for this."

"Sorry to hear that." He clearly didn't give a shit. "Next in line."

In a panic, she decided to try flirting. "Alyssa Jackson is my hero. If I don't get to see her, I will seriously cry." She twirled a lock of hair around her finger and fluttered her eyelashes. "Can't you make one tiny exception?"

"No exceptions."

"But—"

"Next!" He turned to the man in line behind her, who smugly presented his ID.

Bella stood on the church lawn blinking back tears. Had she really spent her hard-earned commission money on gas and a hotel room for this? Lord, what a dumpster fire of a day.

"Ma'am, are you okay?" A skinny guy with curly black hair approached her. Bella noticed a lanyard around his neck and had the fleeting hope that he might be with the campaign. Then she read the badge. He was press.

Still, maybe he could help. "I drove here from Virginia, and they won't let me in because I'm not a resident."

"Oh yeah. Jackson restricts these things to locals. And scumbag reporters like me." He grinned.

"You're from out of town?"

"Yeah. Tom Rossi, *Washington Post*. I'm with Jackson's press pool."

"Oh, that's cool. Um, do you think you could sneak me in? It would really mean a lot to me."

Tom studied her. "You came a long way. Were you hoping to ask a question?"

"Not exactly." Bella thought fast. "I'm a big fan, and I've always wanted to meet her. I finally got a day off work, and I thought this was my chance."

"Hmm." Tom pulled out his phone and tapped the screen. "Are you staying the night?"

"Yes..." *He better not ask for a date.*

"I'll tell you what. I can't get you into the town hall, but tomorrow morning Jackson is speaking at USC Sumter. It's for students only, but she'll stop for breakfast on the way. They haven't said where, but I'm certain she'll be at Guignard Diner, just down the road from the campus."

He held up his phone to show her the location. "Get there before nine. Have some breakfast and wait. You might get lucky."

Well, that was something. "Okay. Thanks for the tip."

When she got back to her car, she looked up the diner on her phone. It was near the college, like he said. Maybe she could salvage the trip after all.

After a restless night at a two-star hotel in downtown Sumter, Bella arrived at Guignard Diner just after eight.

The restaurant was a freestanding building painted hunter green with an expansive parking lot crowded with pickup trucks. Inside, the olive-green walls were cluttered with baseball memorabilia, including numerous black-and-white photos of players and teams from the olden days. The plain furniture and elderly clientele completed the snapshot of small-town America. Bella could see why Tom had guessed that Alyssa would choose it for a photo op.

A bottle-blonde, busty waitress named Darlene pointed Bella to a small table for two. Luckily, it was only a few yards from the entrance.

She sat in the chair facing the door and ordered coffee, then took her sweet time reading the menu to stretch out her visit. Finally, on Darlene's third visit to the table, she ordered bacon, scrambled eggs, and hash browns.

The food was out in a flash, and it looked great. A generous pile of hash browns consumed most of the plate, along with scrambled eggs and thick strips of bacon. Bella was ravenous but forced herself to take dainty bites with long breaks in between as she kept her eyes trained on the entrance. She took tiny sips of her coffee, since she didn't want to risk missing Alyssa during a restroom break.

As the wall clock ticked past nine, Bella lost hope. She had eaten almost everything on her plate, and Darlene's "can I getcha anything else" was beginning to sound strained.

A large man in a suit walked in and scoped out the dining room. He wore an earpiece with a coiled cord that disappeared into his black leather jacket. *Security.* Next, someone with a camera arrived. Soon, the diner was buzzing.

"What's going on?" Bella asked Darlene, feigning ignorance.

"We got a politician coming." Darlene rolled her eyes. "They love this place."

"I can imagine." As Darlene walked off, Bella slid to the edge of her chair and angled herself toward the door.

A thin, nervous-looking young woman entered and held the door open. Alyssa followed, wearing a gray pantsuit and heels. She smiled, showcasing her bright white teeth. An entourage of reporters entered behind her while two photographers jumped in front, bulbs flashing.

Bella stood, but one of the photographers blocked her path. *Damn.*

Alyssa leaned in to speak to an older couple. She placed a manicured hand on the man's shoulder, and then she said something to the woman. They all laughed.

Ha ha. I'm a lying, cheating fraud. Vote for me. Bella fidgeted as Alyssa turned to chat with a few servers—not Darlene, who had steered clear of the entire scene. Finally, Alyssa stepped forward, and the photographer moved to the side.

Bella pounced, reaching Alyssa in two quick strides. "Hi."

Alyssa smiled. Up close, her makeup was dark, almost garish, with foundation so thick, she lacked visible pores. "Hello. What's your name, honey?"

This was it, her one and only chance. But there were cameras in their faces and reporters so close she could smell them. Her heart pounding, she leaned in and whispered, "I work with Nadine Bayani, and she told me what really happened."

Alyssa's fake smile collapsed. She waved the reporters away. "Give us some space, please. This young woman would like to share her story in private." She ripped off her clip-on microphone and shoved it at a nearby staffer.

The crowd ebbed back but only slightly. A photographer aimed his lens at Bella.

Alyssa grabbed her by the arm and hustled her into a corner. She signaled to one of her security guards, who crossed his arms and inserted himself between Alyssa and the reporters.

Venomous blue eyes flashed. "Who are you? What the hell are you talking about?"

Bella gathered her courage. "My name is Bella Clarke. I work at Overstock Oasis with Nadine. She told me it was you who made the deal with Atlas. She had nothing to do with it. I want to know why you let her go to prison for something she didn't do."

"She's lying. You don't know what you're talking about."

"No." Bella's voice was soft but certain. "Nadine isn't lying. She didn't even want to tell me, but I figured it out."

"*You* figured it out. Right." Alyssa scoffed. "What are you, a professional checkout girl? You didn't figure out anything."

Bella's cheeks burned. "I may not be a genius, but I know Nadine. She wouldn't do something like that. And I'm going to prove it." It was an empty threat, but it sounded good.

Alyssa leaned in. "You tell Nadine that if she doesn't stop telling lies about me, the past two years will seem like fucking Disney World compared to what I'll put her through next."

Evil witch! Bella opened her mouth to threaten her right back, but Alyssa spun around and returned to her entourage.

Alyssa whispered something to the security guy, who turned to glare at Bella. Then she moved to greet a family at another table, her smile back in place.

Bella stood in the corner with her mouth open until Tom Rossi pushed through the throngs to join her.

"What just happened?" he asked.

"Um, she got mad at me. I can't talk about it." Bella glanced at her table, which was still surrounded by reporters.

He raised an eyebrow. "I thought you were a big fan."

"I used to be. I'm not anymore."

"Why did you really drive here all the way from Virginia?"

Bella shook her head.

"Come on, I'm a reporter. I know when something's up."

"I'm sorry. I really can't talk about it. But I appreciate you telling me where she'd be this morning."

Tom shrugged. "If you change your mind, give me a call." He pulled out a business card.

"Okay." Bella stuffed the card in her pocket, still watching Alyssa, who slowly made her way to the back of the diner.

The reporters followed, clearing Bella's path back to her table.

She turned to Tom. "I'd better get out of here. Thanks again for the tip."

When she reached her table, she grabbed her purse and pulled out a twenty-dollar bill. She caught Darlene's eye, pointed to the cash, and hurried outside.

Safely in her car, she yelled out, "Holy fucking shit!"

Bella now knew two things for sure. First, Alyssa Jackson was guilty as sin. Second, it was time to go home.

Chapter 28

NADINE SHOOK HER PHONE IN frustration. She was cross-legged on the couch, trying to browse apartment listings on her phone's mobile browser, but the five-year-old device crashed every time she clicked a link.

Normally, she used Bella's laptop. Nadine even knew the password by heart—but she assumed her laptop privileges had ended along with their friendship. Besides, she probably couldn't even find the damn thing—it was usually shoved in some preposterous location like a basket of laundry.

Her head shot up at the sound of keys unlocking the door. *Bella.*

Bella walked in, rolling a suitcase behind her. She wore yoga pants, a wrinkled gray T-shirt, and a pair of cat's-eye sunglasses rimmed in neon pink. Her hair spilled from a ponytail on top of her head.

"Where were you?" Nadine asked.

"Um, South Carolina." She pushed the sunglasses up to her forehead.

"What? Why?"

Bella shot a longing look at the bathroom. "Sorry, I've had to pee for like two hours. I really want to talk to you, but I need a minute. Okay? Don't move. I'll be right back."

As if she had anywhere to go. Nadine racked her brain, trying to figure out what the hell was in South Carolina. Bella had never mentioned a connection to the state.

Bella emerged looking refreshed, her face dripping with water and her eye makeup slightly smeared. She sat facing Nadine on the couch. "I guess I'll just say it. I went to see Alyssa Jackson."

"You did *what*?"

"She was campaigning in Sumter, and I went." Bella held up her hands. "I know, I know. It was reckless, but I was really upset. And I just had to know."

"Had to know what?" Nadine's heart was still pounding.

"The truth about what happened. The whole truth." Bella took a breath. "I found out that Alyssa was going to be at a specific diner for breakfast, so I went and waited for her there. Then I went up to her and whispered that I knew you, and she pulled me aside. That's when I confronted her."

"You *confronted* Alyssa Jackson? By yourself?"

"She didn't admit anything, but for a few seconds, she lost her shit. And I just knew." Bella looked Nadine in the eyes. "She made the deal, not you. Alyssa was the mastermind *and* the one who carried it out. You're innocent. You always were."

Nadine shuddered at the word *innocent*. She saw in Bella's face that there was no point in denying it, and she realized she no longer wanted to. "You're right. Alyssa made the deal by herself."

"I knew it! Did you even know what she was doing?"

"No. I didn't know anything. We received a sudden injection of cash when we needed it the most—an apparent surge of first-time donors—but Alyssa never told me where the money came from."

Nadine thought back to those dark days after Iowa. "After she came in third in the Iowa caucus, Alyssa was a wreck. She'd slump in her seat on the bus, stare blankly ahead. She couldn't even get excited for debate prep, which she normally loved. She had this hopeless look in her eyes. I'd never seen her like that."

Bella nodded. "I remember hearing her say in speeches that she'd never lost an election in her life."

"That's right." Alyssa was many things, but a loser wasn't one of them. "We spent two days in New Hampshire, then came back to Washington for a Senate vote. Afterward, I stayed in the city while she went to her apartment in Virginia to think about whether or not to quit the race. Supposedly."

Nadine pulled at a loose thread at the hem of her T-shirt. "Now I know she went to see Jack Ritter. She covered her hair with a scarf, put on sunglasses, and took a bus to his house. Can you imagine? Alyssa Jackson on a bus with the masses, hiding her face like some amateur spy."

"Wait. Wouldn't there be footage of her on the bus?"

Nadine nodded. "Sure, but no one knew where or when to look. Remember, Jack told the feds I met him at his office. The time he gave was hours before the actual meeting. Plus, Alyssa left her phone at home along with her car, so there was no electronic record of her leaving the apartment. She was smart."

"Smart like a sociopath."

"Perhaps. Anyway, within a couple of days, out of nowhere, she was back to the old Alyssa. Our polling hadn't improved, but she had a spark in her eye. She said we were going all in on New Hampshire, that there had been a flood of online donations."

"But it was really money from Atlas."

"Yes. But we never would have guessed it. The amounts coming in were small—under two hundred dollars, so the campaign wouldn't have to itemize them in reports. But there were thousands of them. None of us knew why it was happening, just that we could start spending money again." Nadine shook her head. "I suppose on some level I didn't want to know. Maybe that's why I never asked."

"But you *didn't know*. Maybe you never asked, but that's not a federal offense."

"No, it's not. Anyway, the rest you know. We bought TV ads and radio spots, paid canvassers, and Alyssa won New Hampshire. The donors came back—real ones this time. We had enough momentum to power through Super Tuesday, and after that, the nomination was hers to lose."

"When did you find out something was wrong?"

"Alyssa came to me one night, a few days after the convention." Speaking the truth out loud took her back in time. She could see Alyssa's sky-blue blouse, paired with the sweatpants she'd changed into at the hotel. Her pale cheeks were streaked with tears and crumbs of waterproof mascara. "She told me she was in trouble, that federal investigators were asking questions about the money that came in after Iowa."

"Is that when you agreed to take the fall?"

"Not then, no. At first, I acted as her lawyer. I told her to tell me everything. She kept crying, saying, 'You'll hate me, you'll hate me.' I finally convinced her that if it was that bad, she couldn't afford to keep it from me."

"Okay. So how did you react?"

"Not well. I started yelling at her. I knew right away that what she had done was bad, really bad. The feds were contacting the alleged donors, who all said they'd never donated to Alyssa. But they did have one thing in common. They all had health insurance through Atlas."

"You knew she was screwed."

"We knew someone was screwed. But we didn't know whether Ritter would flip on Alyssa. There was really no reason for him to keep quiet. He had already been indicted, and he could get a shorter sentence by testifying against Alyssa."

Bella frowned. "But he ended up implicating *you*. How did that happen?"

"I found a way to speak to him alone—which wasn't easy, by the way. The feds were watching his every move."

"Oh yeah? How?"

"He had a meeting off-site, and I pretended to be part of the catering staff. No one looked twice at a brown-skinned woman carrying bags of ice, using the service elevator. Then I hid in the VIP men's room."

Bella laughed. "You're kidding."

"I wish. Anyway, he said he hadn't told the feds anything yet, but he was going to talk unless Alyssa helped him. I begged him to give me a week to think of something."

"And that's when you came up with the story."

Nadine nodded. "Alyssa and I spent a full day and night in her hotel room trying to figure a way out. But no matter what we came up with, when we gamed it out, the result was always the same. Alyssa behind bars, Rob Gunn in the White House. Fucking *Rob Gunn*. If Alyssa went down, that monster was going to become the most powerful man in the world. Unless we gave them someone else to blame."

"Whose idea was it?" Bella asked softly.

"It was hers. She begged me for hours, talking about all the terrible things that would happen if Rob Gunn won the election." In prison, Nadine had replayed that night in her mind countless times.

"Well, she wasn't wrong about that."

"No. I knew people would die. We both knew. It wasn't an exaggeration. Anyway, Alyssa promised to use her position to ensure leniency for Jack— and the other Atlas employee, the one from IT—if he went along with it."

"And he agreed."

"Yes. He told the investigators I came to his office to make the deal. The security footage from that day was mysteriously missing, but Jack's secretary claimed to remember seeing me—after he reminded her, of course."

"But couldn't they prove that *you* stayed in DC that day? What about your cell phone?"

"I said I'd left my phone in Washington. We agreed to say that I went there early in the morning so there wouldn't have been any activity on the phone. Alyssa thought of everything. And once Jack implicated me and I confessed, the feds didn't dig much deeper. After all, why would anyone confess to a federal crime that they didn't do?"

"God, Nadine." Bella's voice broke. "Everyone thinks you're evil, but what you did…what you gave up for this country…it was selfless. Nobody else would have the strength to do what you did."

"I don't know that I'd call it strength." Nadine hesitated. This was the hardest part to explain. "I did it for those reasons. I really did. I wanted to save my country from a terrible fate. But I was also in a low place. My only family lived in the Philippines, and I didn't have any close friends. I just worked all day and night, killing myself for Alyssa's career. And I was in love with my boss who just toyed with me, who made me feel like…"

"Like what?" Bella asked.

Nadine shook her head. "Part of me felt like it didn't matter if I went to prison, that I didn't have anything to lose. Then, after I confessed, the whole country thought I was a selfish, terrible person, and I started to believe it too. Like it may as well have been true. Prison was almost a relief because I was safe from the reporters and the death threats. But the way inmates are treated makes you feel less than human. It's hard to undo. Even now, I don't feel like I deserve to tell anyone the truth."

"But you do." Bella took Nadine's hand.

"I'm beginning to understand that. And it's because of you." She stroked Bella's fingers. "Do you remember my very first day at the store when you brought me that soda and doughnut?"

Bella smiled. "Of course."

"You were kind to me, despite everything you thought I'd done. You treated me with compassion. When I met you, I started healing. It was slow and subtle, and most days I didn't notice, but your friendship made me a whole person again."

Eyes watering, Bella squeezed her hand.

Nadine took a deep breath. "I've made mistakes. Don't get me wrong. I didn't do the crime that everyone thinks I did, but I lied under oath. I kept the truth from the American public. I'm not a saint. But you made me realize that by taking the blame for everything, I'm not only punishing myself, I'm hurting the country. And I'm hurting you too. You deserve the truth so that you can make your own choices. I'm in love with you, Bella. I can't offer you the kind of life you deserve, but if you want to be with me, I want to be with you too."

Bella threw her arms around Nadine, pulling her close. "Yes, yes, yes."

Their lips met in a kiss full of love and promise. When they finally pulled back, Bella's eyes were shining. "I'm so happy."

In that moment, Nadine knew it would all be okay. Despite all her flaws and her fuckups, she made Bella happy. She was enough.

There were new fears in place of the old ones, such as what Alyssa might do if she saw Bella as a threat—but whatever happened, they'd be together.

Chapter 29

NADINE GROANED, STRETCHED HER ARMS upward, then leaned from one side to the other. Her shoulders ached from a long day in the stockroom, unpacking boxes from the latest delivery. Thankfully, the store closed in twenty minutes. Then she and Bella would count the cash and get the hell out of there till Thursday. In the two weeks since they'd became a couple, Bella had managed to get them scheduled for the same shifts on most days. Thanks to her smart planning, they both had two days off in a row.

The doors swung open, and Bella breezed into the stockroom, looking radiant despite the huge yogurt stain on her polo. "Hi." She looked around with a conspiratorial grin, then leaned in for a kiss.

"Not much longer," Nadine said as they broke apart. "Thank God."

"I know. I'm so sick of this place. Especially Jason. He's driving me up the wall."

"What did he do now?"

"He's on shoplifting patrol again." Bella rolled her eyes. "Oh! But one thing was funny. He thought some teenage girl was stealing, so he ordered her to empty her purse at the register. She dumped out a pile of tampons and condoms. He turned bright red."

Nadine chuckled. "I'd like to have seen that."

"We can watch it on the security cameras later. Well, I'd better get back to the front. See you in a few minutes."

Just as they leaned in for another kiss, someone opened the doors. They jumped back to see Kenny gaping at them, his eyes like dinner plates.

"Kenny!" Bella said. "We were just, um—" She waved her hand helplessly.

Kenny blanched, but he kept his composure. "I wanted to ask if I could leave a few minutes early to pick up my…" He seemed to draw a blank.

"That's fine," Bella said at the same time Kenny said, "my grandmother."

"Oh, sure. I'll see you on Thursday."

"Thanks." Kenny turned and mumbled "Jesus" as he stumbled out the door.

Nadine waited until the doors closed. "Did our choirboy just take the Lord's name in vain?"

Bella shrugged. "Maybe it was a prayer."

At closing time, Nadine made her way to the front of the store. Bella was studying the wires hooked up to the sound system. She yanked one out, and the pop ballad that had been blasting from the ceiling abruptly ceased.

"Are we having another dance party?" Nadine smiled, recalling the dance Bella had done a few months ago to cheer her up.

"Nah. I just couldn't take another second of that soul-destroying song."

Bella turned to open the safe. She passed the cash to Nadine and began to count the money in her register drawer.

Nadine counted silently until she caught motion from the corner of her eye. She looked up to see Bella making finger guns. "Uh…?"

Bella grinned. "I'm right on the money."

"Excellent."

"See, here's me"—she walked her two fingers across the counter and stood them on top of a stack of cash—"and here's the money."

They both looked up at the sound of a sharp knock on the glass door.

Bella shouted, "We're closed!" as she turned to look. Then she gasped.

"What? What's wrong?" Nadine followed Bella's fearful gaze.

Alyssa Jackson stood at the door, dressed in a full pantsuit and heels, flanked by a single bodyguard. She rapped on the glass again.

Nadine stared at her former boss, unable to move or speak.

Bella's panicked rambling filled in the silence. "Holy crap. What do we do? Should we open the door? Should we call the police? Crap, crap, crap." She fumbled for her phone.

The word *police* jolted Nadine from her stupor. "No police, and we don't want a scene. Just let her in."

Bella gripped her phone. "Are you sure?"

"Yes. Look, she's not here to kill us. She's a US senator. And we need to get her off the sidewalk before someone recognizes her. Here, I'll open the door."

"No!" Bella said. "I'll do it. Don't move."

Nadine tilted her head, confused.

"Stay here with the cash." Bella pointed to the stacks on the counter. "Don't move away from it. Promise me."

"Okay." Nadine doubted Alyssa was there to rob them, but she didn't argue.

As soon as Bella clicked the lock open, Alyssa barged in, heading straight for Nadine. Bella hurried behind her.

Alyssa whirled around. "Back off. I need to speak to Nadine."

"It's okay," Nadine said to Bella. "Really."

Bella glanced between them, worrying her lip, then slowly backed away until she stood near the entrance, next to the bodyguard.

Alyssa regarded Nadine with eyes of ice. "Hello."

Nadine hadn't seen Alyssa in person for over two years. Her hair and makeup were as flawless as ever, but she looked older somehow. Maybe the smudged-over frown lines were deeper.

Alyssa waved her hand at Nadine's dusty polo. "You look…well."

Nadine bit back laughter. "I'm sure."

"I'm here because I need to know what's going on. That woman over there"—Alyssa flicked her fingers at Bella—"accosted me in South Carolina. She said you told her—"

"—the truth. Yes, she knows what happened."

"What the fuck? What do you think you're doing?"

Nadine's pulse raced, but she stood her ground. "Bella is my friend. I owed her the truth."

Alyssa shot a disdainful glance at Bella, who was out of earshot but watching intently. "You're friends with that disrespectful little hick?"

"She's not a hick. She's smart and talented, and she cares about me. Certainly more than you ever did."

Alyssa stepped in closer. "Of course I care about you." Her voice softened. "After what you did for me, we have a bond that can never be broken. But you know I have to keep my distance. I mean, what exactly do you want from me?"

"I don't..." Just as Nadine was about to say she didn't want anything, she realized that wasn't true. "I want you to announce that it was you who made the deal with Atlas. That I had nothing to do with it."

Alyssa's eyes narrowed as she looked Nadine up and down. "Give me your phone."

"What? Why? Oh." Alyssa must think she was recording her. So much for their special bond. She pulled her phone out of her pocket, unlocked it, and set it down.

Alyssa plucked it from the counter. "Wow, this thing is old." She flipped through the apps, powered it down, and put it back on the counter. "If you start running your mouth, everything you went through will be for nothing. Have you thought about that?"

"The public would know the truth. That's not nothing." Nadine paused to consider her next words. "I'm not out to hurt you, but what you did was wrong. People deserve to know who's running for president."

Alyssa visibly stiffened. "I'm running to help people. I'm going to take action on poverty, on immigration. All the things you care about. All the things we used to talk about."

"But you're not the only option anymore. You're not the nominee yet. The other candidates want the same things, and they're not corrupt."

"Those losers?" Alyssa scoffed. "They could never beat Rob Gunn. I'm the only one who has a prayer. That's why I took the money last time; I knew I was the only candidate who could win." She clasped her hands. "Please, Nadine. Don't do this. Don't throw everything away."

"You mean don't throw *your* career away. But I'm done protecting you. I've made enough mistakes without owning yours too."

Alyssa's eyes grew hard again, and Nadine knew she was done appealing for sympathy.

"No one will believe you, you know. You're a felon now. You work retail." Alyssa made a disgusted gesture at the register. "Your word is meaningless."

"You're probably right." Nadine kept her voice calm. "But I can't control that. All I know is, I'm not going to lie anymore."

Alyssa's blue eyes flashed. She leaned in closer to Nadine. "Listen to me. I am *thankful* to you." She spat out each word. "But if you fuck me on this, if you tell one more goddamned soul, I'm done playing nice."

Nadine arched an eyebrow. "What are you going to do, shoot me and dump my body in the Potomac?"

"I won't need to. I'm a senator. I can send you back to prison with the snap of my fingers. And this time, you won't get out in two years." With that, she turned and marched off.

Bella stood by the door, gawking at her.

"What are you looking at?" Alyssa snapped.

Bella crossed her arms. "Ma'am, we're closed. I'm going to have to ask you to leave."

Nadine snorted. She couldn't help it.

Alyssa turned to scowl at her one last time before she turned back to her bodyguard. "Get me out of this small-town hellhole."

Bella locked the doors behind them, then hurried over to Nadine. "What did she say? What did she say?"

Nadine exhaled. "She's not happy with me."

"But *what did she say?* Did she admit it?"

"What do you mean?"

Bella gestured behind Nadine. "Jason's security cameras! They record sound, and there's one right behind you."

Nadine's vision blurred as she absorbed Bella's words. "That's why you wanted me to stand here. Not because of the cash."

"Yes!" Bella bounced impatiently. "Did she say anything incriminating?"

Nadine couldn't breathe. She managed a grunt, then cleared her throat. "She said she took the money."

Bella inhaled sharply. "Holy shit."

Chapter 30

BELLA SANK INTO GRADY'S CHAIR and booted up his computer. Nadine squeezed into the small space behind her.

"Yuck, the keyboard is full of food." Bella wrinkled her nose. "Um, but that doesn't matter. Obviously." She tapped the spacebar. The screen came to life and prompted for a password.

"Do you know his password?" Nadine asked.

"Yeah, it's right here." Bella pointed to the yellow sticky note on the monitor that said *Password12345*.

"Oh, for God's sake." Nadine rubbed her forehead.

"Could you please sit down? You're freaking me out." Bella had never seen Nadine this wound up.

"Fine." Nadine dragged a chair next to her and sat.

They waited in tense silence. Then the desktop finally appeared. About one hundred icons littered the screen, including numerous games and some that looked like malware. Bella searched through them. "I really, really hope Jason put the software on here."

"What's that?" Nadine pointed at an icon called OO Closed Circuit Cameras.

"I think that's the company security system. The one without sound." Bella kept scanning the cluttered desktop until she found a silhouette of an eye behind a magnifying glass. *Spy Master Pro.* "There!"

"Click on it. Fuck." Nadine sounded about ten seconds away from coming totally unglued.

"I already did." The cursor had turned into a little blue wheel.

The screen filled with three windows against a gray background. The wheel turned again, and full-color images of the store appeared in each one.

"This is it!" Bella pointed at the window showing the front of the store—the feed from the camera mounted behind the register. When she double-clicked, the video expanded to fill the screen. "Damn. It's good quality. How much did he spend on this?" Every detail of the register counter was clear.

Nadine leaned forward. "How do you view the earlier recordings?"

"I don't know!" Bella studied the tabs at the top of the screen. She clicked a pixelated clock graphic, and fields appeared. "Okay, it looks like you can enter a specific day and time. Let's try eight, when the store closed."

The screen jumped to an image of Bella leaning over the sound system. Music played in the background, then stopped when she pulled the wire.

Nadine's voice could be heard from somewhere off screen. *Are we having another dance party?* The audio was crisp and clear.

Bella moved the video ahead five minutes. She saw herself leaving the frame to unlock the door, and then Alyssa appeared in vivid color, striding up to Nadine. "Oh my God."

Nadine's back was to the camera, but Alyssa, captured at roughly a three-quarter angle, was clearly identifiable. No one could deny who it was.

Alyssa began to speak. At first, the conversation was vague. There were references to *the truth* without either woman saying what exactly was a lie. Then, Alyssa called Bella a "disrespectful little hick."

"Hey!"

"Shh! Listen."

And then Alyssa said it. *That's why I took the money last time.*

Took the money. "Holy shit! She admitted it. She confessed on camera. She—"

Nadine shushed her again, placing a hand on Bella's shoulder.

Alyssa stepped closer to Nadine and lowered her voice. Bella turned the volume all the way up. Alyssa's words were softer but still audible as she threatened to use her influence to send Nadine back to prison.

As Alyssa walked away from the camera, her faint voice called Cheriville a "small-town hellhole." That comment alone would be a scandal for a politician, but given the context, it was a mere footnote.

"This is incredible," Bella said. "When this gets out..." A horrible thought occurred to her. "Wait. You *do* want it to get out, right?"

Nadine looked ready to barf on the desk, but she nodded. "I do. I'm ready to tell the truth."

"Okay, now what do we do? Upload it to social media? There must be a way to download the video. Or I could film the screen with my phone."

Nadine massaged her temples. "Let me think. It's not legal to record audio on surveillance cameras."

Knowledge popped into Bella's head. "Virginia is a one-party state." She had learned that a year ago when Raelyn had considered recording a creepy manager at the bank. "And we consented, didn't we? I mean, we kept working here after Jason installed these things."

"That's true. And I'm part of the conversation. But these cameras also record conversations between customers where neither party is aware."

"That's Jason's problem, isn't it?" If Jason got in trouble along with Alyssa, that would be a bonus.

Nadine blew out a breath, ruffling her bangs. "We need a reporter, someone to document everything here. The recording, the surveillance system, everything Alyssa said on camera. Once the story is published, the dominos will fall."

"You must know reporters from your time in politics. Do you still have their numbers?"

Nadine's expression soured. "I do, but I can't think of anyone I'd like to gift with a scoop of this magnitude. My old contacts were...unkind...after everything happened."

Bella clapped her hands. "I know someone! Tom Rossi at the Washington Post. Have you heard of him?"

"Hmm. I don't think so. He might be new."

"I met him in South Carolina. He's the one who told me where Alyssa would go for breakfast. He was there when I confronted her at the diner. He didn't hear anything, of course, but he was curious. And he gave me his card."

"He's not local, though."

Bella bounced in her chair. "But he travels with the Jackson campaign. If Alyssa's here, the press pool must be in town too, right?"

"Maybe...or maybe she's staying in Washington and snuck down here without anyone knowing."

"Washington's only a couple of hours away. He could make the trip tonight. I mean, the footage isn't going anywhere. We can stay here and, you know, guard it."

Nadine pressed her lips together. "Okay. Call Tom."

Bella retrieved her purse from the break room and dug through the contents until she found Tom's business card near the bottom, glued to a breath mint.

She couldn't stop fidgeting as she dialed the number. *Please pick up.*

He answered on the second ring. "Rossi."

"Hi, Tom. It's Bella Clarke. I met you at the church in South Carolina the other day and saw you again at the Guignard Diner. You gave me your card."

He paused, then said, "Right. I remember."

"How close are you to Virginia right now?"

"I'm actually home in DC. First time in weeks."

Perfect. He could totally make the drive. She just had to hook him. "I have an incredible scoop for you. Like, Pulitzer Prize-worthy shit. But I need you to drop everything and come to Cheriville, Virginia, right now."

"Uh, what's the scoop?" Tom didn't sound excited at all. He must get calls from crackpots all the time.

"It's about Alyssa Jackson and what really happened with Atlas Health Source."

"You're going to have to give me more than that. Even if you had real information, I'd need evidence and sources to write a story."

Crap. He wasn't biting. "Can you video chat with me? I can prove this is legit." She glanced at Nadine, who nodded, seeming to guess her next move.

"Fine. Hang on."

The video call came through in seconds. When Bella accepted, Tom appeared on the screen, looking scruffy in his dim apartment.

Bella positioned the phone so that she and Nadine were in the shot together.

Tom sat up, his jaw dropping. "Whoa."

"Hi, Tom," Nadine said. "This is Nadine Bayani, here with my friend Bella. You want to do what she's telling you."

Tom was already scrambling to his feet. "What's the address?"

Chapter 31

BELLA ESTIMATED IT WOULD TAKE Tom almost three hours to arrive, accounting for traffic. They'd have to stay at Overstock Oasis past eleven p.m., but she didn't see another option. The cash was secure in the safe; they'd deal with it later. She refused to leave the store, and their precious evidence, for any reason—not even for dinner.

They snacked on stale cookies from the food section, saving the box to pay for them the next day, but it wasn't much of a meal. After an hour, Bella ordered a large Hawaiian pizza. When it arrived, Bella opened the doors a crack and passed the delivery guy the cash. He slid the pizza in sideways, then scampered away.

Bella took the pizza back to the break room and set it on the table, where Nadine was pacing back and forth. "Mmm, this smells so good—oops." The cheese and toppings had slid to the side. "No problem, I'll just move it back."

Nadine barely glanced at the mess. "I don't know if I can eat."

"Come on, you need something." After arranging the toppings on the crust, Bella scooped out a slice and dug in. She sighed with pleasure as warm oil and carbs filled her mouth. "Mmm, it's so good. Seriously. Just try it."

Nadine sat and broke off a small slice. She took a dainty bite, then another, and soon she was inhaling the pizza alongside Bella. They ate in silence until they had devoured half the pie.

Nadine sat back. "God. I needed that."

"Told you. So, how are you doing?"

"I feel sick. I don't know why. I should be happy."

"It makes sense. I mean, this is huge." Bella felt queasy too but for a different reason. What would happen to them as a couple when Nadine wasn't trapped in Cheriville anymore? Bella wanted Nadine to prove her innocence more than anything, but she was scared.

Nadine picked at a half-eaten piece of crust. "I think a small part of me found comfort in how wrong it had all gone. When I realized there was nothing I could do to make things better, to change anyone's mind about me, it was easier in a way. Does that sound perverse?"

"No, it makes sense. Sometimes I feel that way about flunking out of college. Like, it obviously pales compared to what you've been through, but that year at Mary Washington was really rough for me. When I got the letter that I had lost my financial aid, I felt sad and ashamed but also relieved. I could go home. I didn't have to try and fail anymore."

Bella looked around at the dingy break room where she had clocked into work for the past decade. Ten years of dealing with Grady and Jason. "My job sucks, but it's safe."

Nadine took her hand and squeezed it. "Maybe we're both ready to face the things that scare us."

"Yeah, maybe." Bella squeezed back but then looked away.

If Nadine reclaimed her reputation, there'd be no limit to what she could do. But Bella couldn't see a way out of her own life. She knew now that she was capable of more, that her own fear and confusion had held her back. But she had been stagnating for so long, she worried it was too late to change her life.

Even if she got treatment for ADHD or whatever was wrong with her, she was still ten years removed from her last day in school. Her entire resume consisted of a high school diploma and her promotion to third key at Overstock Oasis.

Bella's phone chimed with a new text message. *I'm outside.* "Tom is here."

Nadine dropped Bella's hand. "Okay." She closed her eyes and nodded as though convincing herself of something.

"I'll go get him. You can wait here." Bella hurried to the front of the store.

Tom stood at the glass double doors, wearing an oversized black hoodie. Somehow the sight of him made it more real. *The Washington Post* had arrived.

Bella unlocked the doors. "Thanks for coming."

Tom looked around the dimly lit store. His face was pale, with stubble and shadows, but his eyes were bright. "Where's Nadine? And what's going on?"

"She's in the back." Bella locked the doors behind him. "And it will be easier to just show you. Come on." She led him to the break room.

Nadine sat with her arms crossed next to the half-eaten pizza. "You must be Tom." She gestured to the box. "Slice of pizza?" Now that they had company, Nadine's walls were up. If Bella didn't know better, she'd think Nadine was perfectly calm.

"Uh, no, thanks. Maybe later." Tom blinked at Nadine as if starstruck. "Are you... Did you ask me to come because you want to make a statement about Alyssa Jackson?"

Nadine pushed her chair back and stood. "Not exactly. We want to show you something."

Bella led the way to Grady's office. She sat at the computer and offered the other chair to Tom while Nadine stood behind them.

Bella pulled up the software and punched in the exact time of Alyssa's arrival. But instead of clicking *play*, she turned to face Tom. "Nadine never made a deal with Atlas. She was completely innocent. What you're about to see—"

Nadine nudged her. "Just show him."

Bella clicked the mouse, and Alyssa appeared on the screen.

"Oh wow." Tom leaned forward to watch. When Alyssa started to speak, he scrambled for his notebook.

Nadine stilled his hand. "Watch first. We'll play it again."

By the time the clip ended, Tom's face had paled another shade. "Holy fuck. Who set up these cameras?"

"That would be the assistant manager, Jason Carson. I can spell his name for you."

Tom turned to Nadine. "Are you willing to speak on the record about this? About what really happened?"

Nadine didn't hesitate. "I am."

He opened his notebook and clicked his pen. "I need to see it again. I want to write down every word. Then I'll call my boss."

"Of course. Take your time." Bella played the clip again while Tom scribbled.

Then he stepped into the hallway to make his call. Bella and Nadine could hear bits of the conversation, including, "I swear to God I'm not fucking with you."

A few minutes later, Tom returned. "They're waking up the lawyers. In the meantime"—he turned to Nadine—"you said you'd speak on the record?"

Nadine nodded. "I'll give you the interview."

"May I record it?"

"You may." Nadine moved to the door. "But I'd be more comfortable in the break room."

"Sounds great." Tom's head bobbed. "And if you don't mind, I think I would like a slice of that pizza."

By the time Nadine finished the interview, it was midnight. By then, a second reporter had arrived from the Post's Richmond bureau.

The lawyers agreed the newspaper could publish the transcript of the video and an image from the footage but not the actual video. This was about what Nadine had expected. While she had never practiced First Amendment law, Nadine knew that courts generally protected reporters who published the contents of recordings. Besides, after it all came out, Alyssa would have more pressing legal concerns than a conflict with the paper.

After the reporters left for the night, Nadine and Bella still had to deal with the deposit they had left in the safe hours earlier. So after they finally locked the doors behind them—five hours after closing—Bella and Nadine drove to the bank on deserted streets.

"Will you get in trouble for this?" Nadine asked as she steered her car into the drive-through. "For making the deposit so late?"

Bella passed her the bag of cash. "Nah. How would they even know? This isn't some high-tech city bank. The bag will just sit in a box along with every other deposit that arrived after they closed at six."

"Good point." Nadine dropped the bag into the receptacle and closed the slot, sending it down the chute.

As they pulled out of the parking lot and headed for home, Nadine decided to bring up another concern, one that had gnawed at her for the past few hours. "What about everything else? I can't imagine corporate will look kindly on what we did tonight, calling in reporters to view security footage on Grady's computer."

Bella chuckled. "I guess they won't. But Jason is going to be in way more trouble. I mean, it wasn't an Overstock Oasis camera." She paused. "Well, I might get in trouble for letting reporters into the store after hours. But come on, this is your life. What other choice was there?"

Nadine pulled into a parking space at the complex, cut the engine, and faced Bella. "Thank you. I'm so grateful to you. I really am. None of this would have happened if you hadn't...um." Tears blurred her vision. After hours of worry mixed with giddy elation, she felt frayed and overwhelmed. "I might have a second chance now. And it's because of you."

Bella unclicked her seatbelt and leaned over to embrace Nadine. "I love you." Her voice was raw, almost sad. Was something wrong?

"I love you too." Nadine decided Bella was just exhausted from the evening. Surely she wasn't questioning what they had done or their relationship. They were together. Everything would be okay.

Chapter 32

BELLA STOOD IN THE SHOWER, the scalding water pouring onto her face and down her body. She felt dizzy and shaky, overwhelmed with the enormity of what they'd done.

How could everything change in a day? Twenty-four hours ago, they were secure in their little world with their shitty jobs and their one-bedroom apartment. It wasn't much, but they had each other.

Now everything was different. If Tom wrote an honest story, the rest of the world would learn what Bella already knew—that Nadine was a hero, someone who had sacrificed two years of freedom to spare the country from a truly terrible leader. Nadine's whole life was about to change, and Bella couldn't imagine her staying in Cheriville.

The scandal had brought Nadine down to Bella's level. If not for her fall from grace, they would never have met, never have become friends, never have shared an apartment. But now Nadine would have new opportunities worlds better than Overstock Oasis. Maybe she'd even get to be a lawyer again.

Bella had no idea what it would mean for their new relationship. She knew Nadine cared for her. But did she care enough to stay in a small, conservative town when she had the chance to leave?

Bella emerged from the bathroom wrapped in a hot-pink terrycloth towel. Nadine sat on the bed in a plain gray T-shirt and boxers, her clothes contrasting with the faded rainbow zebra-print bedsheets.

Nadine looked up from her phone. "There's nothing online yet."

"Tom said it would be hours."

"I know. I just can't stop refreshing the page. God, I don't know how I'm going to sleep tonight." As she spoke, her gaze dropped to Bella's cleavage.

Bella licked her lips. Nadine's rumpled T-shirt exposed a strip of skin above boxers that hugged her slim hips. All Bella wanted in the whole fucked-up world was to be on top of her, to hold her close for as long as she could.

The towel fell to her feet. "Let me distract you."

Nadine straightened her back. "Right now?"

A draft of cool air chilled Bella's exposed body. Was this a mistake? What if Nadine would rather watch the news, and this was foolish or insensitive—

"Come here." Nadine dropped her phone onto the nightstand.

Oh, thank God. Bella climbed onto the bed and straddled Nadine. As she leaned forward to capture her lips, her breasts brushed Nadine's, sending shivers down her body.

The kiss was hot and breathy and charged. While their mouths moved together, Nadine massaged Bella's breasts.

Every caress sent waves of pleasure to Bella's core. She arched backward and ground against Nadine's cotton boxers, soaking the fabric beneath her. "Take off your clothes." She lifted the T-shirt as far as she could.

Nadine pulled it over her head and cast it aside.

Bella drank in every inch of Nadine's muscular shoulders, sleek collarbone, and round breasts, trying to memorize her body. "You're so beautiful."

"Nah." Nadine scoffed. "You're the pretty one."

"I'm the *prissy* one. You're beautiful." Bella didn't know if Nadine believed it, but she would tell her every day—if Nadine stayed. She ran her fingers down Nadine's belly. "Come on. Bottoms too. I want to feel all of you." She shifted to the side, making room for Nadine to slide her boxers down her legs.

Nadine kicked them aside and lay back again, now fully naked.

Heat rushed through Bella as she lowered herself onto Nadine's bare skin. Leaning forward, she compressed her soft breasts against Nadine's firm chest and slipped her knee between Nadine's legs.

Wet curls brushed her skin. Bella couldn't suppress her smile, knowing she wasn't alone in her desire. Soon they were moving in unison, rocking into each other until they were both slick with arousal.

Bella looked into Nadine's eyes. "Can I taste you? Please?"

Nadine seemed to hesitate, then nodded.

Bella kissed her way down Nadine's belly. The skin was smooth and soft beneath her lips. She lingered just above her triangle of curls, wanting to prolong the anticipation for both of them.

At last, Bella slid her tongue into the slippery folds.

"Oh God." Nadine moaned. "Oh hell. Fuck."

Bella explored with gentle pressure. Every shift, groan, and curse caused her own center to pulse. She could have stayed in that moment forever, reveling in the texture, the taste, and the sounds Nadine made just for her.

Suddenly, Nadine grabbed Bella's hair.

Stop? Keep going? Ohhh.

Nadine came so hard, Bella felt the tremors on her face.

"Oh fuck." Nadine panted. "That felt so good."

Bella wiped her mouth on the sheet, then moved up the bed to lie beside Nadine. "You taste amazing."

"Mmm." Nadine was still recovering. Her eyes were closed, and her cheeks were flushed. "Aaah."

Warmth spread through Bella's chest. *I did that to her.* She ran her fingers up and down Nadine's arm.

Nadine finally opened her eyes and turned toward Bella. A slight smile formed as she ran her gaze down Bella's chest and belly, down to her thighs. "God. Your body." She stroked Bella's breasts with her fingers.

"Are you sure?" Bella asked shyly. Every inch of her skin craved Nadine's touch, but she didn't want Nadine to think she expected anything, especially after such an intense night. "I'm sure you're tired after everything that happened today. I just wanted to—oh!"

Nadine pushed her flat onto her back. "Like I said before, I don't feel like sleeping." The hunger in her eyes was like their first time. Bella would never forget the high of Nadine climbing on top and claiming her, so consumed with passion that everything else fell away.

Now, Nadine ghosted kisses up and down her neck, her breath heating Bella's skin until her face, chest, and neck were ablaze. Moving downward, she licked and teased the swell of Bella's breast. When she reached the hard nipple, Bella groaned.

Nadine's tongue was slow and relentless, tormenting Bella until her vision blurred. She moved her hand over Bella's belly in languid strokes that traveled lower and lower each time. Finally, she reached down to cup and caress the damp curls. "Oh my. You're so wet."

"You do this to me. You always have." Bella pushed her hips into Nadine's hand. "Do you remember your first day, when I saw you in the stockroom? You were all sweaty with your shirt sticking to your breasts, and I just"—she gasped for breath as Nadine's finger went deeper—"I've wanted you ever since."

She'd spent weeks at war with her own instincts, trying to reconcile her attraction with Nadine's supposed crimes. Now, as her whole body ached for more, she couldn't believe she'd ever managed to hold back.

"Could you please...ah." Bella sucked in her breath as Nadine nipped at tender flesh. "Um, could you fuck me?"

Nadine's gaze was uncertain. "Do you have something?"

"No. I mean yes, I have toys. But I just want you. Your fingers."

A smile spread across Nadine's face. "Okay." Gently, she slid a single finger inside of Bella.

"Omigod." She was unprepared for the effect their connection would have on her. Her thighs trembled, and heat flooded her core.

"You feel incredible." Nadine began a slow rhythm, gliding in, then pulling back.

The wonder in Nadine's gaze humbled Bella—knowing that Nadine felt safe enough to try something new with her. It was also a turn-on. As Bella lifted her hips to match each thrust, she felt her body opening up from the inside. "Can you use two fingers?"

Nadine filled her with a second finger. "This okay?"

"God, yes." Bella's thighs clenched. "Harder. You're not gonna hurt me."

"Okay." Nadine pushed deeper, increasing her speed.

Bella was close, so damn close to the edge. When Nadine brushed her clit with her thumb, Bella succumbed to pleasure that coursed through her body. "Omigod," she rasped, struggling to catch her breath.

Nadine moved to wrap her arms around Bella and nuzzled her shoulder. "Do you...?"

"Hmm?" Bella cuddled into the embrace.

"Do you mind if I check my phone?"

"Oh." Bella tried not to sound disappointed. "Um, of course not."

Nadine pushed herself up. "I'm going to wash my hands first."

Alone in bed, Bella chastised herself. *Stop being an insecure baby.* This was one of the most important nights of Nadine's life. Of course checking the news was more important than basking in the afterglow.

They'd still sleep together, wake up together...and if it didn't last, well, there'd be plenty of time to feel terrible about it later.

Chapter 33

WHEN BELLA OPENED HER EYES the next morning, Nadine's side of the bed was empty. After a few seconds of groggy confusion, she jolted upright as the events of the previous evening rushed back to her. *I need my phone.*

Notifications cluttered her lock screen—news alerts, missed calls from Grady and her mom, plus a message from Raelyn that was just a string of shocked emojis.

The first alert read, "Alyssa Jackson appears to admit role in Atlas corruption scheme in footage viewed by the *Washington Post*."

Bella tapped the notification, bringing up the story in her *Post* app. The subhead read, "Bayani claims she took blame to prevent election of President Gunn."

The story included a still image of the video, plus a link to the full transcript of what Alyssa and Nadine had said. There was also a photo of Nadine sitting in the break room, staring past the camera.

Bella was transfixed by the snapshot of Nadine in that moment, when she knew her life was about to change a second time. Her gaze was serious, as it had been on the day they met. But now, instead of anger, Bella saw peace in her eyes.

She slid out of bed and walked into the living room. There was no sign of Nadine. Had she left already? Bella pushed down her hurt feelings. This was Nadine's moment, not hers.

But I thought she'd want to share it with me.

Then she heard Nadine's voice coming from outside the apartment. Bella opened the door.

Nadine sat on the porch steps, wearing a jacket over her T-shirt and clutching her phone to her ear. She nodded at Bella but continued listening to the voice on the other end. "Listen, I appreciate the offer. But I've been disbarred in Illinois... Uh-huh... Well, that's good to know, but I need to talk to my attorney."

Bella hovered in the doorway, shivering as the icy December wind blew through her skimpy pajamas. She considered going inside for her coat but worried it might be presumptuous; Nadine hadn't invited her to stay.

"Okay, you can send it over... Same email address I've always had... Yes, that one. But I need to go. I'll be in touch, okay?"

Nadine tapped the phone to hang up, then turned to Bella. "Since I woke up, I've received about a hundred interview requests, plus texts and calls from countless ex-friends, a book deal offer, and now a job offer at an old classmate's law firm."

"That's a lot." Bella rubbed her arms for warmth.

Nadine stood. "Let's go inside. I only came out here so I wouldn't wake you."

Inside, Nadine shed the jacket and turned to hang it in the closet.

As soon as she turned back around, Bella threw her arms around her. She couldn't help it. "Good morning." Then she said into her ear, "I heard a wild rumor that you might be innocent."

Nadine kissed the top of her head. "Is that so?" She sounded light and free.

Bella's eyes filled with unexpected tears. "I'm so happy for you." She buried her face in Nadine's T-shirt, inhaling her scent. She smelled fresh, like soap. This was what she wanted every day for the rest of her life. She was happy—and so frightened that it was all about to end. But she didn't know how to say it.

She pulled away to look at Nadine. "Has Alyssa put out a statement?"

"Not yet. I imagine she's holed up with her lawyer, brainstorming possible defenses."

The thought brought Bella some cheer. "Plan A, I was on drugs. Plan B, I was possessed."

"Something like that." Nadine chuckled. "I'm going to make coffee. Want some?"

"Do you have to ask?" Bella followed her into the kitchen.

"Speaking of lawyers," Nadine continued, "I got a call from mine."

"Oh? What did he say? Does he think they'll reverse your conviction?"

"Maybe. But it won't be simple or fast." Nadine poured ground coffee into the brewer. "I lied to Congress under oath—that's a crime. Amir isn't too happy about that. Or about...well, the whole thing, really. He's quite peeved that I didn't tell him the truth."

"I can imagine." Bella pulled two mugs from the cabinet. "I've heard lawyers don't like to lose."

"We certainly don't." Nadine smiled.

We. Because that's what Nadine was, a lawyer. "Are you... Do you think you'll get your law license back?"

Nadine shrugged. "I really don't know. I could apply for reinstatement in Illinois, or I could apply to the bar in another state—but it probably depends on what happens with my conviction."

"Do you think you'll take that job you just got offered?" Bella held her breath.

"Oh, who knows." Nadine waved her hand dismissively. "He wants to snap me up before other offers come in. I don't know what I'd do there anyway since I don't have a license. He probably just wants publicity for his firm."

Other offers? Bella imagined Nadine courted by high-power law firms and political organizations throughout the country. Miles and miles away. "What about the book deals? Maybe you could get an advance and take your time working on it." *And stay here.*

Nadine scoffed. "I'm not interested in sharing the details of my time in prison, no matter how lucrative the advance. I've been humiliated enough."

"It was just a thought."

"Oh, sure." Nadine relaxed. "I know. But I'm sure I'll have opportunities that don't require me to bare my soul for the gawking public."

This sparked another uncomfortable thought. "Are you going to come out?"

Nadine furrowed her brow. "Come out? You mean...?"

"Yeah, I mean as a queer person. I'm sure people will ask about your personal life. Like where you live and if you're seeing someone."

Nadine shook her head. "They won't ask about that. And if they do, I'll say it's none of their business. Besides, I haven't agreed to do any more interviews."

Bella fixed her gaze on the coffee dripping into the pot, afraid to let Nadine see her reaction. Nadine had dismissed the suggestion so quickly, like there was no point in being open. Did she really think they could keep their relationship completely private, or did it mean she wasn't planning for a serious future together?

As soon as the brewer finished, Bella filled her mug. She added cream and extra sugar, sensing she'd need every ounce of energy she could get. "Well, I should get ready for work. I guess you're not coming?"

Nadine laughed. "Uh, no. I'll write a letter of resignation. Would you mind giving it to Grady?"

"Oh, okay. That's very formal."

Nadine looked puzzled. "Isn't that what I'm supposed to do?"

Bella shrugged. "You can write a letter if you want. Usually people just stop coming in."

"Ah. You know, in a way, I'll miss that fucked-up place."

"Yeah." Bella picked up her mug and walked away, her eyes brimming with tears. The truth had been out for less than day, and already Nadine was leaving her behind.

The first thing Bella saw when she turned into the parking lot was a row of news vans parked in front of Overstock Oasis. The entire lot was packed. She had to circle twice before she found an empty space—a delay she didn't need when she was already running late.

As she hurried across the lot to the store, stuffing her keys into her purse, she realized she should have zipped up her jacket to conceal her purple polo. When she stepped onto the sidewalk, reporters came at her from multiple directions.

A woman with an auburn bob and chunky glasses stepped into Bella's path. "Do you work here?" Her accent was British.

"Do you know Nadine Bayani?" asked a man with a video camera.

"Excuse me." Bella pushed through them. "I need to clock in."

Inside, the store was crowded with people who didn't seem to know what to do. Some stared at their phones while others milled around aimlessly without shopping carts or baskets. Ashley was stationed at a register, but no customers were in line.

Ashley spotted Bella. "There you are! Holy crap, Bella! You are in *so much trouble.*"

A few reporters were still watching Bella, so she walked up to the register and whispered to Ashley, "Why? What happened this morning?"

Ashley leaned in, her eyes glittering. "Oh my God. You missed it. The freaking feds came and took Grady's computer. Of course, corporate asked how we got that video, and Grady threw Jason under the bus. Now he's suspended! And Grady is pissed." She paused to take a breath. "At you, I mean. He's pissed at you and Nadine."

"Right. Thanks." Bella sighed. "What about all the reporters? They don't seem to be doing anything."

"Grady banned us from talking to them. So they just stand around and talk in front of the cameras once in a while. I figured out that it's when a new hour starts." She smiled mischievously. "I managed to get into some shots."

"So they're reporting live from a scene where absolutely nothing is happening."

"Yeah, I guess." Ashley shrugged. "Anyway, Tino is going to DVR the news so I can see myself on TV tonight."

"Cool. Well, I guess I need to find out if I'm fired. Thanks for the update."

Bella walked back to the break room. She clocked in—just in case she got paid for her shift—and then knocked on Grady's door.

"Yeah?" Grady sounded cranky.

Bella cracked the door and peeked in. "Um, hi."

Grady sat behind the desk, which now had an empty space where the computer used to be. He scowled at her, deepening the creases in his forehead. "You. Get in here."

Bella stepped in and closed the door. "I'm sorry I didn't return your calls."

He harrumphed. "Would have saved you a trip."

Oh no. "Am I fired?"

"You should be. You let unauthorized persons into the store after closing. You gave them access to my computer. And you showed them my password!"

Showed them his password? "Well, to be fair—"

"I'm not finished. You showed security footage to a reporter, and now my assistant manager has been suspended pending an investigation. He could face criminal charges."

Bella said nothing. She knew how much Grady valued Jason, who had been kissing his ass for years.

"You know, you're not the sharpest bulb in the box. I took a chance and promoted you because you're a good employee. And I thought you were a good girl. But ever since that felon got here, you've been acting up. First the backsass, and now this. It's a real shame."

"The brightest bulb," Bella said.

"What?" He squinted, wrinkling the skin around his eyes.

"You said I'm not the sharpest bulb. That doesn't make any sense. It's brightest bulb or sharpest knife. If you're going to call me stupid, at least get it right. Anyway, does it matter to you that Nadine was innocent all along? Like, does it matter at all?"

"Innocent? Ha. Sounds to me like she cooked up a conspiracy with Alyssa Jackson. They're both crooks as far as I'm concerned."

Bella clenched her fists. "You don't even know her. From the moment you found out who she was, you treated her like scum when all she ever did was show up and work her ass off. She took shit from you and Jason and customers, unloaded trucks by herself, and never even complained." Bella paused. "Oh, by the way, she quit."

Grady perked up. "Did she? No notice?"

"If she came back here, you'd have to deal with even more reporters. She's doing you a favor."

"Hmm." He leaned back, clasping his hands in front of him.

"Without me, you'd be quite short-staffed," Bella hedged.

"I guess so. And I might think about giving you another chance, now that Nadine won't be here to influence you. But it's out of my hands. Corporate decided to suspend you while they investigate."

He looked irritated, probably because he'd have to close the store more often without her.

Bella looked around the small office where she and Nadine had uncovered the footage of Alyssa confessing. Not even a full day had passed, yet everything had changed.

She'd never forget the rush of power when she realized that she, little hick-town college dropout Bella Clarke, had access to evidence that would bring down a corrupt US senator.

It had been the most exciting moment of her entire life. But now that Nadine was almost certainly moving out of Cheriville, she would probably never have a moment like that again. If she lost her job, she'd never even be able to revisit the scene.

"I guess I'll wait to hear from corporate."

"Yup," Grady said.

Bella left the office, prepared to face hordes of reporters again. On her way to the front of the store, she saw Kenny folding towels. "Hey, Kenny."

Kenny looked up. "You're here."

"Yeah, but I'm leaving." Bella stuck her hands in her pockets. "I got suspended, so I probably won't be back."

Kenny's face fell. "Oh no. I'm sorry. I liked working with you."

She swallowed, choking back a rush of emotion. "I liked working with you too, Kenny. You're a good kid. Text me anytime, okay? If you need anything or want to talk to someone."

Then Bella remembered that he had seen Nadine kissing her the previous day. It seemed like years ago. "About what you saw..." She searched for something to say, but the words eluded her.

Kenny raised his hand. "I've known for some time that you're not on the Lord's path."

"Oh. Um."

"But I can tell that Nadine cares about you. And I'm glad you're happy." He offered a tentative smile.

Bella wasn't sure if that meant *I support you* or *Have fun together in hell*, but she decided to take it as the former. "Thanks, Kenny. I'll see you around."

He was right. Nadine did care for her. She just wished she knew how long it would last.

Feeling at loose ends without her crappy job, Bella drove to Sonic for a watermelon cream slush. As she sat in her car sucking the sugary pink drink through a straw, Nadine texted her. *Lawyer wants to meet with me in Washington. Michaela already gave permission. Leaving now and will probably stay overnight.*

Bella stared at the message. No pleasantries. Not even an emoji. Then again, Nadine had never been one to gush over text.

She started to type back with the news of her suspension but then stopped. Nadine was probably driving. Safety first. That, and she wasn't sure she was ready to hear what Nadine would say in response.

Forget them. Come with me. That's what Bella wanted to hear. But she was afraid Nadine would say something like, *That's too bad. Maybe the grocery store is hiring.*

She couldn't take a reaction like that, not now, so she chucked her phone onto the passenger seat and drove home to an empty apartment.

"So you were fucking innocent."

"Nice to see you too." Nadine stepped into Amir's spacious corner office and closed the door behind her. The office was as sterile as ever with a massive mahogany desk and bland eggshell walls that displayed diplomas, awards, and a forgettable abstract painting.

Amir, however, had aged. His short jet-black hair was now sprinkled with gray. And there appeared to be an extra wrinkle or two around his brown eyes—or maybe that was because he was glaring at her.

"I knew Alyssa was guilty." He rose from his chair.

Fair enough. Amir had pressed her countless times to confess Alyssa's involvement in the scheme. "I admit I never considered that you had nothing to do with it, but come on. You were obviously protecting her."

Nadine kept quiet. Amir needed to get it out of his system.

He paced the gray carpet. "Most of my clients are as guilty as sin. Do you know how hard it is to generate sympathy for a millionaire who raided pension funds or lied to investors? But you—a woman, an immigrant, someone who worked hard to put herself through college. I could have helped you, if you had let me." He stopped in front of her. "Why didn't you tell me the truth?"

Nadine sighed. "I'm sure you read my comments in the paper. If I had told the truth about Alyssa, Rob Gunn would have waltzed into the Oval

Office with four hundred electoral votes. I couldn't let that happen to my country—not if I had a chance to stop it. And based on what he has done so far, I feel justified in thinking that way."

"I get that. Rob Gunn is an abomination. It will take a decade to undo the damage he's done. I'd probably go to jail myself if I thought I could stop him." He paused. "But Gunn won. And you still didn't say anything. Why not?"

"I didn't think anyone would believe me. And...I know it's hard to understand, but by then I didn't think I deserved my freedom, my reputation, my career. But I do now. I really do. What can we do?"

"Let's sit down." He gestured to a corner of the office with two plush chairs and a small circular table. They sat facing each other.

Amir opened a leather portfolio containing a notepad. "The US attorneys want to talk to you. Obviously. They may offer immunity from perjury and obstruction of justice charges in exchange for your testimony against Jackson—especially since you already served two years."

"That's good." Nadine relaxed a little.

"Don't get me wrong. Lying to Congress is serious. But Rob Gunn wants Alyssa behind bars more than anything, and his attorney general will most likely direct the DOJ to make a deal with you."

Alyssa behind bars. Nadine pictured her former boss in a jumpsuit, denied access to makeup and her treasured flatiron. "Okay. Sure."

"As for your conviction, that's a little more challenging," Amir said. "But if they're satisfied with your testimony, the prosecution will most likely support our petition."

"What about my law license?"

"In Illinois, you can't petition for reinstatement for five years after the date of disbarment—so you'll have to wait another three years. Then you'll have to convince the panel that you deserve to be reinstated." Amir searched her face. "Were you hoping to practice law again?"

Nadine pressed her lips together. "Not necessarily. I don't know what I'll do next. Anything would be a step up from my most recent job."

Amir pulled his phone out of his pocket. "Have you ever heard of the Institute for Criminal Justice Reform?"

"Maybe. It sounds familiar."

"Here's the website." He held up the phone, although she couldn't make out much more than the name. "They advocate for prison reform and more support for ex-offenders—housing, education, jobs. Things like that. One of my friends from Harvard is the cofounder. After the story broke yesterday, he called to ask about you. He liked what you said in your interview with the *Post*, and they happen to be looking for a policy director."

"Amazing. All this time I've been scum, unworthy of even minimum wage, and within hours of Alyssa incriminating herself, I'm being considered for law jobs and director positions."

Amir smiled. "People are opportunistic. You're big news right now, and they want to ride the wave. But Kevin is a good guy. He does this work because he believes in second chances. Do you want to talk to him?"

As much as Nadine wanted to take her time and consider all options, her meager savings wouldn't last long. She needed a job. "Yes. Thank you."

"Good." Amir opened the portfolio to a clean sheet of paper and uncapped his fountain pen. "Now, I need you to tell me everything that happened—the fucking truth this time."

Chapter 34

BELLA WAS BARELY THROUGH THE front door of Raelyn's house when Kathy wrapped her in a pillowy hug. "Oh my goodness, honey. Raelyn told me you lost your job. You need some hot tea."

Raelyn appeared behind her mother. "She needs something stronger. Want a gin and tonic? If you drink too much, you can just sleep here."

"Gin would be outstanding." Bella hugged Raelyn.

When they broke apart, Raelyn pulled a bottle of Bombay Sapphire out of the cupboard. She filled three glasses with ice, then added a glug of gin to each one before topping the drinks with tonic water.

"So, cheers," Raelyn said as she sat. They clinked their glasses together.

Bella took a long sip. The drink was fizzy, cool, and potent. "So, I didn't lose my job yet, but I probably will. My boss wants me gone, and the corporate bosses are saying I violated policy by letting reporters into the store. Which I guess I did. It's probably in the handbook somewhere."

"Maybe your friend can help you fight it," Kathy said. "After all, she's a lawyer. And you did it for her." She clicked her tongue. "I still can't believe the poor thing was innocent. All this time."

"Yeah. Holy hell, Bella. You should have seen my face." Raelyn sipped her drink. "Did you know she didn't do it? Tell us everything from the beginning."

Bella did. She told them about Nadine's confession to her, the kiss—glossing over the sex for Kathy's sake—and her trip to South Carolina.

"And now she's in Washington, and I don't know when she's coming back, or if she's even coming back. I don't even know if she still wants to be with me."

"Damn." Raelyn sat back. "I was right. She was jealous."

"Yes, that's the main takeaway here. That you were right." Bella sighed. "I think I'm going to need another one of these. Or two or three."

Kathy smiled kindly. "Honey, you should talk to her. I'm sure she still cares about you. She's probably just overwhelmed right now."

"I know Nadine feels something for me. But I'm scared she was with me because...because she didn't have anyone else. I mean, can you imagine someone like her dating someone like me under normal circumstances? In her old life, she never would have looked twice at some small-town cashier."

"Maybe not," Kathy said, "but I reckon she's not the same person she was before prison. She had to learn the hard way that those fancy friends of hers weren't true. I bet she sees things different now. And if she's as smart as you say, she knows she'll never find anyone with a heart like yours."

"Thanks, Kathy. I really hope you're right."

"What are you going to do for work if you get fired?" Raelyn asked.

"Lord, I don't know." Bella drew squiggles in the condensation on her glass. "I guess another retail gig. In the meantime, I'll try to do more art commissions. I guess I could relax my standards about the work I'm willing to accept."

"Porn and fetish stuff?"

"That's where the money is. I'm not looking forward to it, but at least it will pay the rent."

Kathy tilted her head. "I don't understand. People will pay you to draw pornographic pictures? Wouldn't they rather watch videos?"

"People want really specific pictures. Like they might be in the drawing themselves, or they might want something that doesn't exist on video. For example..." Bella looked at Kathy's kind, curious eyes and reconsidered what she had been about to say. "You know, I can't think of any examples right now."

"You should do graphic design," Raelyn said. "I'm serious. You're such a good artist. This could be the perfect time to go back to school."

"Yeah, maybe." Bella looked at the table. "I guess I could put the tuition on my credit card."

Bella's phone buzzed with a notification. "It's Nadine," she said a little too loudly.

Lawyer working on immunity deal. May have lead on new job. In my hotel room now. How are you?

Bella held up her phone to show Kathy and Raelyn the message.

"You can go in the other room," Kathy said, "if you'd like to call her."

Bella wanted to call. And she would have too, if it weren't for the words *new job.* Nadine was leaving. She was leaving, and she hadn't said a word about wanting Bella with her.

"I'll talk to her later." Bella swallowed. "I just…can't right now."

Raelyn gave her a sympathetic nod. "Another gin and tonic?"

Bella exhaled. "Lord, yes."

Nadine collapsed onto the large hotel bed, sprawling on the plush bedspread and piles of pillows. She hadn't been on a comfortable mattress in years. Literal years. But she found herself longing for Bella's worn-out Ikea mattress or even the lumpy couch.

She picked up her phone again, then dropped it beside her. Still no response to her text from twenty minutes ago. And she knew it wasn't because Bella had lost track of her phone.

Why wasn't Bella responding? It didn't make sense.

When the phone chimed, Nadine snatched it off the mattress. It was Patricia, wanting to Skype.

They had spoken briefly that morning—Patricia's evening—before her sister went to sleep, and Patricia had spent most of the call blubbering tears of joy. Now it was morning in the Philippines, and Patricia wanted an update.

Nadine tapped the icon to accept the video call. Patricia sat at her kitchen table in her dressing gown. Miko was next to her in his high chair, mango pudding smeared all over his mouth.

"Hi, ate." Patricia pointed at the unfamiliar room. "Where are you?"

"I'm at a hotel in Washington, DC. My lawyer put me up for the night."

"Oh wow." Patricia grinned. "You already met with him. What did he say?"

Nadine filled her in on Amir's assessment of her case. Her sister smiled wider with each detail, and when Nadine mentioned possibly testifying against Alyssa, she became giddy.

"That b-i-t-c-h is going down!" Patricia wiped her son's mouth. "Do you hear that, *anak?* The bad lady is going to prison."

"It looks that way." Alyssa behind bars—the thought was still surreal. She didn't feel good about it exactly; she wouldn't wish prison on anyone. But she felt relieved to be done lying. The truth was coming out at last.

"I still can't believe you two pulled it off. Bella is brilliant." Patricia kept smiling as if unable to stop. "When I finally meet her, I'm going to give her so many hugs and kisses."

Patricia would adore Bella. "I'll tell her you said so."

"Is she there with you?"

"No, I'm here by myself." Nadine frowned. "Actually, I haven't heard much from her today. I'm not sure why."

"Why didn't she come with you?"

"I didn't ask her to. She had to work. Amir wanted to see me right away, and I just got in my car and left." At the sight of Patricia's raised eyebrows, Nadine suddenly realized that Bella might have wanted to go with her to Washington. "Oh. Maybe that's why she has been distant."

"You two are together, aren't you?" Patricia asked. "You're girlfriends?"

Was she? They hadn't discussed labels. "We're involved."

Patricia wagged her finger at Nadine. "If she loves you even half as much as I love you, she would want to be by your side today."

Nadine ran her fingers through her hair. "I'm not good at this, Pati. I've never... I haven't dated in years, and men were different. They chased me, and I acquiesced or brushed them off. I don't know what I'm doing." Her voice cracked. "I don't want to lose her."

"You should go home. Or invite her to join you. How far away are you?"

"About three hours. I could make it by ten." Her duffel was still packed. She could be out the door within minutes.

"Good. Tell me what happens. I love you, *ate.*"

Nadine ended the call and checked her text messages.

Bella had responded. *Okay. I'm at Raelyn's. Staying the night.*

Oh, great. Raelyn. The hot friend who was "like a sister" to Bella. Nadine flopped back down on the bed and groaned.

Bella hadn't pictured it like this. She was visibly hungover, wearing yesterday's yoga pants and a borrowed sweatshirt that said *Y'all means all* under a cartoon rainbow with a smiling cloud.

Ideally, she would have a more dignified appearance. But she couldn't wait another moment. And as the third key—holder of a literal key—she had to do it in person.

A lone news van was parked in the crowded lot in front of the store, but it was nothing like yesterday's circus.

Grady was outside the store, taping a cardboard sign to the window that said, *Attention news media: Nadine Bayani does not work here anymore!!*

Bella walked up behind him. "Rough day?"

He turned and frowned at her. "What are you doing here?"

Bella pulled the store key out of her pocket and held it out in the palm of her hand. "I came here to tell you that I'm resigning. Effective immediately."

Instead of taking the key, Grady scratched the back of his neck. "There's no need for that. I think I can persuade corporate that you made a one-time mistake. You know, because of *her* getting in your head."

"You mean you want me to stay?"

"We're understaffed. It's not looking good for Jason, and with Nadine gone…there's no one to cover your shifts."

Ah. That explained it. "Well, I'm sorry to hear that, but I need to move on."

He frowned. "You found another job already?"

"No. But I need to do something different. I might go back to school." The truth was that she couldn't bear to work there without Nadine. Languishing at Overstock Oasis by herself wasn't an option anymore. She needed more.

"Oh, come on. You can work here and go to school."

"No, thanks. I'm going to draw fetish porn for money." She flashed an angelic smile. "It's just better for my schedule." She held out the key again.

This time he accepted it. "Fine. But I'm going to fill your position, so don't think you can come back when things don't work out."

"You should promote Ashley to third key. She acts a bit ditzy, and her outfits can be…extreme. But she's worked here a long time. She's ready."

"Hmph. Maybe." At least he seemed to be thinking about it.

Bella turned away. A light breeze whispered through her hair as she walked to her car. She was free.

Nadine trudged into Bella's apartment, her duffel bag slung over her shoulder. The living room was empty, but she could hear the shower running.

She dropped her bag and sat on the couch to wait. As she leaned back into the cushions, she caught sight of a pencil drawing on the table.

It was a sketch of Nadine from the shoulders up. She picked it up and studied it. Bella had given her eyes a charged, defiant stare with specks of light dotting the irises. The image was all angles, from the brushed-back hair to the peaks and valley of her mouth down to the chiseled shoulders. Was that how Bella saw her? Hard edges?

The bathroom door creaked open. Nadine turned to see Bella emerge in a cloud of steam, wrapped in a purple towel that barely touched her breasts. Her cheeks were flushed from the shower, and her eyelids were pink and swollen.

Bella's eyes widened. "You came back."

"Of course I did. What's wrong? Have you been crying?"

Bella tugged the towel higher to cover her chest. "I'll be right there. I'm going to get dressed."

She returned wearing soft gray sweatpants and a sky-blue T-shirt. Damp strands of hair framed her face and dripped water onto her shirt. She sat, and once again they faced each other on opposite ends of Bella's sofa.

Nadine held up the drawing. "You've made me look rather intense."

"That's you on the day we met. When you, um…"

"When I snapped at you?"

"Yeah." Bella's lips curved into a slight smile. "I'll never forget how strong you were in spite of everything."

"Bella—"

"I quit my job."

Nadine closed her mouth. Whatever she had expected Bella to say, it wasn't that. "Why? Did you get in trouble?"

"Yeah, I got suspended, but that's not the reason. Grady wants me to come back. But I can't work there anymore after everything that's happened.

I just can't." Bella looked up to meet Nadine's eyes. "Before you got here, I was just drifting through the days, earning my ten dollars an hour and trying not to think about how bored and miserable I was. But then I met you. The world-famous Nadine Bayani. And then we became friends and roommates, and my life wasn't small and boring anymore."

Bella folded her legs up and hugged her knees. "Even if you go off to the big city and leave me behind, even if I never see you again, I'm not the same person anymore. You showed me that I'm smart—or at least not stupid—and if I get help for my learning issues, I'm as capable as anyone. I mean, look at what we did. We exposed the truth and brought down a US senator. I was part of that. And now realize I can do more than what I've been doing."

Nadine swelled with pride at the resolve in Bella's eyes. "Yes, you can. You're smart and fierce and brave as hell. There's no limit to what you can do, Bella Clarke." Then the other words penetrated. "But why do you think I would leave you behind?"

"Because…" Bella brushed away a tear. "Because you're getting your real life back. And I'm so happy for you. I really, truly am. But you have opportunities now, and we both know they won't be in Cheriville."

"Oh, Bella." How could she make Bella understand how precious she was to her? "If we're going to do this, I need you to talk to me."

"Do this?" Bella asked cautiously.

"I want us to be together." Nadine took Bella's hand. "If I have an opportunity somewhere else, I'd like you to think about moving with me. If you're not ready for that, we'll figure something else out. I could take a job in DC, visit on the weekends. Something like that. We'll do whatever it takes."

Bella sniffled. "You really want to be with me?"

"*Yes*. God, yes. More than anything." Nadine squeezed Bella's hand. "I have a second chance in my life, but it doesn't mean anything if I lose you."

Bella launched herself into Nadine's arms with a force that toppled them over, bodies pressed together.

Nadine breathed in the scent of Bella's coconut shampoo as warm lips captured hers.

"I love you," Bella said, her voice breaking. "I love you so much."

"I love you too." Nadine ran her fingers through Bella's long, damp hair. "I didn't know what love was until I met you." She had thought she was in love with Alyssa, but now she recognized the infatuation for what it was: a manifestation of her own self-loathing that Alyssa used to manipulate her day after miserable day.

With Bella, it was different. She had accepted Nadine from the beginning, offering kindness when the whole world was treating her like trash. Nadine loved her for that. But she loved her even more for the beautiful, talented person she was.

They lay on the couch, holding each other close. Bella said, "If you get a job somewhere else, I'll go with you."

"Really? You'd leave Cheriville?"

"Yes. I'm ready. It will be hard, but I can do anything if we're together."

Joy overwhelmed her. Was this really happening? Everything she wanted, all at once? "You don't know how happy that makes me."

"Besides, you don't have enough stuff to fill an apartment by yourself." Bella smiled. "You need my clutter and chaos to make it feel like home."

"Indeed." Nadine shifted, bumping her head against the arm of the couch. "You know, considering all the time we spend on this couch, we should get a bigger one."

"Maybe we could go wild and get a chair too."

"Hey, now. Let's pace ourselves."

"Good point, good point. Well, in the meantime, there's more space on the bed."

Epilogue

As the DC Metro train rumbled toward her stop, Nadine noticed the man across from her staring. He was young with shaggy blond hair and green eyes that seemed to ask a question.

Nadine kept her oversized sunglasses in place. They obscured enough of her face to keep most people from recognizing her. A year ago, they had protected her from harassment. Now they spared her from the gawking and awkward questions she received as a minor celebrity.

Lately, she was recognized more often because Alyssa was in the news again. She would be sentenced soon, and most legal analysts expected her to receive a minimum of five years. Many people assumed Nadine would be delighted to see Alyssa rot, but it only made her sad. After her experience, Nadine wouldn't wish a long prison sentence on any nonviolent offender. There had to be a better way.

A robotic voice announced the train's arrival at Clarendon. Nadine stood. The man opened his mouth to speak, but Nadine moved past him, joining the commuters streaming through the exit doors and toward the escalators.

As she walked down the street toward their modest townhouse, she spotted Bella's car parked outside. Her stomach fluttered with nerves and excitement—she was back from the airport.

She opened the door. Bella, Patricia, and the little nephew she had never met were there in the living room. "Hello," she said, her throat thick with emotion.

"Oh my God!" Patricia jumped to her feet and threw her arms around Nadine. "I missed you, ate."

"Not as much as I missed you." Tears filled Nadine's eyes as she squeezed even harder. She didn't want to let go.

Miko toddled behind his mother, studying Nadine with big, curious eyes.

Patricia ushered him forward with obvious pride. "Miko, this is your Auntie Nadine."

"Hi, sweetheart." Nadine knelt down to his eye level. "You're so big! How old are you?"

Miko glanced back at his mother.

"Ilang taon ka na raw?" Patricia asked him.

He looked back at Nadine, holding up two fingers.

"Great job. Can I have a hug?"

When Miko nodded, Nadine embraced him and kissed his head.

Bella sat on the couch, dressed in a smocked sundress, her hair swept up in a high ponytail.

Nadine sat next to her, greeting her with a light kiss.

Patricia resumed her seat on the matching armchair while Miko returned to his toys on the floor.

"I like her." Patricia nodded at Bella. "She'll make an excellent sister-in-law."

Nadine flashed Bella a look that said *I told you so.*

Bella had fretted all week about making a good impression. There was never reason to worry; Bella's Southern charm worked on everyone. Besides, after her part in exposing Alyssa's lies, Bella could be the rudest woman alive and Patricia would still adore her forever.

"How was work?" Bella asked.

"It was fine. They want me to give a speech at a big criminal justice conference at the University of Virginia." Usually, the president of the Institute for Criminal Justice Reform gave this type of speech, but they'd asked for Nadine—probably because she was the most famous employee.

"Ooh, a conference," Patricia said. "They want you to talk about prison?"

"No. Well, a little. But it's more about how we treat people after they get out of prison. How difficult it is to get a job, to find housing. The system sets people up to fail, and it doesn't help anyone."

Bella placed her hand on Nadine's knee. "Nadine works on ban-the-box laws. She worked on a proposal in Virginia that would make employers interview people before asking about criminal convictions. That way, people at least get a chance to make a good impression." She smiled at Nadine. "I'm really proud of her."

"I am too," Patricia said. "And I know she's proud of you too. She showed me some of your artwork over Skype. I hope you'll show me some more."

Bella blushed. "Maybe later."

Nadine pointed to a painting on the opposite wall. "Bella painted that in one of her classes."

"Oh wow." Patricia studied the painting, a red and purple sunset over an open field of grass and weeds. "You're so talented!"

"Thanks." Bella blushed even harder. "It's where I grew up. Out in the country."

"Well, it's gorgeous. I hope you got an A."

"I did. It's just community college, but it's going pretty well."

"As usual, Bella is being modest," Nadine said. Bella had earned three A's and a B last semester. Medication and therapy for ADHD had made a world of difference in both her performance and her confidence, but she was still shy about her success.

"So." Bella shifted. "Would anyone like a coconut? We have fresh ones."

Patricia clapped her hands. "Oh, a treat from home. I'd love one."

Nadine stood. "I'll go open them."

Bella pulled her back down to the couch. "I got it. You visit with your sister." She rubbed Nadine's back.

Nadine had never seen Bella open a coconut successfully, but she sat back down. She locked eyes with Patricia, knowing without words that they felt the same. After many long years, they were finally together again.

Miko walked over to Nadine, holding a small toy car.

"What do you have there?" she asked.

Miko looked to his mother.

"Tell Auntie Nadine what you have."

"A car!"

Nadine hated that she had been in prison when Miko was born. She'd missed so much. But all she could do was move forward. "That's a very nice car. What color is it?"

"A blue car," Miko said brightly.

Something crashed in the kitchen. "Ow ow ow ow ow!"

Nadine jumped up. "I'd better check on her."

Bella was at the kitchen sink, flapping her hand, but there was no visible blood. The coconut wasn't even cracked. "I guess I don't quite have the hang of it."

Nadine touched her shoulder. "I appreciate that you tried. But you'd better let me take over before you impale yourself." She examined Bella's hands and kissed her fingers. Then she picked up the knife and expertly hammered it into the coconut. A few more strikes, and the coconut fell open. "Next one?"

Bella handed her a second coconut. "You look really happy."

"I am. I'm with my sister. And I'm with you." Nadine opened the coconut and looked at it. "This is a meaty one."

Bella leaned against the counter. "How do you say *coconut?*"

"*Buko.*"

"Buko. Gusto ko ng buko. I would like a coconut."

"You're getting good." Nadine gave her a kiss. "I love you."

Bella smiled. "Mahal kita." She picked up a coconut with each hand. "I'll see you in there."

Nadine picked up the third coconut and returned to the living room to join her family.

Other Books from Ylva Publishing

www.ylva-publishing.com

The Love Factor
Quinn Ivins

ISBN: 978-3-96324-377-6
Length: 215 pages (75,000 words)

A smart student-professor romance filled with nostalgia, politics, and the forbidden thrills of lesbian love in the '90s.

Molly is almost thirty, bored, and less into her PhD than her sexy, closeted statistics professor, Carmen, an icy woman with strict standards, and no interest in dating students.

As they work together to expose a scandal, the chemistry builds, making for a dangerous equation.

A smart, opposites-attract, student-professor romance filled with nostalgia, edgy politics, and the forbidden thrills of lesbian love in the nineties.

Never Say Never
Rachael Sommers

ISBN: 978-3-96324-429-2
Length: 220 pages (75,000 words)

Ambitious Camila might have lost her marriage but she doesn't need love to build a TV empire and raise her young son. What she does need is a nanny.

Enter Emily—bright, naive, and new to New York City. Emily is everything Camila is not and that's not all that's unsettling.

Surely she can't be falling for the nanny?

An age-gap, opposites-attract lesbian romance with a puddle of melted ice queen.

Wrong Number, Right Woman
Jae

ISBN: 978-3-96324-401-8

Length: 370 pages (116,000 words)

Shy Denny has a simple life as a cashier who helps raise her niece. Then she gets a wrong-number text from a stranger named Eliza, asking her for dating advice.

Eliza, the queen of disastrous first dates, finds an instant connection with Denny that makes her question everything...like just how straight she really is.

A slow-burn lesbian romance with likable characters and low angst.

Hotel Queens
Lee Winter

ISBN: 978-3-96324-457-5

Length: 319 pages (104,000 words)

At a Vegas bar, two powerful hotel execs meet, flirt, and challenge each other—with no clue they're rivals after the same dream deal. What happens now they've met their match?

Ice meets fire in this opposites-attract lesbian romance, as layered, sassy, and smart as its characters.

About Quinn Ivins

Quinn Ivins has been addicted to reading romance since she was a teenager, when she stayed up late on school nights to read more *X-Files* fanfiction. After romance novels, her top vices include sugar, booze, cable news, and country music.

Quinn lives in the southern United States with her wife, their young son, and their adorable cat. When she isn't working her day job, writing fiction, or chasing her toddler, she gets as much sleep as she can.

CONNECT WITH QUINN
Website: www.quinnivins.com
E-mail: quinn.ivins@gmail.com
Twitter: @quinnivins
Facebook: www.facebook.com/quinn.ivins.9
Instagram: quinn.ivins

Credits
Edited by Miranda Miller, Julie Klein, and Michelle Aguilar
Cover Design and Print Layout by Streetlight Graphics

Made in the USA
Columbia, SC
09 May 2021